The Cowboy's Word

The Cowboy's Word

A Coyote Cowboys of Montana Romance

Sinclair Jayne

TULE
PUBLISHING

Dear Reader,

The Cowboy's Word is book one in a new series called The Coyote Cowboys of Montana for Tule Publishing (thank you always, Tule). I've been playing with the idea of how highly trained and successful soldiers or operatives adjust when they exit their professional realm and return home for a couple of years. The cowboy soldiers are so changed, and for several of them, they have no home to return to, or the circumstances with their families or in their small ranching towns are initially unrecognizable. But my heroes are strong and determined to find their footing and complete the last mission for their fallen brother.

I've had several family members serve—father, uncle and brother—and I was always fascinated by their stories and the impression I had that entering the military was a bit like Narnia—another world with different rules and expectations and language and culture. And when a soldier is discharged, they walk back through the wardrobe and re-enter the world they left. They've grown and changed, and the perception is often that the life they left too has changed. A former soldier and his or her friends and family often must adjust, and that can sometimes be challenging and painful, but this is fiction, based on some research, and I always intend to write to inspire and to entertain.

In my books I often explore the themes of personal transformation and reinvention. In the Coyote Cowboys series, I created men who had all grown up on a ranch—cowboys—who have admirably served their country and now want to go back to the land, but... That is always the fun part—figuring out the hook—what is the conflict each of these cowboy heroes will face as they build a new life and, of course, fall in love.

I want to thank my friend and fellow author Rusty Keller (Kasey Lane), who listened to me mull over my ideas during a weekend writing retreat in early March 2020 right before the world shut down for a scary time. And I also want to thank friend, author and Tule Publisher, Jane Porter, who helped me problem solve so that the series premise finally came into focus with a satisfying pop. My Coyote Cowboys arrive in Montana with one final mission before they rebuild their lives and create new careers. What they aren't expecting—and actively resist—is to fall in love.

I hope you enjoy heading back to Marietta, Montana, for *The Cowboy's Word*. I know I was thrilled to finally find a hero for Shane Knight, one of my five Knight sisters. She's been a bartender at the Graff Hotel for several years, watching her friends fall in love. And with Remington Cross, she's finally found her perfect match.

Sinclair Jayne

Prologue

I T WAS HOT as hell. The sirocco had screamed for days, hurling sand everywhere including, uncomfortably, in his boxers. How was that even possible through the stiff fabric of his dress uniform? He'd been up for fifty-one hours on a mission and only through the mercy of God or fate—something well above his paygrade—had the winds stilled long enough for him to get back to base to participate in this mournful send-off.

Remington Cross, who hadn't been called Remy in over twenty years—only Cross—had less than an hour before he had to turn around and fly out again on another mission that might be his last. Maybe. He didn't usually prognosticate gloom and doom. Not that anyone would describe him as sunny side up, but since he'd enlisted at eighteen, determined to do something good with his life, he'd operated with the deep-seated belief that failure was never an option.

Twenty years he'd served. Fifteen of them in special forces. Twelve of them—off and on—with Jace McBride. And now what? The man who'd convinced him to put in his papers to retire along with the four others standing grim and silent, was finally going home to Marietta—in a box.

Cross gripped the handle on the side of the coffin. The material of the draped flag brushed his fingers, soft and vibrant in a world with so many hard beige edges. He kept his mind blank—Jace had taught him how to do that—fall back on training; don't think, just do; follow orders; complete the mission, no matter how many obstacles loom. He waited for the command of their new team leader—Wolf Conte, who made up their sixth. When it came, he lifted the precious cargo in time with his brothers. Shoulders back, spine ranch-fence-post rigid, face as stoic as theirs, the six men carried their former team leader, the man who had held them together through hell, into the cargo plane's belly.

This was not the first time he had carried the flag-draped coffin of a comrade to the hungry mouth of a homeward-bound plane. But it was the hardest.

Jace had been a much better man than Cross could ever be. And when Cross had been delayed on his last mission—his fault—Jace, though he was due to return home to his family in a couple weeks and off active rotation, took Cross's place.

I should be in the box.

The guilt clawed through him, burning his esophagus and blasting his skin more viciously than any sirocco. Jace had a family waiting for him. A failing ranch he intended to save. Dreams.

Cross had no one and nothing.

As five of them watched Jace's coffin be secured, Rohan

Telford ducked back into the hangar and then returned holding a small cooler.

"Jace would have done it for us," he said soberly, cracking open the cooler and pulling out Jace's favorite beer.

"Damn, cowboy, lost my best friend and now you're going to make us drink Moose Drool." Otis Miller always tried to keep things light when they rarely were. "I hate you."

Rohan handed out the beer one bottle at a time. There was one six-pack and, judging by the waft of cool mist that escaped, Rohan had used dry ice.

"I don't even want to think about who you had to screw to get that here," Cross said, feeling the rare need to say something—anything—because Jace had been a friend as much as a commanding officer and the only one he'd allowed in after a mission went sideways.

Cross had resisted the intrusion, embarrassed that Jace—a man he admired—thought it necessary. He could carry his own baggage and not bitch. But he hadn't taken Jace's 'head checks' personally. Jace had worried about each of his men.

"Got these for Jace," Rohan said his voice tight with the same emotion that all of them were trying to lock down.

In unison they popped off the bottle caps with their thumbs. Cross waited for the words. But no one spoke. No one took a drink. He hated this. Jace was not the first brother he'd lost on the battlefield. He'd stopped counting the men he'd protected, respected and lost. That path led to the abyss. And some days he didn't know why he still fought,

Jace had helped Cross resist falling forever into the shadows.

Would Jace be the last one of his brothers to fall?

Cross looked around the loose ring of men. They must all be thinking the same thing as they eyed each other, trying not to be obvious. Jace would have laughed at their awkwardness—trying to avoid eye contact while they stewed in their snarled silence.

Except Huck Jones. His head was bowed, but not—Cross thought—in prayer even though Huck out of all of them was the most religious. He'd often led the prayers before a mission. Even Cross, who didn't believe in anything except the men standing here, had dutifully bowed his head and let the beautiful words in Huck's rich bass roll over him.

He put his hand on Huck's slumped shoulder and felt the tremble. Regret that he never had the right words washed through him. Jace would have known what to say, how to help Huck let go of something he'd had no control over, but that would haunt him for the rest of his days if he couldn't find a release valve.

Like you've let anything go.

Guilt was a harpy, who flew in, kicked you to the ground, shouted at you to get up even as her talons drove through your flesh pinning you to the hard dirt before she'd eat your dinner. Huck had been with Jace when he'd been hit. Huck was the most skilled with battle injuries, but even he had ultimately been unable to stop the bleeding, though he had helped keep the enemy off the rest of the team until help arrived. Too late.

"Fuck it," burst out of Ryder Lea's mouth.

Cross jumped. Not like none of them cursed. They did, but much less than other teams. It was the cowboy code—a holdover from their days growing up ranch in scattered rural towns across the American west. It was one of the things that had led to the team's nickname—Coyote Cowboys. The moniker had started as an insult, but they'd owned it—even designed a crest that they'd tatted over their hearts.

They'd all been cowboys, who talked about returning to the land, although only Rohan and Jace had had family ranches to return to. Cross didn't know about Wolf. He was from Texas and shut down questions faster than Cross.

Ryder losing control of his mouth should have broken the tension. But all of them were now so steeped in this blackest of moments, and Jace who'd always guided them back from the brink no longer could.

Hit with a rare need, Cross slightly lifted his bottle as they all watched the conveyer belt roll Jace farther into the cargo hold. "Jace. He led an exemplary life in the light, and we need to honor his memory by staying out of the shadows."

"Jace." They all clinked bottles and took a deep swallow.

Damn. That was cold and delicious. And he'd never liked beer.

The plane's cargo door shut and, as one, they stepped back closer to the hangar so they didn't get blasted by the engines as the plane taxied toward the runway.

They had only minutes before they too would have to get back to work. The mission hadn't ended just because a good man, the best man, had fallen.

Cross sipped his beer and watched the plane pause, lined up with the runway. It was a long, long way to Montana with a lot of stops, and though they'd all put in a request for leave to accompany Jace's body home, they'd all been denied.

Cross wondered what he was going to do now. Montana held nothing for him anymore. He'd only put his papers in to retire because Jace had been pushing him for more than a couple of years. Jace had wanted them to muster out as soon as they all could—within the next year as that's when they would have the option to resign or re-enlist. Jace had pitched Marietta as if it were the magical land of Oz where they could all be washed clean—pool their resources, buy land, start businesses and build new lives. Jace wanted them all to start over. Together. Find peace. Build families. Craft a life with purpose.

Cross felt a cold, dark shadow waft through him. Without Jace, there was no plan. No 'together.'

"We can be anyone we want in Montana," Jace had stated more than once as if it were gospel. But without Jace, the Montana dream was dead.

So now what? Did he try to withdraw his papers or muster out in another two months and a handful of days and go where? Do what? His unit, his brothers—they were all he knew. But did he deserve their trust and respect now? He'd missed his extraction point, and it had taken precious days to ghost out and work his connections to return to base. Two days late. And Jace was gone.

He should be the one in the box—of course his mind returned there. But maybe not. He was seven inches taller than Jace. Broader. Maybe the hits wouldn't have been lethal for him. But still, it should have been him.

The plane barreled down the runway. Slight lift and then faster acceleration as the runway ran out, wheels up.

As one, they raised their beers—Jace's favorite brand, favorite flavor though he'd loved them all, and had dreamed of starting a brewery—and why not? He'd certainly tried to brew and distill plenty of beverages both on deployments and on base—secretly, yet not so secret.

Moose Drool. Cross looked at the label. A moose standing upright, skiing.

"He wanted us all to go skiing our first winter out," Cross remembered, a little surprised to hear himself speak—again. Some kind of record.

"He wanted us to do a lot of things," Wolf said. "Jace was full of big plans, and they were always in Marietta. He made that tiny town sound like Main Street in Disneyland."

It was like that in a lot of ways. But Cross hadn't confided in Jace that as a child he'd lived in Marietta, because then Jace would have wanted to know why he'd left, and Cross did his best to forget his past.

The plane had taken off and was fading into the hazy air and fuzz of heat, looking more like a mirage than a plane carrying precious cargo.

"Jace made going back home sound so easy." Rohan's lip curled.

"Don't you got a ranch to get back to in Marietta?" Otis asked, his freshly shaved angular jaw pale compared to his deeply tanned face.

Rohan, looking unusually kempt—his sandy-blond hair freshly cut and slicked back—said nothing, just wiped his mouth with his forearm, and pocked the bottle. His vivid green gaze never stopped tracking the progress of the plane.

"Maybe we can build a future in Marietta," Ryder Lea said. His thick dark hair was, for once, combed. "The Montana summers could warm our souls."

"Yeah and the winters will freeze our balls," Rohan said.

No one laughed. The silence felt toxic, choking off Cross's air.

"He made Montana sound like salvation." Otis stared at the empty, shimmering sky. "Like we'd pool our resources and start a church."

"We do got Cross," Ryder said casually. "Churches don't get taxed."

"We'd get smited walking into a church. I'm thinking cult." Wolf Conte laughed grimly.

"Amen." Cross finished his beer and stared at the bottle, not sure what to do next.

"Jace said something," Huck finally spoke, his voice a tortured whisper.

The air around them went electric. Huck stared mutely at Wolf.

"Jace had a list," Wolf said, his voice going leader on them. "Things he needed to do."

Chapter One

ANYONE WHO PREDICTED Cross would be in an Irish-themed hotel bar on a Friday night in Marietta, Montana, would have been hostilely dismissed as a liar. But here he stood. A few days out from his exit interviews. Three days on his Harley driving west like Marietta had a homing beacon trained on him. Weirder still, the bar and the hotel had been conspicuously renovated and remodeled—upscale and historically accurate to his untrained eye.

The Graff Hotel had been a fenced-off, boarded-up eyesore when he'd lived in Marietta. The roof leaked, the walls wept water and black mold, the windows sagged, jagged with broken glass. The once grand building had become a dark, broken hulk taunting residents about better days during the brief copper boom, the arrival of the railroad and then finally ranching. The only sway the hotel held when he'd been a kid was over the imaginations of residents. Ghost stories had been swapped during school lunches. Dares had been issued by teens on weekend nights.

Now the Graff boasted suites and single rooms, each one individually and historically decorated to showcase the glamour of a long-ago era. Globe sconces glowed golden throughout the lobby and antique-looking mirrors reflected elegance and history. It was a world Cross doubted had existed as it was portrayed. Still, he felt the pull of nostalgia and resented it.

Marietta wasn't Disneyland. And he wasn't on a movie set.

None of the Graff seemed real including the long, highly polished dark wood bar that had a plaque detailing how it had been shipped over from an Irish pub that had closed its doors after four hundred years.

People like him didn't belong in a place like this.

Why the hell was he here?

Dumb? Insane? Dangerously curious? Take a pick.

Coming into the hotel bar had nothing to do with honoring Jace's memory, and it sure as hell had nothing to do with his vow to his brothers when they'd each pulled a task to complete out of Jace's damaged helmet.

Coming to the Graff felt all wrong. A waste of time and he was verging into stalker territory. A grim smile ghosted his lips. Stalking was his brand. Cross had stalked targets across the globe, and he'd been in high demand. But he still didn't trust the side hustle he'd been handed. He'd been heading to Marietta when he'd been summoned, and wanting Jace's death to have some meaning, he'd answered the call, but now he wasn't sure what he wanted to do.

Shane Knight had been absurdly easy to find. And working and living in Marietta—where he'd been heading. Cross wasn't a believer in coincidences. But twenty-five thousand dollars had been dangled by a former army major Cross had rescued, if Cross could return an expensive heirloom watch. Cross didn't care about the money, but Jace's friend, Alex Holt, whom Cross was in Marietta to meet, would likely appreciate the extra cash since he was a single dad.

Remy still wasn't convinced this errand wasn't one last middle finger of manipulation by a master, who'd already created havoc in Cross's life. So here he was, curious. Stalking.

"Can I buy you a drink?"

Cross dragged his attention away from his sour musings back to the dark wood, green leather booth seats and soft golden lights welcoming him to the pub if he'd take one more step inside. A breathless blonde wearing a tight pink T-shirt proclaiming her to be the maid of honor was hitting on him.

"No." He made no effort to soften the rejection.

Her mouth dropped open and her eyes rounded. Had no man turned her down before? Jace would have flirted. Cross didn't know how and didn't care to learn. His life had been geared toward survival from a young age.

He was in Marietta to complete a mission for Jace. And maybe one for the former major he'd rescued like an idiotic hero in an action movie, from a cartel prison. Then he'd ride out of Marietta for good a free man. No expectations. No responsibility.

No direction.

"Why not?" she demanded.

"Drink's not on my list." He scanned the bar one last time, wondering if perhaps the bartender he was looking for was on a break.

"Who has a list in a bar?" she demanded.

"Me."

Was he blowing it again? Allowing himself to be distracted? The last time he'd deviated from his primary mission, it had set off a cascade of disaster, resulting in Jace's death. If he could go back in time, he'd stab his own eardrums instead of listen to the former major's hoarse siren's whisper about needing to survive for true love, needing to get home to a woman who shone like the sun and whose eyes were as turquoise as the Adriatic Sea.

Cross had seen the Adriatic. No woman in the world had eyes like that. He'd been a fool, and now Jace was dead, and Cross was wasting time in a hotel bar when he could break in and steal the watch whenever he wanted—or not. He was still on the fence. He didn't need to be wasting time looking for Shane Knight. He needed to find a place to camp and then search out Jace's friend, Alex Holt, tomorrow. Tell him that he would serve as his kids' godfather in Jace's stead and give him his contact info and then blow out of town.

Cross had little doubt that Alex—seeing his six-four, two-thirty of hard-packed muscle, harder, expressionless face, and scared, tatted skin would say 'thanks no thanks.'

Coward.

Jace wouldn't run. He'd commit. Persuade. Stay. Damn Jace and his big heart for dying.

No. Damn him for kicking off the whole disastrous chain of events by briefly going rogue because apparently, he had a previously unsuspected sappy, romantic streak that had reared its ugly head at the worst possible moment. If it weren't so tragic, he could have told his brothers, and they all could have laughed their asses off—with Jace—while drinking his latest beer concoction.

But there would be no more beer brewed by Jace. No more team laughs. Cross had deviated from a mission for the first time in twenty years, and Jace had returned home in a box. And now each of the Coyote Cowboys had a year to complete a task from Jace's homecoming list because he couldn't. At the end of the year, they would meet again in Marietta to have a proper memorial for Jace and then...? Cross didn't know. Would any of them stay in the small, impossibly cute Montana town in the aptly named Paradise Valley?

He knew without Jace he wouldn't. Too many ghosts.

"Are you just totally rude or maybe on the autistic spectrum?"

Was the bridesmaid still here and talking? Why? Cross looked down—way down—at the diminutive but pushy bridesmaid, who was weaving on her dainty, high-heeled feet.

"Or are you gay?" She thrust her chest closer so that her very pert breasts in an overachieving push-up bra brushed his abs.

"Those are my choices?" He felt a whisper of regret that he felt nothing looking at her. No arousal. Not even irritation. It was like he'd died alongside Jace.

"You're in a bar alone on a Friday. And you're like smokin' hot." The bridesmaid held up her hand and ticked off the points. One. Two, and now a third finger. "My bestie is getting married next weekend, and I'd love a plus-one for her wedding, but if you're only passing through, I'll settle for a cowboy to ride tonight."

He'd been gone from the States for a long time. Was it really this easy to hook up?

"Find another horse." He spun around to leave, but the bridesmaid grabbed his belt and dug in her stilettos.

"I want a cowboy." She jutted her chin forward.

Did she think she could Amazon-Prime a cowboy straight from the bar to her bed? He didn't have the time or inclination.

"I haven't been a cowboy for a lotta years, ma'am," he said, watching her chocolate-brown eyes narrow and spark.

"Don't ma'am, me," she said. "I'm only twenty-five."

His heart crunched. So young. So sad. About five years younger than his sister would have been had he not failed her.

"Ma'am." If he had a hat, he'd tip it, just like he'd seen

Sam Wilder of the Wild Wind Ranch do a thousand times when he'd been growing up, until fate had slapped him stupid and spun his life thread into something unrecognizable when he'd been twelve.

"Jerk." She kicked his shin and stamped on his foot. He barely felt any of it as he still wore his motorcycle chaps and steel-toed boots from his ride. She huffed and stomped off, and Cross took one last look at the bar. What he'd expected to find here, even if Shane Knight had been working, he wasn't sure. It's not like she would wear a six-figure stolen watch to work in a bar. She could have sold it, but he was damn good on a computer and hadn't been able to find any records of private sales of the watch he was maybe looking for.

His lack of commitment should concern him. Waffling got you killed fast.

While he mused his next step, realizing he was actually hungry and the smell of food was a tempting lure, a door he hadn't noticed swung open and another bartender, crate of whiskey resting on her hip, glided behind the bar. Her long, white-blonde hair glinted in the lights and, for Cross, the rest of the bar and the people in it disappeared. What was happening? Was Shane Knight the former major's true love?

'I love a woman, a woman with a smile brighter than the sun. Her eyes are a crystalline aquamarine...' Cross nearly clapped his hands over his ears so he didn't hear that seductive whispering voice ever again. He could repeat the tale the

prisoner had woven verbatim. He still had nightmares. But what was the major's 'true love' doing in poky Marietta? She was supposed to be getting married next month. She was supposed to be expecting her and the former major's first son.

'True love,' the prisoner had said. He had to live for his true love. Make it home for his true love and their child. How had Cross been even dumber than he'd imagined?

"True love my ass."

He hadn't realized until this moment how scaldingly stupid he'd been, how he'd been utterly ensnared in a make-believe drama. He'd desperately wanted Jace's death to have meaning. But he'd been tasked with returning an heirloom from the woman that the major had vowed to love forever. So, who was the major marrying in a few months?

True love was a lie. It didn't exist. He'd known that, and yet some dumb, childish part of him must have wanted to believe. True love couldn't be in Marietta while her lying lover lived in his family's legacy plantation-style horror of a mansion in Charleston.

Cross shifted position so that he was in a more shadowed area of the bar. It was a warm, welcoming room, decorated to set a mood, not to hide in, but Cross had made a career out of hiding in plain sight. He watched Shane Knight smile and chat and all the while he tried to make this situation make sense. When Cross had mustered out, former Major Brandon Montgomery Huntingdon III had contracted him.

He wanted to thank him for his service and thank him for saving his life, especially as Cross had kept his mouth shut about the rescue. The Third was not supposed to have been in that country, much less captured. Cross had arranged his care and his trip home.

He'd not expected to see him again, but curiosity had bested him again. The former major had offered him a job as a bodyguard plus. Cross was pretty clear what the plus meant—errand boy to do all the dirty work. A fixer. Rich men liked to pretend their hands were clean. The salary offer had blown his mind. He'd even been offered health insurance and 401K options. WTF?

Cross would rather snip one of his nuts off than be a lapdog digging around in the criminal world for an entitled man, no matter how much money was dangled. His mother had done her best to raise him right. And Sam Wilder had been an exacting man. Hard. But honest.

It was embarrassing to admit to himself he'd felt invested in the woman who shone like the sun's happiness. He'd thought the major was a tool, but he'd wanted the woman to have her man, her comfortable life being adored and her child a father, a family and a legacy.

But now he realized what his naïve hope that true love existed had cost. Jace had lost his life. His family would never have him home. The brothers had lost their best friend. All the people on Jace's list were never going to be able to look him in the eye and forgive him or welcome him back into their lives. His sacrifices had meant nothing. True love. Cross wanted to smack his fist in the major's smug face.

So what should he do now?

Cross's agile brain kicked up one plan after the other, but he still felt hollowed from the shock of seeing the woman who'd taken root in his imagination even when he tried to rip her out. The sun had become an impossible-to-acquire ideal—beauty, kindness, loyalty, love. And now the dream had morphed into a nightmare of another life wasted. Just like his mother's and his sister's.

Had the former major played him for a sucker? Possibly. Was the sun a deceptive thief? Maybe. Was someone or something operating behind the scenes orchestrating the "coincidence" that Cross would have two tasks he needed to carry out in Marietta before he went off-grid?

Cross and his team had made many enemies around the world, but they were beyond top secret. All of them were ghosts. Coincidences raised his suspicions, and his instincts blared. His brothers were all going to be arriving in Marietta over the next six months or more. Cross needed to ensure they'd all be safe when they arrived.

He watched the sun shine behind the bar, mixing different cocktails, chatting with the staff and customers seated at the bar. She seemed to know everyone, charming them all, and Cross was forced to accept that this detour had not been wasted. It was another lesson. He would not be escaping Marietta as quickly as he'd planned.

SHANE KNIGHT POURED out the six cosmos and added alternating fresh raspberries, blueberries and a slice of a peach to each penis-shaped toothpick that the maid of honor had proudly provided. Shane had tended bar for several years of college and grad school. She'd thought she'd left her shaker and encyclopedic knowledge of alcohol behind when she'd entered her profession as a therapist, but after she'd flamed out at twenty-eight, she'd picked herself up, driven west and returned to the psychological safety and creativity she'd always found behind the bar.

She'd thought she'd seen it all. It wasn't that the penis toothpicks were particularly shocking, but they'd better fit the vibe of Grey's Saloon though she was confident though that there weren't many women who'd be brave enough to hand owner Jason Grey a pink box of penis-shaped tooth-picks to use for cosmo garnishes.

"Apparently I am not intimidating," she muttered, traying the drinks to carry over to the table, since both servers were busy.

Shane handed out the drinks, covertly checking the bridesmaids' level of intoxication. She knew they were staying in the hotel, but in case they had plans of driving anywhere tonight, she'd warned the valet, Joseph, to check in with her before handing over any keys.

"Do you want to play a game with us?" asked a petite,

busty blonde with sparkling brown eyes, who'd returned after striking out with some mountain of a man, who'd stood stoically in the shadows just inside the bar's entrance.

"Yes, play," the bride-to-be sang out. "You must have a lot of experience with men." The women cheered and toasted with their cocktails. "The game is about how to find your soul mate. It's a party game, but it's based on science. The game maker has a PhD in psychology and a podcast."

"Compelling." Shane smiled, bored already. She didn't play games—especially at work and definitely never relationship games using artistic tarot-looking cards. The women had been drawing cards for a while and had seemed highly engaged and amused, even the bride who one would assume had already found her soul mate.

"I was going to suggest some food," Shane encouraged. "Ranch-spiced cauliflower? Rodeo tater tots? Cowboy nachos?" The appetizers weren't normally called that, but the rodeo was less than a month away, and since Marietta relied increasingly on tourism, the chamber of commerce and downtown associations teamed up early and hit the promotions hard.

"Nachos with the cowboy," the bride shrieked.

"And the rodeo tater tots with a side of cowboy," the busty blonde maid of honor fist-bumped the bride, who giggled as if her bestie had said something hysterical.

The maid of honor didn't seem too discouraged by her shutdown earlier, but her eyes continued to stray to the entrance of the bar as if looking for the man. Shane blinked. It looked as if he'd melted into the gleaming dark paneling at the entrance. Her curiosity spiked. Hard for a man that large to disappear.

Nope. She shut her curiosity down harder than the maid of honor had been earlier.

"Maybe we should get all three," the bride said. "We need our veggies."

Everyone laughed and they all toasted. Then the bride stood. "I'm going to see if Mr. Tall, Dark, Handsome and Broody will join us."

For a moment, she wobbled but took a fortifying sip of her cosmo. Shane made a note to fast-track the food and push sparkling water. She'd even impale more fruit on the penis toothpicks and jam them in the bubbling water.

The maid of honor also stood, clutching the bride's arm. "We'll double-team him. He won't say no to me twice."

"Appies coming up," Shane said, turning away, not wanting to see the poor girl get shut down twice by the same man. His body language screamed 'move on.'

Riley Telford, a local cowgirl, who'd tried her luck in an LA band and had slunk home a couple of years ago, returned from her break, picked up her guitar, plugged it back into her amp, and sat down on the stool Shane had placed for her.

"Another water with honey and ginger?" Shane switched directions to ask. "Or are you ready for me to start brewing tea?"

Riley paused, tuning her guitar. "Water, but tea at the end of this set."

"You got it."

"Thanks, Shane. You going to ride rescue for the lost hottie?" Riley indicated the man who was leaning against the wall, not even looking at the two women talking to him.

Shane's mouth dried. He was looking at her. And how.

"He doesn't need rescuing," she stated. Shane's father, a former LA fire marshal, had taught her to read a man and a room by puberty. "The only rescues I stage now are when I foster dogs for Whiskers and Paws."

"He's gorgeous and looks like all kinds of bad news." Riley's slightly husky voice, which was so compelling when she sang, ached with longing.

"Don't do it," Shane advised. And then she made the mistake of looking back in his direction.

His charcoal stare was fixed on her, and she felt as if he could touch her soul, but instead of feeling threatened, she was intrigued. Who was he? Why was he here? But her days of reaching out or offering rescue were so far in her past she didn't want to remember them. If only she could time-travel and return to slap some sense into her silly, arrogant, early twenties heart.

"He looks like an Aztec god," Riley murmured. "Did the Aztecs have gods?"

If she'd been an Aztec, Shane would definitely have worshiped him. His face was angular, bony and had an uncertain ethnicity that intrigued her. Everything about him looked hard. Wide, flat forehead with a widow's peak of dark silky hair that fell to his shoulders. High cheekbones with deep hollows. An angular jaw that thrust out. And his nose looked like it belonged on a coin or a cathedral wall.

And then there was his body. Broad shoulders. Black T-shirt stretched across his chest, narrow waist and…

Don't look down.

She felt dizzy already.

"See," Riley whispered, amusement in her voice.

"Too well," Shane tried to joke even though the blood in her brain had migrated south. Even her vision fuzzed. God. It was like he was a homing beacon of testosterone tempting her with reminders of how long it had been.

"Told you," Riley whispered.

"Eh." Shane shrugged a shoulder in the biggest lie of her life. She was not in the market for a man, but if she was, he looked like a neon billboard sign advertising a decadent, sinful night of hot, slightly edgy sex. His whole vibe was fast and dirty and out the door before the sheets cooled.

She could be in the market for that since she was no longer looking for forever—love, marriage, baby in a baby carriage.

But a one-night stand? What would that even be like?

The bride-to-be and her sidekick had struck out again.

So he wasn't here for short, busty, slightly buzzed and

easy.

I'm none of those things.

"In or out?" Riley asked.

"Out." Shane pulled back from the brink. What the hell was she thinking? That man might scream temporary and a very good time, but he also screamed volcanic explosion—definitely not a starter stud for a one-night stand. But maybe next month she should give one of the cowboys coming in for the Copper Mountain Rodeo a shot.

"You can extend your break and whisper sweet nothings," Shane suggested dragging her attention away from him, with a rather heroic effort. But now she could feel his dark gaze drilling twin holes in her ass as she walked back to the bar.

Riley followed her. "So out of my league," Riley said.

"You perform in front of audiences," Shane reminded her.

"So do you."

Her few and far between jazz jams and gig fill-ins were continents away from what Riley had done, and still did.

"Is it a competition?" she asked as she prepared Riley's water. "Start a song. That will grab his attention," Shane advised.

She should go jump in an ice bath.

"No thanks." Riley shook her head, making her red-gold curls dance. "My taste in men sucks sour lemons full of seeds."

"That's quite the sensory description." Shane laughed, even though the spell the man seemed to have cast over her body made every nerve hum in excitement—even her nipples chafed against her lacy A-cup, mostly unnecessary bra.

She got another drink order, and as she moved to make it, she'd be lying if she didn't put an extra swish in her hips. She didn't mean to. Her hormones were just objecting to her brain's decision to not cast her line. She'd never been so aware of her body, the way the air felt on her skin. Even her useless womb clenched in hot excitement.

He needed to leave her bar. He shouldn't be here. He might be casually posed, but Shane wasn't fooled. That man had seen Life with a capital L. He pulsed a similar vibe to Colt Wilder even though he was several years out of the Rangers.

"Cop?" Riley speculated. "County sheriff department?"

Shane poured her some still mineral water and added some ginger and a splash of cinnamon tea and drizzled honey on top. She handed the glass to Riley. "Military. Special Teams. On leave or recently out," Shane called it. She knew that look, and beat of her heart wanted to help him, while every brain cell urged her to keep her distance. And her stupid body whimpered 'welcome home.'

She held his gaze. This was her bar. Her people. Her domain.

"Oh." Riley's voice eased. "Maybe a friend of Colt's."

"Maybe," Shane agreed.

It was possible, but since Colt was not here—not that she'd ever seen him come into the bar or hotel lobby without at least one of his brothers or his wife—she felt there was another reason for the soldier's presence.

Riley took a sip of the water. "Wolf Den seems more his vibe."

"Definitely," Shane agreed. He could find trouble in the dive bar if he was looking for it. "Play one of your new songs," Shane urged, wanting Riley to act naturally, but also to encourage her. Since Riley's return from LA, she'd had a hard time regaining her confidence. She'd holed up at her family's ranch for months. Lost a ton of weight and her sparkle before she'd started working with horses againand then finally, with Shane's and her family's encouragement, she'd picked up her guitar and started composing and occasionally singing at the Graff and sometimes FlintWorks.

Shane deliberately strode over to the table directly in the path of the man. Yup. He tracked her movements, whereas he hadn't given the bride or the bridesmaid a single look.

"I'm not a gazelle on the savannah," she stated as she breezed past him to let him know she'd noted his attention and wasn't intimidated by it.

She checked on a table that she knew didn't yet need anything. But when she stepped back to return to the bar, her body hit a hard wall. Him. She knew without looking. Her heart jerked in alarm. She hadn't felt his approach. Somehow, he'd contained his energy, even though Shane had highly honed instincts. She'd had to with her job as a psychologist with the army. And her father, an alpha male of alpha males, had made sure all five of his daughters knew how to read every situation for danger and how to fight dirty, incapacitate and escape if they ever had to.

Every nerve in her body tensed, but it took only a second for her to realize that she felt no threat. However, she was experiencing sexual heat. Hers. She was six feet in her cowboy boots, and he was taller. She felt the most male part of him below the small of her back. He was long and thick and fully erect. The thrill that coursed through her was hot and carnal. Yes, please.

No.

"If a gazelle is not your spirit animal," he murmured in her ear. "What is?"

His voice was low, more of a sleepy growl that tingled her cheek, and slid like heated molasses down her spine.

"Not that stupid game." She looked at him over her shoulder and sucked in a shocked breath. He was beautiful. Rough. But so masculine. "The maid of honor finally lassoed you in?" she teased.

"Never. I prefer a challenge."

"Really." Her lips twitched at his flirt. She turned away to head back to the bar and the illusion of safety.

"Impala? Roan antelope? Ostrich?"

Ostrich? Shane spun around to face him holding her now empty tray against her chest.

Mistake.

She looked most men in the eye. Not this one. And she couldn't read him at all. Nothing in his charcoal-gray eyes but cool distance.

"Ostrich?" she repeated, both outraged and amused by his suggestion. "This is your stab at charm?"

"Swing and a miss?" He didn't look like he cared.

What was he doing here? Professional interest stirred, and she mentally slapped it back down. Nope. Nada. Never. She'd burned her therapist shingle.

"I'm not wrong, Shane. You are running from something."

She stifled her jolt. A man like this would feed on it. So, he knew her name. There could be innocent reasons for that, but this man was far from innocent. She stuck out one black cowboy boot with golden sunflowers on them.

"You are speaking metaphorically since I'm not wearing my running shoes," she stated.

He didn't answer or change expression, as if his silence could coax a reaction.

"Order a drink or get out. The Wolf Den's more your vibe."

She strode back to her bar. She was the boss. Her boots clicked on the polished hardwood floors that Graff owner Cormac Sheenan's crew had stripped and smoothed and refinished to a gorgeous shine a handful of years ago when he'd purchased the dilapidated hotel and refurbished it. The

Graff was on travel destination top-ten lists, and Shane was proud that the bar also topped many top-ten lists for innovative cocktails and interactive cocktail-making classes. Since she'd started bartending several years ago, bar business had quadrupled.

The man would not throw her off her game. She didn't want him to think he'd gotten to her—so again, she put an extra cowgirl swish to her hips. Not to flirt. *Liar.* Because if she were going to flirt with a man, he would be the one she chose. He had complicated and secretive and hard-edged engraved into his bones. And she wanted everything he had—just for tonight.

She expected him to follow her. Push the spirit animal theme.

He didn't. Instead he leaned against a column and watched her without looking like he was watching her. And the energy he exuded was crazy quiet. How did a man like that fade into the background? He had to be six four minimum. And the way the black leather motorcycle pants hugged his body and framed his package shouted sinful and should be outlawed in all fifty states. His shoulders were massive slabs of granite that she wanted to grip while she rode him and forgot about everything for a while.

She really needed to stop lusting. Poor Lachlan continued to make drinks while she was practically drooling.

Riley began to sing a Bonnie Raitt song, and Shane drew in a deep breath to reset.

"Hey how's my bridal party?" Walker Wilder, the special events coordinator, entered the bar, business suit still looking neatly pressed. Her hair was up in a smooth chignon, and her second pregnancy had yet to show on her trim, but curvy figure. As always, Walker held her tablet in her hand, looking like she was about to delegate a list of tasks.

"They're good," Shane said. "Happy with their drinks and penis garnishes and their appetizers are next up."

"I'm trying to ignore the penises," Walker said. "Tell me they aren't drunk."

"I'm monitoring."

"I know," Walker said. "I'm just wanting this weekend to be perfect. It's the first wedding we're hosting at the Wilder ranch, and Langston and I have crammed in a lot of activities this week—I don't want a hungover bridal party. Laird is doing a whiskey tasting and cigar bar tonight with the men in some man cave he designed under his tasting room. We have an early morning hike and goat yoga at Talon and Colt's—I kid you not—so I made him promise to behave," Walker said about her cousin.

"Nice pun." Shane bleated softly. "It's all going to go swimmingly," she promised, seeing the alarm flare on Walker's classically beautiful features.

"It will." Walker smiled. "I have a great family and a great team. But I'm still me—a type A control freak. Fully owning it. We have hired a professional photographer to film the bridal events, and Langston and I went all out planning the events so that we have plenty of ammo for the Graff and Wilder websites, brochures and online adds and also for the chamber of commerce. With the economy and post-pandemic world we have to think outside the box to keep Marietta on the map and compete for tourist dollars. Not just ranching anymore." Walker practically sang the last sentence.

"I'll be sure to make T-shirts."

Walker typed something on her tablet and then checked in with the bridal party, who cajoled her to also join their game. Walker skillfully dodged and waved good night to Shane.

Shane wondered what she would have planned for her own bridal party. She hadn't been allowed to get that far, but she didn't think a party game or goat yoga would have made the cut. She was so lost in the past for a moment that when she looked up and saw the man seated directly in front of her, she nearly dropped the shaker with the ingredients for two dirty martinis.

"Ready to order that drink." He sounded as enthused as if he were showing up for a colonoscopy.

"What can I get you?" She used her driest, most professional voice, the one she reserved for customers she suspected were contemplating behavior that wouldn't fly in her bar.

"Surprise me."

"That's a wide-open door."

A ghost of a smile touched his lips, making her stomach

plunge. The charcoal of his eyes lightened to quicksilver for a moment, and she was so shocked that she couldn't quite catch her breath.

"Don't act so surprised. I'm sure men always leave the door kicked wide open for you," he said.

"I'm not looking for trouble," she warned, not sure how to take his last comment, but wanting him to know that she could handle him no matter what.

"First lie of the night," he noted.

"You think there'll be more?"

"Probably."

Shane tried to shut down her rush of excitement.

"I'm prepared. Just looking at you, Shane, promises a heap of trouble."

"You're confident you're prepared?"

"Trouble I can always handle."

"Sure about that?" She loosed the challenge in her voice.

"Always." His gaze didn't waver. "Your move, cowgirl. Make that drink."

Chapter Two

"WE PLAYING MENTAL chess?" She watched him, apparently assessing.

She was smart. Thinking the entire time, and he'd watched her assess the mood of the room and the people in it with a savant-like quality. True bartenders were socially gifted. Shane was so much more.

"I don't play games."

"I don't believe that."

"Good for you."

His admiration grew. It had nothing to do with her beauty, which was jaw-dropping. Her platinum-colored hair looked natural and was pulled back in a messy braid. Her creamy skin tone gave credence to the hair color. She was tall, almost a little too slim. Her features were small-town farm-girl beautiful, but her eyes elevated her beyond beautiful. They were an impossible color, similar to an aquamarine stone he'd seen in a jeweler's shop window in Iraq. She must be wearing colored contacts.

I have to live for a woman with eyes the color of the Adriatic...

The hated voice again mocking him for again veering off

mission. He'd seen the Adriatic in many lights—smooth as glass, turquoise or a fathomless blue green that was so beautiful it seemed alien. But he'd never once been able to let his guard down and swim in the sea, let its beauty wash over him, soothe him. And he couldn't do that now.

Though Shane was an incredibly beautiful woman, she didn't seem to be wearing much makeup—perhaps a swipe of mascara to darken her pale lashes. No lip gloss adorned her voluptuous, slightly pouty lips. She might glow as if lit by an ethereal light, but she was still just a woman. And a thief. And ballsy. Her eye contact remained direct and unwavering, almost too intense, which made him feel like she was hiding something more than the vintage Patek Philippe strapped face inward on her wrist.

Stolen goods in plain sight.

Challenge accepted.

The thought hit him like a bullet to his skull. The fascinating enigma of Shane Knight and her strength and unearthly beauty was not why he was in Marietta. Shame felt like he'd bathed in an oil slick. He didn't owe the former major any more than he'd already given him—the sacrifice of the best man Cross had ever known. But still, Brandon Montgomery Huntingdon III had wanted more—the heirloom watch should be passed from father to first son for his October wedding. And if not by then, before the birth of his child in March.

Cross knew he should get off the damn barstool and walk

out into the night.

Huntingdon could retrieve his own watch if he wanted. And that stopped Cross cold.

"I want the watch. It means the world to me. To my family. Use any means necessary to retrieve it," he'd said.

And then he'd dangled enough money that could help Alex Holt raise his child—set aside money for college or music lessons or whatever kids needed.

The former major had not only pointed Cross, once a top military asset, at a thief, but he pointed a honed and dangerous weapon at the woman the major had once professed undying love to.

Why?

Cross watched Shane move gracefully and deftly behind the bar, clearly skilled and at home as she made his drink. The glimpses he caught of the watch added to her mystery and, honestly, her allure. Why had she taken it? She didn't seem like a woman with any pretense. Why wear a six-figure watch to work but not show it off? None of it—her, the theft, the major's request—added up.

Cross knew he should walk away. Not his fight. If Shane had stolen a six-figure watch, she could deal with her own consequences. But with a sick feeling in his gut, he knew he couldn't leave her unwarned. The former major would send someone else.

"Interesting watch."

She didn't look at him. "A reminder."

"Of what?"

Shane ignored him and spooned ice into a copper cock-tail mixing glass. She deftly measured bourbon, sweet vermouth and Campari and poured them over ice with flair. She stirred the drink ten times clockwise and then ten times reversed, each movement quick and graceful. She strained the liquid into a squat, old-fashioned cocktail glass.

Cross looked around the room while he pondered her non-answer. Marietta was technically what he could consider his hometown though he hadn't been back in nearly twenty-five years. Would anyone recognize him? The thought curdled in his gut. He'd practically been invisible as a kid. No one had fought for him or his sister back then. No one would take an interest now. Besides, being invisible was second nature now.

"This is a full-mouth experience." Shane's voice was twinged with amusement as if she knew he'd been trying not to obsess about her.

And on cue, his fixated gaze swiveled back to her. She boldly held his regard while she peeled off a thick slice of orange peel, dipped it in something and then, holding the orange slice low over the drink, she stuck two cloves into the orange peel and dropped it into his drink and slid it across toward him.

"A touch of sweet and spicy and smoke, and the bourbon rounds it all out. First one's on the house, cowboy soldier."

He stifled his surprise and reached for the beverage, noting the bloodred color. It was beautiful, but one more reminder of his past. So much blood. Death.

"I'd call it fishing," he said.

He looked rough, dangerous. It was a hard thing to hide, and he didn't often try.

"No you'll call it a damn good drink."

He tilted the drink in her direction. "The drink have a name?"

Challenge and something else sparkled in her eyes, and her sexy mouth tilted in a smile that nearly knocked him off his chair. Whatever she'd made, she was far more potent.

"I'm still thinking on it. This is new, just for you."

He didn't often drink. He'd lived a dangerous life and needed control, but tonight he loosed his leash and held the drink to his lips and took a healthy sip.

The explosion of flavors was unexpected and more delicious than he'd anticipated.

"Surprise," she said and walked off to fill another order.

SHANE CLOSED OUT the bar and sent Lachlan home after they'd cleaned and restocked. It had been a good night for tips. The hotel was full—it often was, but when she'd started adding seasonal drink specials; bringing in local wineries, breweries and distilleries for tastings; and teaching cocktail classes and instituting game nights in the alcove near the gift store, the business had picked up.

A sense of pride filtered through her even though she knew her parents and sisters, try as they might, didn't understand how she could be happy working and now managing a bar, when she had worked so hard in college and grad school to become something else.

Sort of. Not really that different. A smile touched her lips as she looked at the gleaming bar in the soft lighting. Shane enjoyed the creative freedom she had at the Graff, the privacy she had from her lovingly nosy family and the beauty and space of Paradise Valley. The mountains and farmland and so much space and sky allowed her to breathe. Nature felt fierce and dominant, putting people in their place.

As if Mother Nature agreed, it was pouring—sheets of warm rain hurtling out of the sky in an end-of-summer display when Shane opened the door to leave through the hotel's garden. The rain bounced up from the pavers on the meandering path. She wondered about the soldier who'd left hours earlier after finishing his drink and leaving a crisp fifty-dollar note on the bar. He'd been wearing motorcycle leathers and boots—not conducive to rain or curving mountain roads.

"He doesn't need me worrying about him." Shane mocked her concern.

She stood in the doorway of the hotel, took off her watch, and placed it in her waterproof backpack, and after a moment of consideration, she shrugged out of her silky

Johnny Was boho style off-the-shoulder blouse that her sister Sutter had sent her for her birthday—all of her nice clothes were from Sutter or her documentary filmmaker and producer sister, Blue. She rolled up the blouse and added it to her backpack, leaving her in her thin, royal-blue tank.

Smiling, Shane stepped out into the night and was immediately soaked. She walked through the garden, taking a moment to savor the trellised area with the climbing roses and party lights. Often the garden would be set up for events in the summer—the hotel had stylish tents to protect against uncooperating weather, but tonight—since the wedding was booked at the Wilders' ranch—there were just the few tables tucked into various verdant nooks for guests to enjoy morning coffee or tea or afternoon wine or cocktails.

Shane pushed through the gate all but hidden behind a wall of ivy and wisteria and walked out onto Front Avenue. She tilted her head back to look at the midnight sky. The rain looked silver as it danced through the glow of the replica gas lights. She spread out her arms, palms up, and stuck out her tongue to catch the drops. The first chill shivered through her, a reminder that summers in Montana were short and autumn days could be warm, but the night temperatures would start to dip, preparing everyone for the long, bone-chilling winters.

Shane loved all the seasons. They marked time. Reminded her she was alive. She loved the traditions each season delivered, and she was quick to create new ones, with friends and colleagues.

She breathed in deeply, loving the smell of the wet asphalt mixed with the tang of the wet wood and leaves of the oak and aspen trees. She often walked to work except during the winter. She savored the movement and the silence of the streets as she walked home to the small house she'd recently purchased on Church Avenue. The walks helped to clear the work chatter from her brain. Marietta always felt safe, even tonight as she'd flirted with the hot but broody former soldier. She tried to push him out of her mind once again, sighing at the effort and her lack of discipline.

Deputy Logan Tate cruised by and paused. He rolled down his window. "Need a ride home, Shane?"

"Nah. I love the rain." She reluctantly drew her arms back to her sides and looked at Logan instead of the sky. She probably looked a little woo-woo to the upright officer of the law, but his photographer wife Charlie had definitely softened many of his hard edges as had fatherhood.

"Sure? You're soaked."

"I'm warm enough," she said, not wanting to give any of her neighbors any topics for gossip if Logan dropped her off on the quiet street. They already obsessed about her job, late hours, lack of a husband or kids. And since the probability of kids for her was one in some fantastically high number, she didn't see the purpose in a husband.

Maybe. She knew enough to never say never, but of all the magic she'd seen in childhood—the orange-red glow of a rising Strawberry Moon, the feel of the ocean waves under her surfboard during her teens in Southern California, the first green poking up from the wild flower seeds she'd planted, the way the light would catch the iridescence of the red head of an Anna's hummingbird as it drank nectar from a trumpet creeper vine—she couldn't believe that she'd be blessed with a child.

She didn't deserve to be blessed.

Logan waited, his chivalry and responsibility warring with her independence. Shane smiled and waved and then crossed to First Street. The deputy waved back and drove off. Humming one of the Adele songs Riley had sung tonight—'Turning Tables'—Shane hadn't even made it a block when she felt the hair rise on the back of her neck.

She spun around. It was him. He stood by a gleaming motorcycle under a gold light. Black bike. Black leathers.

"It fits your vibe to lurk in the shadows," she said, loosening her body, but rising a little onto her toes, arms free, even though she didn't feel a threat from him.

He noticed her change in stance. A smile tipped his lips, and the change in his face was breathtaking.

"Good move." His voice was smoke and gravel and her tummy hummed in hope. "You have some instincts of self-preservation. Not trying to hide tonight. Wanted to make sure you got home safe. It's after midnight. Should have taken the ride from the cop."

"How'd you know I didn't drive?"

He hesitated. She braced for the lie.

"There were only a few cars in the employee parking lot, but none that looked like one you'd drive."

"What do you think I'd drive?" she asked intrigued.

"Sporty but practical. You'd want something with storage because you look active. I'd say smaller SUV-type car. First guess a Jeep. You'd want a bright color judging from the shirt you had on earlier, but you'd tell yourself you should be practical so I'm thinking a brighter blue. But the cowboy boots could mean smaller truck."

Surprise tinged with admiration filtered through Shane. She loved private guessing games about people. She was already racking up impressions about him.

"Not bad. I wanted the orange Gladiator, but I need a top for cargo so I went for a Jeep since I play upright bass and gig a bit and can't transport it if it's raining. I went with Hydro Blue."

This time the smile lit his eyes so that they looked silver. God, he was beautiful in a hard and rough masculine way. And haunted though he wouldn't admit it.

Not your job anymore.

"Your bike's sweet, but not any more practical than me walking in the rain."

"I have skills."

"So do I," she said softly, enjoying their byplay and vain enough to enjoy the fact that while all the other women in the bar had struck out tonight, he wanted to walk her home.

But he'd known her name, so she couldn't get too comfortable.

"Head home. I'll follow at a discreet distance."

"Like a dad?" she teased.

He jerked a little before he covered it. "Don't know," he admitted, his voice a little rougher now. "I never had one."

Why had he told her that? Suspicion edged out curiosity again.

"I had a great one. Still do. The best. And he wouldn't want me leading a stranger to my home."

"I'm not wild about the idea either," he said, surprising her. "Here," he offered and wheeled his bike slowly toward her. He held out his ID. "Take a picture of my license and the license plate on my bike. Text it to a friend, and I'll follow you to your street—won't look at which apartment or house is yours."

"Why?"

"Because I had a great mom and she taught me how to do the right thing." His gaze shuttered. "Didn't always do it after I lost her, but I got back on the right path at eighteen when I enlisted in the army."

She felt his energy dip. He'd lost his mom young, it sounded like. And he'd never had a dad. Shane was lucky. She still had both of her parents and four sisters.

But I won't move back home.

For a moment guilt pressed on her chest, tangled the air in her throat. She'd always been so tight with her family, had always been in the middle of everything, but she was too different now to go back.

Shane glanced briefly at the license—Washington State. Yup. That's where the special forces base was. For a moment she didn't want to look at his name. Keeping him anonymous made their little back-and-forth more exciting. She liked the way he looked at her—like she confused him, and he was hungry.

I'm starving.

But her dad had trained her too well. Her gaze lit on his name. She tilted her head, indicating he could follow.

Would he truly walk behind her like some chivalrous knight from a long-ago era?

"I've never seen a woman walk in the rain like you," he said, closer now. The gravel in his voice raised the goose bumps on her skin that had nothing to do with the rain.

She turned around, walking backward so she could watch him. "I love the rain. I love the snow. I feel like it washes me clean."

He didn't respond, and her gaze lit on his mouth— sensuous for such a hard man. The fire in her core flared hotter in interest.

"You don't seem much bothered by the rain either."

"The weather stopped bothering me a long time ago. Part of the experience."

"You on leave or out for good?"

"Doesn't feel good yet," his voice rumbled after a long

pause.

Shane's heart pinched.

Don't do it. Don't do it. Don't do it.

"Adjustment to civvy life can be hard." Shane to the rescue, her never quite dormant counselor persona bossed forward, the assertive do-gooder she couldn't exorcise. "Is Colt Wilder why you are in Marietta? You served with him?" She knew Colt. Well, knew his family. One of his sisters-in-law was her bestie, and his wife volunteered her vet services at the shelter where Shane volunteered.

"Colt Wilder," he echoed, stopping.

"If we're going to talk and walk, we might as well do it together," Shane said, practically. She didn't want to raise her voice in her sleeping neighborhood.

"It's late. I want you to feel safe." His expression was stubborn. Of course it was.

That was it. She did feel safe. And she shouldn't, but she'd always trusted her instincts—too much so. Temptation had stopped whispering and nudging. It now yelled and kicked.

A sexual connection with a man had been off the table for so long. One-night stands in a small town could be fraught with social complications—the men wanting her number, wanting more. So she'd kept herself aloof, but even though her body had betrayed her, she couldn't quite turn it off the way she wanted. But this man shouted one booted foot already out the door, keys jingling, cell phone already tucked in his pocket, back turned, gaze on the open road.

Should I?

"Why did you think I would come to town for someone named Colt Wilder?" There was reluctant curiosity in his voice.

"You're not local. Lewis-McChord is a joint base for Army Rangers and Green Berets. Colt was a Ranger who left the service a handful of years ago to move home to Marietta, and he and a few locals help vets settle in, find jobs, receive services if they need them."

And she'd said no to helping his program over and over. But Colt, typical special forces soldier, never gave up. He just came at her a different way.

"Don't know him."

"Typical badass. Keep it tight," she teased. "Name and rank only."

"I knew a kid named Colt long time ago in Marietta's elementary school. He was a few years younger. He joined the Rangers. We ran a few missions, but he wasn't Colt Wilder."

"Oh, duh." Shane laughed, nearly slapping her head. "That's right. He discovered his birth mother a few years ago. And he has a twin and two half-brothers. He took the family name when he married and adopted his wife's son, Parker. He's Colt Wilder now."

"You seem to know a lot of people in town." His voice held a slight edge of speculation, and Shane's radar zinged.

She turned around at the entrance to her street, stood in the middle, hands on her hips, like she could block him from going further.

"Cut to the chase, Remington Cross. Who are you looking for and why?"

Chapter Three

"HOW DO YOU know I'm not looking for a what?" he dodged.

By her unimpressed expression and the wait time that tick-tocked while the rain fell steadily, he learned more about Shane Knight than he would have learned in an hour of conversation at a bar. Not that he'd ever done that. He knew his strengths. Chitchat and closed rooms with a lot of people would never make the cut.

Her lips that he'd been battling to kill a fierce fantasy of being stretched around his painfully swollen cock, tipped up in a smile. "Tell me what you're doing in town, and maybe we can…talk about it at my place."

"You have no sense of self-preservation." He heard the disbelief and outrage in his voice. "Anyone with a brain can tell I'm dangerous," he practically growled that last line. The ex-major could send someone else after her and the watch. He'd not been able to think of much else while he waited for her to finish her shift.

"I'm not proposing," she said. "You got a place to stay?"

This was not how he'd envisioned his first night in Marietta playing out. He knew he'd arrived too late to visit Alex

Holt at his workplace—the community center—so he'd planned to camp along the river tonight and touch base with Alex tomorrow morning after he got a coffee and finally something to eat.

She looked at him, hands on her hips. "I'm not afraid of you. I'm not a quivering Regency-era heroine. I grew up with a badass firefighter dad, his work buddies and add in my bush firefighting uncles in Australia and that's a lot of chest-thumping testosterone I've had to wade through."

"I stand here. You walk home."

"I don't even think you want to intimidate me," she said thoughtfully. "But you think you should. That would feel safer."

He nearly choked on his spit at her bold spirit and the way Shane looked at him. He felt like for the first time in what felt like forever, someone was really seeing him. All of him. He had to fight the urge to get on his bike and ride. But he was stuck. He had to carry out his vow to Jace. And now there was Shane to protect and convince to return the watch.

"I know you're a badass, *Remy*, but I've been raised to trust my instincts. I can tell you can be dangerous, but it's training for you. Not your core, and you're not cruel or violent to women unless they are a threat."

She was the biggest female threat he'd ever faced—and he'd twice had a female assassin make a run at him.

"You may not want to tell me why you're here. I respect

your privacy, but the end of summer rains can be fierce, and often have thunder-boomers, though the storms are usually short. I've got a covered area in my backyard and a gas firepit. My dad helped me build it when I bought the house this past spring. You can sit out the storm and dry off and warm up. I've got tea, coffee, fresh-squeezed juice or water."

A wave of...something washed over him. Exhaustion made sense. He didn't want to dig any further.

"Stay until the storm passes," she urged, her voice a soft caress in his ears, and her expression more welcoming than any he could remember. What would it feel like to belong, to have someone waiting for him—not just his results?

Cross was not usually given to useless self-reflection. It brought an ache to his sternum that he hated. All the more reason to get on his bike and ride.

And yet, duty. Guilt. Both effective manacles.

He looked into her eyes. She was fearless. And dangerous because the pull she had over him was already a force of nature.

He should say no. Stick to the shadows and his mission—all he was good at. How the hell was he going to play godfather? Cross felt like his skin was curling off his body. He was the last man suited in his unit to draw that task, and yet the rules—no switches, no complaining, no failure.

But he was tired of his thoughts, of his aloneness, of his life so far on the fringes. And cold. Shane Knight made him feel how iced over he was as a man. He inclined his head yes, and followed her down the pretty, treelined street. Small houses. Simple. Some craftsman style with wide covered front porches where a family could sit after dinner and chat, play games, read bedtime stories. His stomach twisted.

Shane was quiet as she walked beside him.

"Where's home originally?" Maybe her father was local. He could warn him she might be in some trouble before he left town.

"Sweet Tea, Tennessee, originally. Doesn't feel like home anymore. It's pretty, but…" Shane shrugged her slim shoulders.

She had secrets. He had nothing but.

"All your family there?" Despair seeped in.

"My parents moved back there from California a couple of years ago. When I was eleven, my dad wanted a change and moved us to California. He worked in the LA County fire department, and he finally retired. My mom's an artist. Two of my sisters are now in Sweet Tea, married. Sutter has a little girl and a baby boy on the way. Tyler's expecting her first. They're both musicians."

She slowed down in front of one house. Craftsman. Dark green, brown trim. Porch with a porch swing with a cushion on it—cream and brown pattern—and a vintage globe light illuminated it in the night.

"Sutter, Tyler, Shane," he mused—he'd heard of Sutter Knight. She was a country music star. "Your dad wasn't trying to send any sort of message with those names."

Shane smiled, still looking at the house, a warmth in her eyes that he hadn't yet seen. "My other two sisters are Dare and Blue. Blue's the oldest. Gotta give it to my dad, he's persistent, but he was a great dad for daughters. He got us all out in the woods hiking, learning about nature, survival, sports. He coached our teams. When we moved to California we all learned to surf..." She broke off.

He waited.

"We'll go in around the back," she said. "Bring your bike."

Shane walked like she mixed and poured drinks. Fluid. Spare movements with an underlying grace and an impressive confidence that he felt was hard-earned.

"Hang on." Shane walked up a short flight of stairs to a landing, spilling over with potted flowers. She unlocked her back door and keyed in a code on an alarm pad.

Pretty sophisticated alarm for a small-town bartender. Paranoid? Or was her father—as a first responder—extra cautious? He'd have to check into the security system at Alex's place. The memory of the list of tasks, written out in Wolf's familiar all-caps and the rules niggled his conscience. He owed it to Jace and his brothers to do his best, even when he thought he had nothing left in his tank. He just wished he'd done more research. All he had was a name and a place of employment. Never before had he set off on a mission so slapdash.

For the first time he thought about the kid. Baby? Toddler? What the hell was he supposed to do for a small child, although he'd often taken care of his sister when she'd been a baby, changing her, feeding her, holding her when she cried, playing with her.

And look how that turned out.

Edgy, looked up and down the street, noting hiding places, escape paths, sniper and ambush positions. He was the first to muster out, though Huck Jones had been reassigned and out of communication. How long would it take for him to be normal? To be able to help the others?

They'd given themselves the year, before they'd meet late next summer for a memorial for Jace where he'd wanted it— fishing, camping and a cookout to swap memories on the shores of Miracle Lake about twenty minutes outside of Marietta.

He remembered Miracle Lake from when he was a kid— ice-skating in the winter, and hiking and playing in the woods in spring and summer, finishing up with a quick dip. One year his mom had bought Brianna a big swan floatie and she sat ensconced like a princess while he paddled her around the lake, watching the hawks catch thermals far above in the brilliant blue sky, so bright it hurt his eyes.

He hated being back in Marietta. No mom. No sister. No ranch to work a hard but honest day. All the memories swarming like hornets stinging him.

Shane hit some party lights that lit up the covered area, and Cross took stock of his surroundings. There was a vegetable garden—raised beds, whiskey barrels of flowers, and six rough, white birch branches held up an A-frame green metal roof that comprised the covered area. The rain played an upbeat song as it hit, bounced on the green tin roof and slid down the copper rain chains into green ceramic cistern pots. The back of the structure featured what looked like a living wall—a vertical herb garden maybe.

Cross had never seen anything like it. A small water feature added to the aqua symphony. He walked into the yard, and inhaled deeply; scents of basil, rosemary, lavender, thyme, cilantro and other things he didn't recognize co-mingled and kicked something out of his memory—him and his mom wresting a couple of old wine barrels out of the back of her Subaru and up to the porch of the double bunk house they called home at Sam Wilder's ranch where she'd been the cook. His mom had wanted to grow herbs to season the food for the ranch hands.

He'd felt so important helping her. She'd been so happy when he'd positioned the pots, filled them with composted soil and planted the herbs for Mother's Day. He hadn't thought about his past in decades. His eyes stung and blindly Cross reached out to touch a feathery leaf with a tiny yellow petal—mustard?

"My vertical garden." Shane's voice guided him back to the present. "The yard is pretty space-challenged for what I'd like to do, but considering it was a dirt lot with half-dead grass when I bought it, I'm pleased with the progress." Shane looked around. Her unusual-colored eyes shone with pride and happiness.

I want that.

He wanted to build something. All he'd built was emptiness. Heartache. Death.

Maybe Jace had been right. They could rebuild their lives. Well, Jace couldn't. He'd been robbed, but Cross and the others could build lives to be proud of. Honor Jace's memory.

"Genius hack," he commented. "Never seen anything like it."

"My sisters and I used to garden with our mom. We ate what we grew. Montana doesn't have the best growing season but..." She looked around. "I make...well, I make bitters and essential oils, I sell them in Miranda's gift store at the hotel, and this year I'm trying out a booth at the farmers' market. This is my test year. Next spring I'm going to build a greenhouse."

He nearly offered to help.

Idiot. He'd be long gone.

She didn't need him.

He was deviating from his mission again. Alex and his kid were primary. He was here for Jace. Not the former major. He had one task. One problem, one ghost at a time. It was madness to spend time with Shane, although, a justification seeped into his consciousness. Shane might know Alex. He could learn more about him and the kid, casually. Two birds. One stone.

And maybe he could find out more about the watch—warn her or... Since when had he become such a Boy Scout? He could imagine the other Coyote Cowboys laughing at him. Wolf threatening to kick his ass. And Jace urging him to go for it—whatever it was.

"You want to go inside?" Shane invited. "There's a bathroom off the laundry room. You can change into these and put your clothes in the dryer." Shane handed him a stack of clothes she'd retrieved when she'd entered the house and had come out the back to let him in.

He took the clothes. Men's sweats—definitely not the usual baggy drawstring navy blue or camo he'd worn for as long as he could remember. They were tailored and impossibly soft. The T-shirt was a faded college one. An Ivy, he thought—Brown. He wondered whose they were—the major's? His blood recoiled.

Shane too had changed into dry clothes—a coral-colored sheath-style sleeveless dress that fell midway to her ankles. There were buttons on one side, and she'd left the bottom four undone so he could catch flashes of a couple of inches of her slim, golden-toned thighs. The dress had a racer-back style—sleeveless, with a generous portion of her back and side showing, and Cross immediately wondered if she was wearing a bra or not.

"They are my brother-in-law's. They visited earlier this summer for a few days, probably trying to discover why I've told them how the Smoky Mountains aren't enough of a draw to lure me back when I have views of the Gallatins, Absarokas and of course Crazy Mountain with its mythology." Shane's skin seemed luminous in the night, lit by the moon.

"Dawson and Sutter are obsessed with hiking or trail running sections of the Appalachian Trail all around Gatlinburg and Sweet Tea and communing with nature. So I gave them some western joy. We went off-roading and picnicking the day before they left. We got pretty grubby, and I washed everything, but after we made dinner and then walked over to catch a concert in the park, I forgot about the last load in the dryer."

Not the major's clothes. More relieved than he should be, Cross walked up the stairs to the house, briefly pausing. "Can I catch a quick shower?" He was used to roughing it, but also quick to take advantage when he didn't have to.

Shane nodded. "Everything you need is in the downstairs bathroom next to the laundry room."

"Thank you," he said after a long pause and entered her house cautiously, telling himself he was once again playing the fool.

SHANE MADE CINNAMON and orange tea in the electric kettle as well as strong, black coffee with her French press. She focused on each task so that she wouldn't think of the hottie badass in her house peeling off his motorcycle leathers, so different from the rodeo cowboys that were designed to hold audience's attention—and then his jeans. Boxers? Briefs? Commando?

Shane's hands trembled and she gripped them together, not wanting to burn herself with the hot water. Was she insane? Why had she brought him home? Offered him a change of clothes? She'd like to think she was just a Good Samaritan, but she knew her motives were far from pure.

Take a pick.

Lonely.

Empty.

Bored of leashing her libido and adventurous spirit. She was exhausted by the sadness that had dogged her for so long even as she'd battled it back. She'd rebuilt her life. Changed her dreams. Accepted that there were things she would never have and had moved on. She was thriving. Even had moments of incandescent joy.

And yet... She added a little local honey in her tea, stirred it and tried not to wait for the sound of the screen door opening and closing.

Her body ached to be held, turned into liquid fire, the empty places filled temporarily.

Why not him? He was a soldier or former soldier passing through.

He returned, so quietly that if she hadn't been anticipating him, she would have missed him.

"A plus on water conservation," she said lightly trying to leash her unruly libido.

"You and your father created something quite beautiful," he said.

Shane continued to twirl the honey in her mug, loath to break the spell the night and rain had woven. She should— her hookup days, nothing much to brag about—had been abandoned after her first couple of years in college. And at her age, she couldn't give a man who wanted to settle down what he wanted.

But Remy Cross was not anyone's idea of home and hearth.

She stopped fussing with the spoon. She was a strong woman. She took charge of her life and her happiness. She wanted to see where the night could take her.

"You going to keep dancing around my question?" Shane asked, handing him the strong black coffee because she knew herbal tea or cream and sugar wouldn't cut it with this man. "Or are you going to tell me why you're here?"

SO MANY LIES ran through his head, each one more plausible than the last. But as he looked at the woman standing in front of him—her beauty and inner strength like a flame— he didn't want to utter anything easy. His career had been built on stories—some he told, some written by others, lies, partial truths—all in the effort to assist him to complete his mission.

He sipped the coffee and nearly closed his eyes as pleasure washed over him. He hadn't had coffee so rich since he'd been in Istanbul, but he could hardly share that could he. There was actually very little he could share with her or anyone. The separation tugged at his bones.

Tiredness washed over him. He felt sixty-seven, instead of just thirty-eight yet his last mission was just beginning. He couldn't look beyond that. Not yet. He'd always imagined he'd ie on a mission. It hadn't occurred to him that he could have a scroll of empty years roll out limp and crumpled in front of him.

Jace had made him believe. He'd made all of them believe. And then he'd been cut down leaving them all hanging.

"I grew up in Marietta—for a few years anyway," Cross confessed and sat down at the picnic table even though Shane had a circle of Adirondack chairs with brightly striped cushions arranged around a gas fireplace. The cold, unyielding wood would keep his senses more alert. Looking at those comfortable chairs reminded him of all the things he'd briefly had but lost.

Shane didn't speak. She was restful to be around, although her beauty made him long for things he had no business considering. She bent down and got the gas fireplace going, yet then she stepped back and joined him at the picnic table, sitting across from him. A large mason jar of sunflowers and greenery provided a bright accent that made him think of the day conquering the night, although the glow and promise of the woman did that with an exclamation point.

"I don't remember much before Marietta. My mom was a barrel racer. She toured with the Montana rodeo circuit before I was born and then for a few years after. We lived in the living quarters of the horse trailer. In the off-season, we were usually in a bunkhouse on a ranch somewhere. She'd train horses or give lessons, or whatever, but when we lived in Marietta, we lived on the Wild Wind Ranch. That was the most normal time of my life, I suppose."

He took another sip of his coffee and let it heat his body.

"Sam Wilder's spread," she mused. "I've heard of it. So you've come home," she said softly.

"Marietta hasn't been home since I was almost thirteen," he said. "So not home."

Why was he spilling his life? His past was not why he was here. Nor should a beautiful woman wearing a stolen watch intrigue him almost to the point of obsession. He might be a civilian now, but he was definitely uncivilized.

"Is that why you're here, to find a home?"

No. But the question felt like a direct hit, and him with no Kevlar.

"Do you often sit outside during the witching hour with

a strange man?" he volleyed back.

"It's past the witching hour." Shane had the secret smile again. She sipped her tea, and the fragrance of cinnamon and citrus and something floral wafted his way—the woman or the drink?

"The next witching hour, when the witches have strong powers to cast spells is between three and four a.m. That's when things will really get interesting."

Amusement lurked in her eyes, but so did desire. And questions. It hit him then that she was willing. Was he willing to toss out his discipline and caution his first few days of freedom?

Hell yes.

Not the answer he wanted to hear from himself. That right there should cause him to drain his coffee, stand up, get his damp jeans and T-shirt out of the still-spinning dryer and get the hell out of here.

"Home can be anywhere. It's more an attitude than a place." Shane kicked off her boots, peeled off her socks and wiggled her toes. Her toenails were a brilliant deep and sparkly blue. Her fingernails were short, rounded and bare. "When my sisters and I were kids in Sweet Tea, we lived in the woods along the Pigeon River. We were practically feral, always out running around barefoot, sometimes naked or in our underwear swimming in the creek. Eating the bounty in the woods. The town kids called us witches. We would play into it—stare at them, pretend to speak some magical language, and do things with our fingers like we had an invisible wand or were casting spells.

Shane tilted her head back and looked up at the green metal roof with the thick beams strung with party lights. The lights highlighted the planes of her face, and the small flames dancing in the firepit behind her highlighted the white blonde of her hair.

"I bet the god-fearing families of Sweet Tea wet themselves in terror," he said. She was casting a spell on him, and what was truly dangerous, there was a part of him that wanted to be ensnared.

Shane laughed. "It wasn't nice," she admitted. Her mysterious eyes held the faraway look of a pleasant memory. "We were always into music. We had our own band and would stand on the lunch tables at school and break into a cappella versions of Destiny's Child, Britney Spears, Faith Hill, No Doubt, TLC, and Shawn Colvin hits. True devil-worshiping music."

"I think Sweet Tea wasn't big enough for you," he said.

"Marietta's not that much bigger." Shane sighed, her light dimming. "I learned to become smaller." She stretched out her legs on the bench and raised her arms up over her head, inviting him to note the irony.

Nope, not wearing a bra.

"My point is, Sweet Tea was home because of my family and nature," she said after a comfortable pause. "LA was home because of my family and the ocean. When I was in college my friends and routines and decorations created a home for me. Same when I was working. Marietta's home because of the beautiful views, the hiking trails and nature and the people. I've made my home here by finding a job I love and making it mine, making changes that I want, by making friends, by buying a house and changing it with my own labor, money and time so that it suits me. You too, Remy, can make a home wherever you want. It just takes the will."

He felt like one of those poor trapped frogs in a high school biology class. "I think you can still cast a spell, Shane Knight." His voice was rough, exposing him.

"You think I can?" She looked at him.

"Do you want to?" He could barely breathe. Damn. He should be good at this part. He was a big man, had a danger-ous edge. Women in dangerous parts of the world and rougher bars responded to that. He'd never had trouble sealing the deal without much conversation.

But he'd never met a woman like Shane.

"Still thinking on it."

"Don't." He took another long draft of coffee. Got up, helped himself to the rest. "You're not that kind of woman."

"What kind of woman?" Her eyes flashed. Good. He needed to piss her off. She was getting under his skin. Making him want.

"A hit-and-run kind of woman." His voice sounded as rough as he felt.

"Hit?" Instead of standing while he stood, with the fire-pit between them, she drew her mile-long legs into what he dimly remembered his sister proudly calling criss-cross-applesauce after her first day of preschool. "My aren't you masculine." Her voice went syrupy Southern, and she fanned her face with her hand.

"So you think of sex like a hit on a woman and then you run?" She looked up at him. "Like a military op." She smiled. "Women do serve, as I'm sure you know. Besides I was hitting on you."

She'd confused him. No faux denial. No fake outrage.

"And you seem like a man who would stride away, no backward glance, not a man who runs."

Where was all the air in this part of town?

"You got that right." For some reason his mouth kept moving. "I'm here to carry out a task for a fallen brother. Then I'm gone."

"Understood, Remy." Her gaze was kind, the desire still there, but she'd made her own decision to back away and disappointment crashed into relief.

"No one has called me Remy in years," he admitted.

Now she stood, approached him casually, but slowly as if he were a wild animal she didn't want to spook. He supposed he was.

"How's it feel?" Her fingertips skimmed his, and he had to fight the urge to hold her hand.

He was weak. Wanting a connection he absolutely could

not have. He would let her down. Destroy her like everyone else he'd cared about.

"I don't know," he said, too restless to sit, too off-balance to leave.

Shane walked around him to pour more hot water into her cup from the outdoor kitchen. Somehow, not having her so close loosened more words so they could fall out.

"I could say that I'm not that man anymore, but Remy was never a man. I enlisted at eighteen. Was called Cross in basic and every day after that. But I was Cross long before I enlisted," he remembered, hating bringing up the images, the turbulence, the rage that had stormed through him. "I was placed at a ranch for troubled teens a few years after my mom died when I was twelve." His voice mocked the words because trouble hadn't begun to cover the damage: to him, to so many others "I'd bounced around foster care for a few years before being sent to the ranch when I was fifteen. I was never called Remy again after that. Just Cross."

Shane blew on the water steaming from her mug, her crystalline gaze locked on him. She closed the distance between them, moving more like mist than a flesh-and-blood woman. Maybe she really was a witch because his body came alive in a fierce fire that burned and belonged to her more than him.

"I don't think you're just anything, Remy," she said.

Anger stirred, saving him. "What do you think I am?" He invited her scrutiny.

Bring it on, headshrinker.

"What?" She sounded thoughtful. Her beautiful gaze, lit by the glow of the party lights, was open, searching, whereas he, with his back to the lights, was as always in the shadows. "Not who?" With her thumb, she stroked along a scar that feathered out from his left eye, and then down his temple and jaw and lingered on his bottom lip. "You are anyone you choose to be," she said. "But I think you are lost."

That was a hard hit. "You going to find me?"

Women. Always thinking they could save men. They couldn't.

"No. You are."

Chapter Four

"D EAD?" HE REPEATED as if he'd never heard the word before.

"Ummmm, yes." The young woman's face creased in nervous sympathy. "I'm so sorry," she whispered. "Was Alex...Alexandria a...a friend of yours?"

Cross was hyper-aware of every noise behind him in the rec center. A group of men in pretty decent shape were playing pick-up basketball, and in the classrooms down the hall, he could hear a guitar lesson in one and little kids singing 'Happy Birthday' in another.

And Alex Holt—Jace's friend from high school, the one he'd promised to serve as godfather to his fatherless kid—was dead. And a woman. Not a man as he'd been assuming, and that was kicking up a suspicion that Cross didn't like at all. What man had a best friend for a woman that he hadn't banged? Was the kid...

He let the thought hang. He couldn't do anything about that. But the dead part was a problem.

How had Jace not known? Just how close had they been? A godfather sounded pretty damn close. Was guardian part of that equation? The question kicked up desperately, prickling his nape with sweat.

"Alex was a woman?" He couldn't quite grasp how he could have set off on a mission so blindly.

The young woman had gone from nervous to uncomfortable to alarmed in the time he'd been standing here silently stunned.

The questions would have to wait. But the task was not completed although…decision snapped straight his spine.

"What about her kid?"

"Who?"

"She had a kid."

Crap. He didn't know the name, gender or age. Impotent fury washed through him. Damn Jace for just scrawling a four-word task on a list. Agreement but no details. Cross had never been so unprepared for a mission. His fault for dialing it in because it was stateside—in frickin' Marietta, Montana, where people all played nice, but turned their backs when life went to hell.

And the former major had been one more distraction he should have eighty-sixed.

He pinched his nose and closed his eyes to center his thoughts. He was taking this too personally—letting his past resentments creep into his present. But how could he have gone off half-cocked, never mind not even aiming? He should have probed Shane for details last night instead of fantasizing about her naked, digging her nails into his shoulders and screaming his name—his first name—before rolling out his sleeping bag on her patio and falling into a surprisingly restful sleep.

Jace deserved his best, not his half-assed.

It would have helped if Jace had put more information alongside each of his going-home goals, but why would he? He knew what each one meant. He hadn't been anticipating that his brothers would carry out the five tasks he'd jotted in a small notebook he'd always kept in his left thigh pocket of his pants.

Cross didn't know what the other tasks were. Wolf had wanted it that way—private. Fair. No trades. Each brother had his own private mission chosen by fate. And for the first time, Cross wondered if any of his brothers had their own make-amends list. He didn't have anyone or anything to take care of.

"She had a kid," Cross repeated.

Please not a daughter.

"I didn't know Alex. I'm sorry. I…she got sick. It was fast. I'm actually her replacement. She went on…on hospice before I started, but she kept her health insurance," the young woman said in a rush, "until…you know…the…end so that…"

She paused, stared at him mutely. Her fear expanded like a deep breath. Christ, did he look that scary?

"That's good," he said, trying to calm his rioting mind. The kid wasn't in imminent danger. She was probably with family. He'd just need to check in, introduce himself, tell them about Jace's wishes and…

And then what? He hadn't let himself think that far ahead. He didn't know what a godfather did. And he was a million miles away from Jace's open heart, his 'everyone's a friend' approach.

What was he supposed to do now? His chest felt hot and constricted like the last time he'd been shot. Sure, his vest had stopped that round—barely, but he'd felt like he was having a heart attack.

"Thank you." He forced the absurdly unfamiliar words out of his mouth.

She nodded, looking even more uncertain.

"Thank you." He tried the words again. "I apologize for interrupting your day."

His mom had been big on manners—not that she'd had many directed her way from what he'd seen. But she'd been a great mom, loving, determined to raise her kids to be strong, self-reliant, kind, generous to others. She'd been a big believer in finding joy in big and small moments.

A despair he hadn't felt in over a decade or maybe longer washed over him. He was a failure. He'd failed his mom. He'd failed his sister. And now he was going to fail Jace. Cross dipped his head like he was still that kid wearing a cowboy hat and doing his best to be a man on the Wild Wind Ranch so that he and his family could finally have a home.

He'd be a stranger if his mom could see him now. Not a

man she would admire. Not a man who found joy in any-thing—except the magical moment stolen last night. He'd sat in Shane's backyard and had a conversation. One of the first 'normal' things he could remember doing.

Acid curdled his stomach.

He was the wrong man for Jace's task. And the wrong man for a woman like Shane. He stalked out of the rec center, passing by the high school he'd never had the chance to attend. He walked down treelined streets, turning a variety of next-move ideas over and over until he saw a group of colored tents, flapping gently in the breeze. The market. He stopped on the sidewalk and stared at the incongruous sight—his thoughts so dark, but the tents so bright.

Shane was a vendor. She'd told him about selling her essential oils and bitters. He'd helped her pack the table, supplies and boxes into her Jeep after he'd slept on her patio—using the extra-large yoga mat she'd provided after he'd turned down the twin bed that she'd converted into a swing off one side of her covered patio, convinced he'd break it. Or it would ruin him for life in the rough.

Shane had woken him up when she headed out for a run. He'd joined her—although him running in his motorcycle boots had caused a raised eyebrow, and he'd dryly reminded her that soldiers didn't change into their Nike Air Zoom Alphaflys when they had to run across mountain passes trying to get a better position to take down the enemy.

He'd taken another shower, dressed and then had been

handed a breakfast burrito that had been as welcome as it had been delicious. And healthy too judging by the green stuff he hadn't asked about loaded into it along with the eggs and colorful veggies. They hadn't spoken over the breakfast, but when she'd started loading up her Jeep, he'd helped. It had been disturbingly difficult to climb on his bike and head out to clear his head before waiting for the rec center to open.

Even though Shane wasn't part of his plan, he continued to walk toward the grouping of tents. He needed to learn more about Alex Holt—her life, her family and her kid. He paused. His trajectory was eerily familiar to last night—a detour to check out Shane Knight. Was he rationalizing his need to see her? No. Small towns. She might have known Alex. Or know someone who could help.

Seeking her out again had nothing to do with her beauty or the almost bewitched feeling she stirred in him. This was business. She might have insight into the kid's whereabouts or could help him devise a strategy to approach the kid because if today's reaction at the rec center was anything to go by, he was scary to civvies.

He wished he'd taken her up on her offer last night, but no, he'd tried to channel some 'gentleman code of honor' that he'd imagined Jace would employ.

He wanted to kick his own ass because if they'd slept together, she'd be more inclined to help him—maybe. Cross laughed at his own hubris.

Carrying out Jace's wishes was now more complicated, but he'd made a vow. Shane was part of his solution. End of story.

SHANE BAGGED UP several different bottles of cocktail bitters, one of her handmade diffuser bottles—she'd started glass blowing two years ago at a studio in Livingston—and one bottle of essential oils—cinnamon bark blended with bergamot and orange for an invigorating feel in winter, for a customer. It was mid-August, and winter was far from anyone's mind now, but Shane had to think ahead. Today was the first day she was selling this autumn-themed mixture.

Many of the locals thought her scents were pretty, but they didn't want to pay what they considered the steep price. They didn't believe in aromatherapy any more than they believed in the tarot card reader Miranda Telford invited to her gift shop at the Graff once a month, but tourists loved the scents and the tarot and aura readers. Selling her bitters and oils at Miranda's gift store had been a good decision, as had renting a space at the first year of the farmers' market.

Miranda had been encouraging her to start an online business and to hire staff—both to help her with making the oils and blowing the glass and with the shipping and marketing, but Shane was hesitating. It would be a lot more work, and her life seemed wonderfully balanced now. Work she enjoyed. A hobby that was creative and mildly lucrative, friends and a house and backyard garden she loved. She even regularly saved for retirement.

I sound fifty, not thirty-two.

She ran her customer's credit card through her Square for payment, and then wrapped their purchases in the bandanas she sewed from scraps of fabric she collected.

"Your summer cocktail samples, are as usual selling my bourbon and gin today without me having to open my mouth," Laird Wilder said. They always had their booths next to each other's because he used her bitters to create the sample tastes for prospective customers for his spirits.

She laughed. "Your mouth is plenty open, Laird. You are the consummate salesperson. I notice it's mostly women who swish up to your booth, tongues hanging out with thirst, or maybe—" she cocked her head, pretending to consider "—they come to stare at your pretty face."

"It's all your smelly goo that attracts the women. Not my face or hot body that you accidentally on purpose forgot to mention." He flexed and made a goofy face. "Besides the women are always buying my sh...products," he said enunciating each syllable, "for their boyfriends or husbands."

"I didn't mention your hot body because your wife terrifies me." Tucker Wilder was one of her closest friends.

"That would be a fun idea—her a little jealous," Laird mused, watching a group of women approach them. "But never going to happen. I'm so crazy about Tucker that I'm a pathetically sure thing. I follow her around the house and ranch, devoted as a family hound dog, offering to cook things, move things, run errands, massage her feet."

"If a family hound could do that, maybe I wouldn't only foster." Shane laughed. "And you'd better be waiting on my bestie. She told me the good news—twins."

"I am an overachiever." Laird smiled, but she saw the worry as well as happiness in his eyes.

"I like the idea of you as a hound," Shane teased to keep his spirits up. She was thrilled for Tucker, but she knew once her friends started having babies, the friendship dynamic changed, and she had to make more of an effort to stay in the picture. And seeing the babies, holding them, always filled her with an ache of desperate want that seemed to swallow her whole.

Laird dropped his head back and quietly bayed like a dog. That reminded her of her coyote cowboy last night.

Nope. She didn't want to think about him. He'd rejected her tentative offer of a one-night stand, and his shrug-off hadn't stopped the wistful and frustrated fantasies last night. She'd gotten no sleep and tonight would be another long and busy shift at work. She wasn't going to waste her day wishing.

How many rejections did a woman have to be handed to receive the message—he's not that into you?

Loud and clear, buddy.

But that was not the message his eyes, his body and his barely contained sexual energy had been radiating last night. She'd kept fantasizing about her coyote cowboy…

Not yours.

But her imagination did care because she'd kept picturing him in a Stetson and cowboy boots and nothing else… A flush rushed over her body. She could not think like that. Remy had 'complicated and dangerous to her hard-won peace of mind' branded onto his very cut chest. He was gone for good. She needed him to stay gone.

But then he wasn't. Shane nearly stumbled over her own feet when she spotted Remy walking toward her, tall and fluid with a purpose that would be slightly scary if her traitorous body weren't already clamoring hello as heat pooled between her thighs and her nipples perked right up. Fabulous. She hadn't bothered with a bra because she barely needed one—a complaint she'd heard more than once from boyfriends past. Shane reached for her thin denim shirt that had a sun embroidered on the back and casually shrugged it on.

What was he doing here? With the sun behind him he looked like a…like a…her imagination failed her. Marauding pirate. Or a Viking—if he'd been blond like her, but no he was dark, a man in the shadows.

You can pull him into the light.

She stomped down that thought.

"That is a man on a mission," Laird noted. "In desperate

need of a present to keep his ass out of the doghouse?" Laird laughed. "He looks a little like Colt only...do you know him?" Laird turned toward her, eyes wide with questions as Remy continued to bear down on them.

Shane's mouth was too dry to speak. The effect Remy had on her body was overwhelming. It was like she wanted to full-body jump him, leaving only her inconvenient brain behind.

Laird jumped to his feet beside her, looking all kinds of protective.

"I do." Shane found her voice. "He's a..." She had no idea how to finish that sentence.

"Remy, what's up?" She exited her booth so that the table was between Laird and Remy, which would hopefully chill his Mr. Protective act. Laird might be easygoing compared to his soldier fraternal twin brother Colt and cowboy brothers Luke and Kane, but he was still a Wilder. And he led a search-and-rescue volunteer team, so definitely not a beta.

"She's a woman," he said. "She's dead."

"What? Who? How?" Shane felt like a high school reporter.

Intensity and pain rolled off him in waves and, without thinking, Shane wrapped herself around him like she could hold all his broken pieces in place. Her hands ran up and down his bare arms, and his heart slammed against hers. She rested her cheek against the pulse she could see strongly fluttering in his neck.

She breathed in deeply and slowly, held and released as if she had some magic power that would calm the storm that churned inside of him.

"Talk to me," she encouraged, her voice going husky with tension.

His arms didn't hold her back. Instead, they hung loosely at his sides. Shane eased away, resting her palm flat on his chest, where his heart still pounded. She could feel Laird staring a hole through her back. He was worried. She should be worried. What was she doing? Shane to the rescue? That had ended in disaster more than once.

"I'm sorry for your loss." She grabbed at the conventional phrase.

"Dead." His voice cracked. "She's dead. I didn't..." He ran a hand through his hair. His voice broke. His hand shook. "How can she be dead? How did Jace not know?"

None of it made sense, but his bewilderment was tangible.

"I got your booth," Laird said in a low voice. "You take care of..." He looked at her eyebrows raised, clearly expecting some information.

"Thank you, Laird," she said even as she felt her soldier cowboy's tension kick higher. His attention shifted to Laird.

"Who's that?"

Did he just growl at her? "No. You. Did. Not," Shane tried to walk him backward palm still owning part of the real estate of his chest that was as hard as she had fantasized about, but he didn't budge. That just kicked her temper up another notch. He'd rejected her last night. He didn't get to ask about other men.

"Are you trying to push me out of here?" he asked mildly.

"Yes, pretend it's working." She glared. She worked out. She was tough. "Who died?"

"Alex Holt."

"Alex?" Icy dismay washed through Shane, and she ceased trying to push Remy away from the milling shoppers. "You knew her?" Shane could barely get the words out. "Is Alex why you came back?" Shane's throat was so dry she could barely speak. "Were you..." An even more horrific idea bit her brain. "Are you...oh my God." She covered her face with hands that shook. "Are you..." She peered at him in horror. "Did I practically proposition Arlo's father last night?"

SHANE HANDED HIM a lemonade with sprigs of lavender and three blueberries in the bottom of the icy glass that he hadn't asked for.

"Okay." She sat down at the picnic table in her backyard after they'd packed up her booth at the farmer's market. "Why don't you start at the beginning," she invited.

"You don't need the beginning." He was on edge, pacing with the adrenaline and trying to hold off the crush of failure. He'd held it together in far more dangerous situations. He had to keep it tight now. Arlo might need him. God help her.

Not a young girl. Please not a young girl.

Who was he praying to? When had his prayers once been answered? God had turned His back on him decades ago, and Remy had returned the perceived slight. He couldn't get his mind to quiet. It was like without the structure of his unit, he was a burst of molecules and atoms rocketing around.

"The beginning would help me to understand the situation so that I could better help you, *if* you want my help." Shane took a sip of her lemonade and hit him with that unwavering aquamarine gaze. Her voice was skillfully neutral, reminding him of a couple of the army shrinks his commander would sometimes send him to after a particularly difficult mission to get him 'back to base,' was the term used.

He doubted his baseline was any shrink's ideal.

"I just need information." He didn't need to drag her into his last mission and his F-up to end all F-ups.

"As do I," Shane said. She sounded reasonable while he sounded cold and clipped.

Gone was the sexy, intriguing woman from last night, her eyes lit with desire. This Shane was analytical and determined to get answers. But Cross had been honed to hoard information.

Shane palmed her lemonade, her eyes flinty. "You came to me, Remington Cross. You interrupted my day. Keep your secrets, soldier, or don't. I can try to help or leave you swinging." She swallowed more lemonade, and he watched the long line of her throat work.

Shane stood up fluidly. "I have to get ready for work. You know the way out."

She walked into her house but left the door open.

Years of relying only on himself warred with his duty to Jace and his utter incompatibility to be the type of man suited to the task.

He either asked for help or he didn't.

Chapter Five

CROSS PAUSED ON the threshold of the kitchen, not wanting to interrupt Shane in the intimacy of her bedroom where he heard the rustle of clothing. He tried not to picture her peeling off her jeans and tank and imagine what she'd slip into.

Idiot. She wasn't 'slipping into' anything for him. She was heading to work, but if he did take her on a date... Cross shut that stupid thought down. He hadn't been on a date in the traditional sense in his life.

Would Shane be a hike and picnic kind of date or candlelit dinner?

Stay in your lane.

"How did you know Alex?" Shane called out.

"I didn't," he admitted.

"Huh?" She stepped out of her room just as she slid both of her arms into a rose-colored loose pantsuit, and yeah he caught a glimpse of a matching lacy rose-colored bra. Did her panties match? God, he was a masochist.

"Why were you looking for her then?" Shane asked. She smoothed a dab of moisturize on her fingertips and feathered it over her skin. Her feet were bare.

He stared, fascinated. He'd never seen a woman get ready for work or anything. He'd taken off a lot of clothes, but had never helped a woman put them on, and he had an uncomfortable urge to brush her beautiful mane of hair, feel it fall across his body. Inhale her feminine scent.

"She was the high school friend of my team leader," he said. God, he was tired of dodging questions, of feeling so off-balance. "Jace McBride," Remy added and leaned against the farmhouse sink. He watched Shane roll on some socks—a bucking bronc with a cowboy holding on.

"Jace...died," Cross said, damming up the rest of the words that wanted to spill out. "He left a list of things he intended to do when he got home—a list of amends he wanted to make to people who mattered to him."

Shane had bent at the waist and was running her fingers through her hair. God the color was beautiful. He actually took a step forward wanting to feel all that silk. Shane stilled and then straightened. Her hair fell well below her bra strap. She gathered it up and twisted it into a low knot at her nape. Cross watched, fascinated as she stuck two sterling silver sticks with pink jewels at the tips and worked them into her hair.

A memory surfaced. His sister, Brianna in a pink leotard dancing around the house, her arms waving 'graceful as a swan swims,' she'd said. She'd had black elastics on her skinny wrists, her expression pleading for him to fix her hair. She needed a 'smooth top bun' for her Saturday ballet class.

The class was always a rush—her mother finishing the cooking and cleaning at the Wilder ranch and racing the clock to make it into town in time for the Saturday morning class.

He shoved the memory back where it belonged, but not before the guilt lodged another arrow in his chest. Had her foster family let her continue with ballet? Had her adoptive parents? Had she dreamed of being a dancer before her time and dreams were snipped short?

"The brothers in our unit each drew a task from Jace's list—sort of a bucket list of amends or promises to people. He never got the chance so we…"

The loss hit him hard all over again.

Shane walked across the open floor plan, light streaming in the large windows. Her pantsuit flared gracefully around her calves, out almost like a skirt. She went to the refrigerator and poured him a glass of water. Lemon and cucumber floated in the water from the jug. She handed it to him.

"And your task, Remy?" she asked in a low voice.

"You don't call me Cross," he noted.

"Should I?"

He paused. He was out of the military. He needed at some point to stop somewhere and build a life. Become a different man. But first he had to find Alex Holt's kid and make sure they were all right.

"My mom and sister called me Remy," he said, remembering. Sam Wilder too. But his childhood and his name had pretty much died with his mother on that highway so many years ago. "I was Remy when I lived in Marietta, but that was so long ago I'm pretty sure no one will remember that kid."

"You might be surprised, Remy. It's a small town; people care. They remember."

He hadn't experienced that caring when his life had fallen apart. Hopefully Alex's kid was getting a better deal. Not knowing had him on edge.

"You going to help me?" It felt like a dare.

Shane twisted her wrist to check that damn stolen watch, and the practiced move felt like a punch. She slid her feet into pink ankle cowboy boots with red roses embroidered on them.

"Depends on what you want," Shane said carefully, tension in her voice.

"I need to find Alex's kid and make sure they are all right."

"Why?"

"The list. Alex had asked Jace to be godfather to her kid, and obviously he's out of commission so I'm stepping up."

Shane had been in the process of pouring herself a glass of water as well, and she dropped the jug, which bounced and rolled and, as she reached for it, she tipped the glass off the countertop where it shattered.

It was the first awkward thing he'd seen her do, but when he stepped forward to help, she waved him off.

"I got it," she said.

She picked up the jug and righted it. Mopped up the water with a tea towel and swept up the glass and put it in the trash.

"What I said upset you?"

"No." She tossed the tea towel in the laundry basket in the small utility room off the kitchen. "No, I was just clumsy."

But she didn't meet his no doubt hard stare. He wished for a moment he was a different man. That he… No use for wishing. Action was all that mattered.

"My mom wasn't much of a churchgoer. I don't even know what a godfather does exactly," he admitted in a low voice.

"They don't introduce themselves and then ride out of town," Shane said flatly.

"You're pissed."

"No." She crossed her arms. "Yes. No. I don't know." She huffed out a breath. "I have to get to work."

"I'll walk you."

"Remy." She finally made eye contact and he felt like he was drowning in her aquamarine challenge. "I know you want to honor your friend—" she seemed to be choosing her words with care "—but I don't think it's a good idea for you to introduce yourself to Arlo and then just ride off to live your life."

"I didn't ask your opinion."

"You asked for my help. My opinion is a package deal."

He liked that she felt comfortable taking him on.

"And what kind of a name is Arlo? It sounds…old-fashioned or something out of one of those black-and-white movies."

"I always liked the name," Shane noted. "It's cute and unexpected. Arlo was first mentioned historically in a 1590 poem 'The Faerie Queene.' It was a fictional place that might mean—in Irish-Gaelic—between two highlands. Or a hill. Alex wanted Arlo to be strong, make her mark in the world."

Cross's throat was as dry as the deserts he'd spent so many years in. Every curse word he'd ever heard scrolled through his head. A girl. A daughter. Another female he'd no doubt let down.

"I didn't say I would be riding out of town right away," he objected, although that had been his plan, and he had no idea how he'd stay. "I mean to see this through."

Shane pushed past him and swung a small brown leather backpack up over one shoulder.

"Are you her father?"

"No," he said. His voice was loud in the room. "Told you, I never met Alex. I don't have any kids I walked out on." Like he'd been walked out on. Outrage churned in his gut as well as fear over his total inadequacy for the task ahead.

Shane refilled her silver water bottle and put it on a netted cup holder on the side of her small backpack.

She held open her door, silently ushering him out. This time he didn't take a last look around, wanting to memorize the warmth and comfort of her home, because he was very sure he was coming back.

"Were you friends with Alex?"

Shane hesitated for a moment. "Not really. She was friends with Miranda Telford, who owns the gift shop at the Graff."

Cross opened the garden gate and closed it after Shane walked through. She locked it.

"Alex got sick. Brain tumor. It spread so fast. She was gone in a few months."

He winced. Life was cruel and unfair. "And Arlo?"

"Social services were searching for her family. She stayed with Miranda's family when her mom was in hospice and for a couple of weeks after the death. Miranda has a daughter, Petal, who's friends with Arlo. They were in the same grade. That's how I know Arlo a little. The two girls would sometimes come in after school and work on homework or craft projects in the boutique. Miranda has a lot of cute community events in the store for different holidays, and I develop themed cocktails and mocktails for the celebrations of holidays. Petal and Arlo like to help 'create the magic brews.'" Sheer agony flashed across Shane's features, before her features smoothed.

But he had too much training to miss or dismiss it.

"And?"

"And?" she challenged, her boots clicking decisively on the sidewalk.

"You never followed up?"

"Bartender."

She didn't look at him.

"What the hell does that mean—you're no longer human?" He got in front of her, set his body.

"Oh, because I'm a woman I need to save the world?" She dodged him with an efficiency of a running back with the ball.

"Where's Arlo now?"

He walked alongside of her. Damn she had a long, fast stride that he really would have appreciated more if she hadn't been intent on walking away from him.

He wondered what her reaction would be if he swooped her up and tossed her delectable tight body over his shoulder.

She'd probably clock him, and he shouldn't like that idea so much. But he'd get arrested. Hard to offer fealty to a child and her guardian from prison.

"Do you know?"

"No." Shane chewed her bottom lip. "I don't. I... Miranda has a young son in preschool, and she recently found out she was expecting again—twins. She has difficult pregnancies so..." Shane shrugged.

He had a sick feeling in his stomach. "There's no family?"

"Remy, I don't know, and before you Velcro on your cape and fly off to play hero, you really need to think about this."

"I. Made. A. Vow."

"I know." She stopped walking. "God." She closed her eyes. "I know. I know." She placed her palm on his cheek, her expression worried. "Soldiers." Her voice lacked heat. "This is all kinds of complicated."

"I can find her. I can find anyone."

"Remy." Now her other palm was on his cheek, soft, warm, and he wondered what she'd do if he kissed her palm.

"This isn't the military," she said softly. "You can't just ghost in, do whatever you want to do and ghost out again."

"I'm dedicated to ensuring that Arlo has anything she needs," he said, offended that Shane would doubt his purpose or character. True, he looked intimidating as hell, or so he'd been told, but Shane didn't look like a woman who was easily scared or backed down.

"I am the opposite of a threat to that child," he said stiffly.

"I don't think you're a threat," she said. She grabbed her water bottle, unscrewed the lid and took a deep swallow. And then another.

"It's just…how long have you been out?"

"First week after my debrief."

Her hands shook and she took another swallow of the water. A few drops spilled and chased down her cheek. He wished he were the water. He wished he could lick the liquid from her skin.

"Remy." She spoke his name like a prayer, and he liked how it sounded on her lips. "I know you have good intentions…"

"I only wish to introduce myself to Arlo's guardians and give them my contact information if they ever need anything and inform them that I will be acting on behalf of Jace McBride, a friend of Arlo's mother and her godfather."

Shane started walking again. He could see the hotel now.

"I have skills. I'm good with my hands."

For digging my own grave.

"I have money saved if her guardians need anything."

He paused at the side entrance of the hotel that had a key code. Shane started keying in the code, blocking it. Not that he was looking, but he saw the motions of her hand so he could tell the code. He'd have to teach her how to be more secretive later.

"But since you know Arlo, are familiar to her…" he ground his teeth together, hating to ask "…I would appreciate it if you could meet her with me to ease the way if she is not too far from here."

Shane's shoulders drooped, and she sucked in a deep breath, pausing before she swung open the door.

"Shane?" Her reaction shocked him. He'd imagined that she'd immediately agree. Shane had such an innate warmth and kindness that he was surprised that she hadn't followed up with the orphaned child herself.

"Let me think about it, Remy," she said softly, slipping through the door, without looking at him.

It clicked definitively behind her.

SHANE WAS IN the post-dinner lull of her Saturday shift. A few people were straggling in from other restaurants to have dessert since the Graff had added a new pastry chef and a chocolatier consultant to the staff, and they had a lovely selection of ports, dessert wines and specialty coffees.

Riley had been trying out new music tonight, and her family—parents, two brothers and their wives—had been here to support her. Shane had vacillated about asking Miranda about Arlo. Surely the young teens would have kept in touch. But that would have meant getting involved and failing again so she'd dredged up one excuse after another to stay silent.

She received an order for three Irish coffees and one Spanish coffee when Remy walked in the door. Her stupid hormones cheered, and the rush of heat, flushed cheeks, elevated pulse and breathing and dancing nerves was humiliating because Remy looked cold. Haunted. She needed to maintain her distance. Fantasizing about Remy when he had one leg straddling his bike to ride out of town was unacceptable. If he stayed, that would be even worse.

But she was helpless to ignore him when he walked in all broody and moving like a predatory animal on the hunt. He turned her legs to melted butter and her mind to mush. Even her dang, betraying body angled toward him like she was a sundial and he the rising sun.

She made the coffees and delivered them personally to give her body time to calm and her brain time to focus.

"Arlo's thirteen," Cross said, barely sitting down on a barstool. His features were tight, and tension radiated off him like a star about to supernova.

She tried to school her features into calm and failed utterly. Why had she imagined she could ever morph into a woman comfortable with a one-night stand? She was all about connections even when she didn't want them.

"She's in the system. We have to go get her."

Shane saw an order pop up for another two Spanish coffees in the restaurant, but Remy's use of *we* short-circuited her brain and body connection. She bobbled the stainless-steel milk steamer. Milk sloshed out on her hand.

"Ouch." Reflexively she brought her hand to her mouth, but he was there first, palm flat on the bar and hurdling over it like he was in an action movie. He took the jug of hot milk from her, and wrapped ice in a clean bar towel and laid it over her hand, just as her brain registered the pain.

She looked at him, but he was focused on her hand. His sensuous mouth tight with tension like the rest of him.

"I'm fine," she said, not pulling away like she should.

He looked at her then; his darkly silver gaze felt like a hot touch.

"Men always, always get the best eyelashes," she grumped to distract herself from his touch.

She should be telling him no. There was no 'we.' No, she would not get involved. No, she was no longer Shane to the rescue. If she tried to play surrogate mom for a motherless girl and then lost the connection… Shane shook her head, not even wanting her thoughts to play with that scenario.

"When are you off?"

"I close the bar," she said firmly. "And I sold my white horse."

He still held her hand. "We probably can't show up after midnight. And I don't have a helmet for a kid yet."

"Remy, what are you talking about?" Shane stilled. "You can't kidnap a child," she said slowly, enunciating each syllable. "And you can't be back here." Although that was the least of his potential digressions.

Lachlan was giving her a WTF look, and Just—Justine Justus, the new bartender Shane had hired so Lachlan had time to finish his business degree online—was staring at Remy like he was dinner, and she was hungry.

"You're hurt. My fault."

"My own fault for being distracted by you." She shooed him away. "And no more Captain America moves."

"Captain America?" For a moment his mouth softened. Then his eyes glittered silver, and the hard planes of his face went harder than granite.

"Remy." She touched his arm. He all but quivered with tension like a hunting dog waiting for the signal. "Tell me you're not going to do something crazy."

"I made a vow." His voice rang with determination, and Shane's heart sank. "Do you know what happens in the system?" he demanded. "Do you know how kids are shuffled around, neglected, mistreated? Do you have a clue?"

He was so fierce, so intense, that Shane wrestled with the urge to hold him and the instinct that she needed to step back. She couldn't get involved. Put her heart out there. She couldn't save anyone. She'd proved that. She hadn't even been able to save her unborn child.

"Remy, you need to go." She spoke softly, pouring authority into her voice. She smiled at Lachlan, holding up her hand wrapped in the bar towel as if that were the excuse for Remy rearing up and going alpha action man.

"I. Made. A. Vow."

"I know." Without thinking about it, her forefinger stroked along his hand that now rested on her hip. "I know you are committed." Her air crashed out of her. Damn this man. But damn her because she was getting involved. Someone had to be the voice of reason. "But there is a process you need follow."

"We…"

"Other side of the bar. Now. Sit."

Was she a dog trainer now?

"Is there a treat attached to that command?"

Somehow his voice had deepened even more and was both silky and rough.

"I am part coyote," he reminded her.

"More like an alpha wolf," she said under her breath. The thought of this man having a commander—respecting and trusting another man enough to follow orders—had her all kinds of curious. Her heart clenched. So many good men and women lost.

"I'll make you a coffee," she said softly, suddenly desperate to keep him at the bar so he wouldn't stalk off and commit a federal crime and terrify a child before the end of her shift. This man got results. He'd found Arlo in the short space of time after walking her to work. She hadn't done that.

You didn't try.

"Or if you'd prefer to wait for me at my outdoor patio, you can go there. We can talk…make a plan," she promised rashly, "after my shift."

That sounded normal, when she felt anything but. His nearness set her on fire and scrambled her brain. Why did she find his 'man of action' persona so dang hot? Something was clearly wrong with her. She was a strong woman who solved her own problems, but this alpha hero chest-beating 'I made a vow' man had smashed through her defenses.

She half-expected Remy to hop over the bar again. More than a few of the people in the bar had been watching them curiously, no doubt wondering if he was an irate worker, or a pushy or overly romantic boyfriend high on love, lust and drama.

"Keep your hand iced for another ten minutes," he bossed and then tamely moved around her, lifted the hatch, and perched on a barstool directly in front of where she preferred to stand when working.

Of course he did. Nothing slipped by the ex-soldier.

Shane turned her back on Remy, winked at Just and spread her all fingers out low at her hips and mouthed 'total ten, right?' hoping to make Just laugh.

She shook her head and muttered, "Fifteen at least." Lachlan shook his head and flipped a bar towel over his shoulder and walked to the other end of the bar away from the crazy.

"Yes, to coffee?"

"One of your fancy ones," Cross said, looking around the bar.

"Which one?" she asked, swiveling the QR code in his direction so he could download the menu. "I can..." She trailed off as he spun the QR code back around.

"Surprise me."

Chapter Six

"YOU'LL NEED A plan," Shane said after they'd walked to her house shortly after midnight. Remy had loaded up on coffee, but he'd also helped her to clean the bar—tidying the bathrooms, taking out the trash, unloading the last dishwasher load and wiping down all the tables, chairs and floor.

They hadn't once mentioned Arlo.

"Never go into battle without one, well, except for this one."

Shane looked up at the ethereal sky. There was no place better than Paradise Valley for stargazing—probably why she hadn't been tempted to move back to Tennessee even after going 'home' to help Sutter's husband, Dawson, set up the bar at the hotel he'd designed and built.

"Maybe you should start by not thinking of it as a battle," she suggested.

"I have no wish to terrify the...girl. Why couldn't she have been a son? This would be so much easier."

"Why?" Shane couldn't help the spurt of feminism.

"Can you imagine me with a girl?"

"Remy, I think there's very little you can't handle," she

said honestly, but then wanted to kick her own behind. She was getting involved. Someone had to be reasonable, but she needed to establish rules to keep her heart safe. "But we really need to talk about..." she made a gesture with her hand "...everything."

She wasn't even sure what 'everything' involved, but she did know Arlo and her needs must come first. Shane's breath tangled in her chest and guilt clogged her throat. She wasn't mother material. Her body and fate had painfully proven that.

"I'll listen to any advice you have," Remy said tautly. "But I made a vow. I am a man of my word."

Her air leaked out. "Remy, I know you made a promise to your brothers and to Jace's spirit, but the situation has changed," she said gently.

"Yeah. Her mom's dead. I googled godfather." Impatience chased across his face. "The information was mostly about religion." He made a face. "I'm not remotely suited for that role, but I can learn." He squared his shoulders. "Take her to church."

Shane had an inappropriate urge to laugh. Remy sounded like he would be standing in for Arlo in front of a firing squad.

"A godfather doesn't have legal standing, or financial obligations, but there was something about showing interest in the child's development and education."

He had done his research. They had reached her gate,

but she'd reached no insights. Her mind spun like a crashing Mac. She unlocked the gate. The night was chilly, but she didn't want to bring him inside her house. Too dangerous for her self-control. He was too tall, too muscular, too potent. Too everything. He'd take up all the air and make her long for things she couldn't have.

"I can…" She hurried forward intending to turn on the fountain and the firepit, but his hand stayed her.

"You've been on your feet all night. Let me take care of you. What would you like to drink? What can I get you to eat?" Remy led her to a chair, and she sat, suddenly feeling her exhaustion from her restless night and worry about Arlo.

"Tea," Shane said. She opened her mouth to tell him where she kept her supplies in the outdoor kitchen, but he was already on the move, turning on the electric kettle, pulling out a mug, riffling through her tea bags and finding the lemon ginger brand she'd had last night.

Then he was in the fridge, pulling out a couple of apples and slicing them. He peered suspiciously at the almond butter, which made her smile. Then he sliced a banana and added it to the plate with the apple and added a generous scoop of almond butter and some cheese slices. By the time he'd served her the food along with a napkin, the water was boiling.

"Thank you. You know your way around a kitchen."

He shrugged. "My mom was the cook for Sam Wilder's Wild Wind Ranch," he said. "I used to help her. And I've had to fend for myself during missions all over the world. Tell me about Arlo." He settled in the chair across from her, his body angled slightly forward, gaze on her like she was about to spill state secrets, and he didn't want to miss a one.

"First tell me your intentions?" she parried.

"Not sure yet."

"Not sure?" Shane, about to sip her tea put it down with a plunk. "Not sure? You can't just burst into her life, ta-da here I am, and then when it gets tough you're back on your bike."

"You seem to have strong feelings about Arlo's well-being," he noted, his voice so silky soft it was like melted dark chocolate. Her outburst hadn't fazed him.

He was setting a trap. Shane knew mental and emotional manipulation when it walked in the door and said hello. She picked up her tea, and leaned back in her chair.

"I know her slightly from her interactions with Petal and Miranda at the hotel." Shane didn't exactly lie, but her stomach was so knotted with conflicting feelings that she felt she was going to hurl up the small sip of tea.

His eyes narrowed.

Who was playing psychologist now?

"Arlo is not a war prize," Shane said firmly, meeting his hard stare. "She's a young, vulnerable, grieving teen whose had her life turned inside out and upside down. Alex died less than two months ago..."

Remy jerked in his chair like she'd shot him. He was on

his feet pacing the small patio like a jacked-up leopard. She could practically smell the adrenaline.

"Less than two months," he breathed, turning to look at her, his expression tortured. "So recent." His voice was like torched gravel.

"You had nothing to do with Alex's death." Shane kept her voice steady. Her other hand rested between his shoulder blades, and he trembled like a wild animal caught in a trap. "You got here as soon as you could."

"I wasn't supposed to be here." He pulled away from her, his hand raking through his hair. "I was supposed to lead that mission where Jace died. Me." He slapped both hands on his chest hard. "Jace had less than two weeks of active duty. He was off the roster. Just wrapping things up, handing all the intel over to Wolf who was taking over. Then Jace was golden, heading back to McChord for his exit interviews and to finish up paperwork. He would have been here. He would have seen that Alex was sick. Dying. He would have…"

Remy stopped talking, clearly realizing something that Shane didn't.

"You are not Jace."

"Don't army-shrink me."

She felt like he'd sprayed her with a garden hose, his comment was so quick and unexpected.

"How did you know that?" She didn't even sound like herself.

"Told you, I don't go into battle without a plan. I need to know the players on the board."

"I'm not a player. Arlo is not a game."

"You're right about that."

"How did you even… Why would you even…" What had he done? "Did you research me?"

DAMN. THIS WOMAN, this whole train wreck of doing a good deed for Jace had morphed him from a man who rarely spoke to one who had a big mouth.

"My past is off-limits. And Arlo's future is not a game."

"We agree on that."

"Explain." She faced him, and he had the impression of two cowboys on a dusty main street facing off at high noon.

He thought of subterfuge. Half-truths. Lies. But the kid had to come first. He had no idea how, but he was going to have to ensure that the kid—Arlo—had a good home. A family. A good life. Security. Maybe it would be easy. Her family could already be on the way. But Cross's life had never once stepped foot on the easy path.

"I had a specialty in the service," he said. He had several, but no need to freak her out. "Classified, but I heard about you from a prisoner I rescued a few months back. Can't go into more detail."

"Or you'd have to kill me," Shane mocked.

He didn't joke about things like that, but as she stood toe-to-toe with him, her arms crossed, her expression searching, he knew like a lightning strike that he was going to stay in Marietta not only until he got Arlo's future settled, but also until he knew Shane was safe from the former major. And that meant he needed the story on the watch.

"How did the prisoner know me?" Shane asked skeptically. "I haven't worked as an army psychologist for nearly five years."

"You really don't know?"

"Not psychic," Shane said. "Unfortunately."

She surprised him by sitting down in a suspended egg-shaped chair with large, bright paisley cushions and pushing off with one foot to set the single swing in motion before crossing her legs.

"Major Brandon Huntingdon the Third ring a bell?"

Both feet went flat on the ground, and she nearly tumbled out of the swing. "Brandon was the prisoner?" She gaped at him. "Impossible. He put his time in for his West Point commitment and left. I didn't even meet him until years after he'd been out. When did you say you 'rescued' him?" She actually pulled out the air quotes on him.

"Few months ago."

"Bzzzzz," Shane made a dismissive buzzer sound. "Try again. Brandon hasn't given me a thought in years."

"He gave you a lot of thoughts," Cross said, his mouth as sour as his tone. "Said you were his fiancée."

His gaze lit on her watch.

"*Was* being the operative word," Shane snapped, and pushed off on the swing again. "Brandon wasn't my only mistake," Shane said, glaring at her bare feet that were tucked up on her thighs in some sort of pretzel pose. "But he is the most mortifying. Five years ago, I was twenty-seven, too trusting, but professional and definitely should have known better. And that is all I'm going to say about that."

She swung harder. "I'm determined to believe he was an aberration."

Like it was so easy to dodge future mistakes. Cross couldn't make the facts compute, but her body and expression were so closed off he knew if he pushed, she'd toss him out on his butt.

"Let's talk about Arlo."

"Okay." He allowed her to shift the conversation, but he wasn't done discussing the major or the watch.

"You can't just charge to Arlo's rescue like some blindly devoted feudal knight, just because of a promise you made to a fallen comrade," she said. "You don't even know her. You don't yet have a..."

"You do," he interrupted before she could poke too many holes in all that he lacked.

"In passing," Shane reiterated, but she didn't meet his gaze.

"It was more than that," he accused. "You're minimizing your closeness with Arlo. Why?"

Shane popped to her feet. The chair wobbled wildly. He too rose and caught the chair, standing close enough to her that their chests nearly touched.

"I'm asking for help," he said, pretty sure those four words in that particular order had never exited his mouth. "Not for a lifetime commitment."

He heard her swallow, and the desire to stroke her throat, to tilt her chin up so that she looked at him and he could drown in the warmth of her aquamarine eyes nearly overwhelmed his common sense.

He was so cold, and she could warm him.

"But a child is a lifelong commitment." Her skin looked translucent in the night.

"First steps. I need to meet her. We need to know what we're dealing with."

"You, Remy, you. And *you'll* need to tread softly," Shane said. "You'll need permission to meet Arlo. And if she's happy and doing well, you'll want to back off."

Shane dragged in a deep breath and finally looked at him. "But if you want to just meet her to give her your cell number and a wad of cash before riding out of town, it's better to leave now."

"Is that what you'd do?"

Her body jerked, and her expression collapsed as if he'd struck her.

"Hey." He pulled her into his arms, not even aware that he did so. "Hey," he whispered again, kissing the top of her head. Her hair caught in his evening stubble. He never seemed to be able to get a close enough shave, even if he did shave twice a day, which he had today.

"I'm sorry. I'm wound up," he confessed. "Everything is so new. So different. I'm feeling my way."

"Me too," she whispered. Her voice sounded confessional. "I don't know the right thing to do," Shane said. "I've failed so many times."

That was BS. The words danced on his tongue, but he bit them back. He couldn't imagine Shane failing anyone, but if she believed it, then likely nothing he could say would change her mind.

Could she change yours?

It was the first time it had occurred to him that there could be a different way of framing an outcome. Probably not, but he didn't have time for theoretical philosophizing now.

"I can't just drive away, Shane, but I admit part of me wants to. I'm not the man for this. I don't see the end. But I can't walk away, and not just because of my promise to Jace. I've failed people badly. And I have to see this through even if I have no idea what it looks like."

The whole time he spoke, her palm rested over his heart, and her clear gaze searched his. And he let her see him—all of him. His doubt. His frustration. His determination.

"Okay, Remy. I'll help you."

SHE DEFINITELY WAS not enthusiastic about it.

The next day, in the early afternoon, Shane drove north, both hands tight on her Jeep's steering wheel. Her expression was neutral, but her lips were tight. He thought she was probably doing breathing exercises to calm down so she wouldn't hit him over the head with the book she'd put in the fancy gift bag with shredded dark pink whatever bursting out of it. She'd also tied a sparkling gold ribbon on the handle.

They'd shopped this morning in the hotel's gift shop that Shane had opened up after a whispered phone conversation with someone. The book had gone into the bag, a sketch pad, a leather-bound journal and watercolor pencils, which he hadn't even known existed. Then they'd gone to the Copper Mountain Chocolate Shop and Shane had created two shimmery copper gift bags of milk and dark chocolate cowboy boots. He'd paid again after a scowl contest, and one bag went into Arlo's gift bag and the other was for 'the other girls.'

He hadn't even thought about other girls in the group home. His stomach cramped with each mile.

"There are so many ways this can go sideways, Remy," she choked out.

"I'm aware." He looked at the blurred scenery.

"You do know how crazy this is," Shane finally said.

"Thought shrinks weren't supposed to say crazy."

"Recovering shrink." She drummed her short nails against the steering wheel twice as if she had to release a highly pressured valve. She shot him an emotive look that if she truly had had any witch powers as a kid should have poofed him into a toad.

'Shines like the sun. Burn your flesh off your bones. Sears your soul clean.'

The words whispered in that dark hole still burned his brain, mocking him, only now a flame fiercely flared in his chest. Jealousy.

"You want to talk about the major?"

"Former. And no."

As a shut-down, it worked…for now. His gaze shifted to the watch. She always wore it, tight, facing into her body.

"Tell me what you're planning for today," she demanded.

"Just two people talking to a kid."

"Really? You have no other agenda than to tell her about Jace? Does she even know about Jace?"

Nervous tension clawed through him. "Why'd Arlo have to be a girl?" He couldn't censor the question.

"Why are you hung up on gender?"

Damn this woman. She could let very little go. He knew he'd needed guidance but fileting himself open for her perusal…

"I had a sister." He tried to keep his voice a flat, nothing-to-see-here tone.

Shane didn't react except for a blink, and her fingers clenched on the steering wheel. She said nothing, and if she thought he was suddenly going to emote like a patient in therapy, she'd be cooling her heels until the earth imploded.

He saw her swallow, waited for the follow-up question—a spoon scooping out his heart.

He blinked against the sting in his eyes.

"She loved dandelions," he said, desperately wanting to stave off more questions. "When I was done with my chores, I would put her on the front of my horse and ride out to a pasture. She'd pick fistfuls of dandelions, and I'd put her on my shoulders and run around with her while she blew the seeds. They'd drift all around us like we were in a snow globe."

"A dandelion storm." Shane smiled; her eyes glowed.

"Something like." He tried to cram the memory back into its box but releasing it had given it life. It had expanded, no longer fitting easily in the dark, crammed spaces in his mind. "I was eight when she was born. Different bio fathers, but this one didn't stick around either. Another rodeo cowboy." He ran his damp palm down his thigh. What was up with men, taking their pleasure but leaving when they were needed? And there was an ugly irony that all he'd ever wanted to be was a cowboy on the Wild Wind Ranch.

"I bet you were a fun big brother."

Shane's comment eased some of the bitterness. His mom

said he'd been the best. But he hadn't—not by a long shot. Brianna would be alive if he'd been smarter. More determined. Less selfish.

"Maybe…" He coughed out the word.

"Was your sister Arlo's age when she passed?"

"Head-shrinking again." He looked out the window, determined to pull himself together.

"Bad habit. I'm blaming you since you keep bringing up the past." She moved her hand that had been in her lap to cover his, and the tension that had been clawing through his body backed off enough that he could breathe until the sign announced Bozeman.

His fingers tightened on hers.

SHANE STOOD OUTSIDE the faded gray house. Weeds choked the small yard, but there was a hammock strung between two trees and a couple of books on the brown grass. Not inspiring, but anyone running a group home for teens likely had their hands full. Shane remembered that Arlo had loved flowers—that's why she'd brought the book that Arlo and Petal had started of the flowers they'd pressed. They'd researched the flowers—their history and meaning and where they grew, and then had tried different writing styles—block letters, shaded, even trying calligraphy they'd learned from a library book. She had even taken Arlo and Petal on a hike

looking for flowers to press, when Miranda's pregnancy had
started taking its toll with nausea and exhaustion.

There wasn't one flower in the yard to offer a pop of col-
or.

Remy—she persisted in seeing him as Remy even when
he seemed to be in soldier on a mission Cross mode—beat
her to the door and rapped with three resonant knocks.

"Have you thought of what you're going to say?"

Not your problem to solve.

Before he answered, a woman in her midthirties wearing
a too tight western-style shirt opened the door. She straightened out of her slouch and touched her limp brown hair, and
took a long drag on her cigarette. Her gaze appraised Cross
and ignored Shane.

"Yeah?" She put one hand on her blinged-out jeans. Her
feet were bare, and her toenails painted a sparkly red. She
blew smoke out in a steady stream to the side of her.

"You the folks the social worker called about? Friends to
Arlo?"

"Yes, ma'am." Shane jumped as Cross spoke.

His voice was soft, almost like a late-night DJ. Mrs. Potter, who ran the house with her sister, stubbed out her
cigarette in a planter of dirt just outside the front door.

"I was best friends with her godfather. We served in the
army together. He passed away a few months ago in the line
of duty, and he'd asked me to keep an eye on Arlo—see if
she needed anything when I retired and returned home to

Montana."

Shane felt like she was in an alternate universe. She'd never heard that warm, rolling tone out of Remy, nor that many words.

Not your business.

"I wanted to introduce myself." Remy smiled, and Shane could practically see Ms. Hammond's eyes roll back in her head as she fluttered her blue mascaraed eyelashes. "My name is Remy Cross, Ms. Hammond, and this is Shane Knight. Shane's taught Arlo and her friends some botany and cooking classes," he added. "She put together a little present for Arlo and brought chocolate for the other girls."

It took total concentration for Shane to keep her jaw hinged shut. Who the heck was this man? And if Mrs. Potter wasn't about to combust as she drank in Remy in a blend of lust and awe, Shane felt she was about to.

"We were hoping for a short visit with Arlo like the social worker said on the phone," Cross said.

Mrs. Potter cocked her hip, her body still blocking the entrance.

"Social worker didn't say what time you were coming." She angled her chest out toward Remy. "But that's not surprising. Dump the kids off and maybe show up for the follow-up visits but sometimes not, and usually never on time like I got nothing to do but hang around all day waiting for someone from the county to grace us."

"Government." Remy struck the perfect 'what can you

do' tone. "Elaine, may I call you Elaine?" Again, with the smile, and Shane wanted to hit him—how did *he* manage to look deferential and shy? "We know you are a busy woman with many responsibilities. Shane and I have no desire to impose on your valuable time. We can talk to Arlo outside. The afternoon is pleasant, and the breeze from the mountains is refreshing."

It was hot, stifling, and in a state known for its stunning natural beauty, this faded house slipping into disrepair with everything dead in the yard that was mostly dirt was an unhappy place to visit. Still Remy was trying his best and as an accomplice, she was falling down on her job. First up, snap Elaine out of her Remy-induced sexual stupor.

"We brought refreshments." Shane smiled. "I baked some chocolate chip and also peanut butter cookies for the other girls. And bought an assortment of chocolates for you and your sister and the other girls."

"That so?" Elaine flicked her a hard look. "Y'all married?"

"What?" Shane yipped in surprise.

"Not yet, Elaine," Remy said earnestly.

"Whaaa…" Shane's lips pursed. What game was this?

"Shane is stubborn." Remy kissed her temple. "Playing hard to get." He looked at Elaine appealingly, and she wondered if he'd keep that Boy Scout smile if she stomped on his toe.

"That's dumb." Elaine lit another cigarette and sucked in

deeply and then blew out the smoke again, this time to the side of Shane. "You blind? He's fine. Better than."

She couldn't argue that point, but she kept her mouth shut. Remy must be running some op, which of course he hadn't shared with his 'partner.' She would have a lot to say on the way home.

"Thank you, Elaine," Remy said. "May we see Arlo now for a spell?"

He was talking like he was some Southern man from the thirties or some ridiculous time, and Shane thought about kicking him somewhere higher. He'd better pull out his real personality with Arlo, or she'd blow his cover wide open.

Elaine narrowed her eyes back on Remy drinking in his height, musculature and angular face with a strong jaw and brow and high cheekbones that screamed masculinity. Add in his shaggy black hair that grew back from his strong features and he was beyond appealing physically. He was deadly sexy. And today he'd worn an open western-style shirt over his black T. His sleeve of tats was covered. Instead of his motorcycle boots he wore cowboy boots. They didn't look new.

Was this new look part of his ruse or did Remy truly intend to return to his cowboy roots? She again thought of Colt Wilder and his family's ranching operations. He might be able to hook Remy up with a job.

"You said you had cookies for the girls and chocolates?" Elaine demanded, hand out.

Shane held out the larger of the two tins and Elaine opened it and poked around.

"Arlo," she bellowed. "Get out here."

Shane handed her the bag of chocolate cowboy boots. Elaine took a milk chocolate one and bit into it.

"You need to stay in the yard where I can see you. Supervised visit." She picked through the cookies next, choosing a chocolate chip.

"Of course," Remy said smoothly as if he hadn't hinted at kidnapping Arlo last night.

"But she can walk Beast around the block if she wants," Elaine said through a mouthful of cookie. "It's the only job she's any good at, useless girl. Just sits on her bed and stares at the wall holding that ugly stray dog I was mental enough to let her keep. Won't eat much. Won't talk. Doesn't do her chores and looks right through you when you try to talk sense to her." She took another bite of cookie. "Arlo, folks here to see you."

She finished the cookie and took another—this one peanut butter. "Remember, just a walk around the block with that mangy dog, then sit yourselves where I can see you."

Shane couldn't decide if Elaine would spy on them because she thought Remy was hot or if she was scrupulously responsible for her charges. Shane knew she wasn't being fair, but the sad and rundown appearance of the outside of the house had her worried about the inside.

"Arlo just lost her mother," Shane reminded the woman.

"Yeah." Elaine shrugged. "We all lost someone and something. Happens. These are good," she admitted, grudgingly. "Didn't think skinny supermodel types could or would bake. Live and learn."

She stepped back and partially closed the door.

Remy skewered Shane with a look that stabbed her bones.

"You were saying I should back off if she's happy and doing well." His voice was like a whip.

Shane flinched but kept her attention on the bright ribbon of the gift bag instead of Remy who held the cooler with the other snacks and drinks for their picnic. He had a blanket from her house rolled up under his arm.

"We shouldn't jump to conclusions," she cautioned feeling like a phony because she definitely was high-jumping to a lot of them. "And you—" she couldn't contain her irritation a moment longer "—really should consider Hollywood with your 'ma'am,' 'visit a spell' and aw-shucks smile. And what was that kiss and the implication that I'm too stupid to marry such a prime example of a man?"

"That's what bothers you in this situation?"

She pressed her lips together.

"You do think I'm prime?"

"Stop fishing for compliments." Her embarrassment gave way to annoyance again—much easier to handle. "You asked me to help, but you rogued way off script."

"Going with my gut."

"You're lucky I didn't punch you in it, but I probably would have broken my hand."

A smile ghosted on his lips, but instantly fled. "I know everything I need to know."

"No, you don't." Shane was aghast, wondering how she was going to drag his six-four or six-five body of smoking hotness back to her Jeep without braining him first.

"You don't know anything," she whispered in case Elaine was still listening. "Arlo is an adolescent deeply grieving an enormous loss. You are just coming off multiple deployments and a long-term military career. You have no stability in your life yet. None. You have no plan. No housing. No job. This is not about you or your vow." She poked him in the chest with each point. "This is about Arlo. Only about Arlo and what's best for her—not what's best for me...I mean you."

She bit her inner lip to keep the swear word in.

"Thank you, Dr. Freud." He rubbed at his chest.

She pressed her finger against his lips. "Not one more word."

"Or?" His eyes lit up, and he sucked her finger into his mouth. His tongue licked along her length and heat curled her toes.

And then the door slowly squeaked open. Shane pulled back her finger with a pop and wiped it on her jeans. Remy's smirk locked her breath in her lungs.

"Shane?" The astonished voice jerked her back to their

mission with a power that jarred her bones.

Arlo stood there in skinny black jeans with rips in the knees and thighs, a sky-blue tank with a bucking bronc that read *Copper Mountain Rodeo* from the previous year. Gut punch. Shane had attended the rodeo with Alex and Arlo along with Miranda and Petal and the rest of the Telford family. It wasn't even one full year later, and yet Arlo's life had blown apart. And like a character in a Greek tragedy, Arlo had cut off her hair—badly so that it was chunkily cropped unevenly all around her head.

There wasn't a TikTok produced that could make that mess look trendy. Shane could barely swallow, but she sure tasted bile in the back of her throat.

"Arlo." Shane dug for a smile. She'd seen worse, but they'd been clients. Not personal.

"Hey, Shane." Arlo's blue eyes had been flat but now they lit up with a hopeful desperation that was another fist to Shane's gut. "Petal texted me you were coming. Did you come to take me home?" She turned to Remy, and her eyes widened. "Are you my real dad?" She breathed the question into the stale air that still smelled like cigarettes and dead lawn.

Chapter Seven

BEAST TURNED OUT to be a beat-up bichon frise and maybe some other breeds with a fierce attitude, wearing a cone of shame after a run-in with a racoon. He was partially shaved and the stitches on two places on his back and underbelly were still in. The skin was still pink and looked a little greasy.

"Tea tree ointment for antiseptic just like you told me about, Shane," Arlo finally said into the silence as they walked around the block after Remy's disconcerted mumbled 'no' had killed the sudden light in Arlo's eyes.

It had reminded him too much of holding on to his mother as the snow had swirled around them. She'd been alive—barely, bleeding internally, which he hadn't known about, and externally, which he'd tried to stop by ripping off his jacket and pressing it to her wounds. She'd been desperately trying to talk, and it had been hard to hear over his sister's shrill screams. He hadn't wanted to listen, hadn't wanted to believe she was dying, but she'd known it. He'd held her as the light faded from her eyes, and her features went slack, even as he heard the distant wail of a siren.

He didn't know what to do or say to make this painfully

awkward walk that felt like a death march easier. He was a man of action not words. But Shane was talking. He needed to listen and banish the roaring in his ears.

"Tell me about Beast," Shane asked as Beast lifted his leg on a random patch of dead lawn.

"I found him in an alley the second time I ran away."

"You ran away? What the..." Remy just managed to shut it in time. The look Shane shot him—admonishment tinged with resignation and he thought humor—took his mood from black to gray streaked with yellow, maybe even some pink. Shane could probably tame a rampaging bison.

"He was lost?" Shane's voice was soothing—probably something she learned in shrink school.

Shane's calm vibe as she pet the ugly dog even relaxed him, but it also made him want to rile her a little, get her to see him as a man, not some animal to tame.

"Yeah. No collar. I took him to a vet." Arlo was looking at the ugly, ragged Beast as they walked, not at them. "They scanned him for free. No chip. I snuck him back into Elaine's, but of course she noticed. No privacy. But because he's so ugly none of the other girls tried to take him like everything else."

Remy stopped walking. Shane's fingers lightly brushed his, steadying him. He drew in a deep breath. She was right. He couldn't ride off with Arlo. Fix her on his own. Jace had intended to be a presence in Arlo's life. Make a home and new life for himself and his brothers. How was he going to do that without Jace—and now with a grieving thirteen-year-old girl?

Cross didn't have a home to return to…unless old Sam Wilder was still alive and needed a ranch hand. That had been a spread. For a moment, memories of the ranch—the pastures of golden wheat and other grasses, the grazing cattle, his excitement when Sam Wilder had increased his chore load before and after school—filled his head. For the first time since he'd left the service, he felt a flicker of hope. Maybe he could craft a different life in Marietta. Quiet his ghosts. Build instead of destroy.

"Why'd you think I was your daddy?" Remy interrupted Shane. "Your mama say Jace McBride was your daddy?"

Shane's exhaled sigh was nearly silent, but he heard it. He noticed everything about that woman far too much and he doubted his fixation had anything to do with his rigorous training.

"Nnnnoooo?" Arlo drawled out after a long pause.

Beast's energy was beginning to flag even though they'd only made it halfway around one neighborhood block. Arlo scooped Beast up and cradled the panting pup in her arms. She turned around to head back to the group home, her steps slower than before. He and Shane walked with her, though the slow pace was maddening—not that he wanted to return to the depressing house, but he wanted an action plan.

"We brought drinks," Shane said. "And some snacks.

Maybe we can sit on the…lawn and have a picnic."

"Like we did at Petal's? Miranda and my mom used to…" Arlo trailed off into silence.

He zipped it, trusting Shane, yet she didn't immediately fill the silence. Instead, she put her arm around Arlo and pulled her close as they walked and fussed over the dog a little. When they were back at the house, Remy could feel curious gazes on them. He had the same itch on his skin that he'd felt on occasion in the field when he knew the enemy was stalking him and his men.

He should not still be on such high alert with a few adolescent girls and a sexually bored caretaker watching, but he was. And he was out of his depth. The one sentence on the piece of paper he'd drawn from Jace's helmet had sounded deceptively simple.

"Maybe I should proceed how Jace would have proceeded," he mused aloud as Shane encouraged Arlo to help her spread out a blanket.

"Why didn't Jace come?" Arlo asked.

"Sh…" He broke off and ran a hand through his hair. "I'm all sorts of bad at this…talking thing," he admitted.

"Think you can rig us up some shade, man of action?" Shane gracefully sank onto the blanket tailor style and began unloading the cooler and the other bag that she'd brought. "There might be something in the Jeep that will work with the hammock." She handed her keys to Arlo. "Maybe you can help Remy. I'll pour Beast some water."

AS FAR AS picnics went, Shane couldn't imagine one less gloomy. Arlo seemed to shrink inside herself when Cross—hard to think of him as Remy when he was so still and watchful—gently told Arlo of Jace's heroism, death and desire to ensure that she and her mom were happy and safe.

"But we're not," she whispered, balling herself up, thighs to chest, arms wrapped around her legs, chin on her knees. Beast pressed close to her thigh.

"That's why I'm here," Cross said, and Shane winced.

She shouldn't have come, but someone needed to inject reality into this sad situation, because Cross didn't seem to acknowledge all the hurdles and potholes in their...no his way.

She poured out some lavender lemonade, adding a strawberry and a few blueberries to the glass. She held it out toward Arlo, who stared at it blankly. Shane wished she could swallow the lump clogging her throat. She didn't push Arlo to take the blue plastic glass.

"My mom and I used to picnic by the Marietta River in the park by the courthouse," Arlo whispered.

"It's important to remember the good times," Shane encouraged. "It will create more good times and help you on the days that are harder."

"Every day is hard," Arlo murmured.

"It is at first," Shane said, wishing Remy would open up

something of himself. He'd had loss. He could share. He and Arlo could start to connect if he truly meant to stay and be a presence in Arlo's life.

"Some days are dark," Remy said, his deep voice firm, cutting across the gloom like a knife. "You don't know how to take the next step, but you do. And you keep going because there will be more riverside picnics ahead."

"You can't promise that," Arlo whispered.

"I can and I am." Cross didn't hesitate or break eye contact even when Shane handed him a lemonade that she was tempted to splash into his arrogant 'I can do what I want' face.

What part of caution did he not understand? Shane had counseled teens in the system during her training. There had been success stories—many of them. But it was the failures that had dragged her down, and she'd struggled to maintain her objectivity. Remy's jumping in with both feet was not helping. She too wanted to scoop Arlo up and drive her back to her house. Miranda had been so relieved when Shane had called her about the plan. She'd want an update, and Shane had no idea what to say.

Cross waited until Shane had her glass of lemonade. "Cheers." He tapped his glass against both of theirs.

The confusion tinged with hope in Arlo's eyes, as she stared at Cross, filled Shane with unease. He shouldn't promise the girl anything. Silently she urged him to realize the precariousness of his position.

"Cheers, Beast." Cross lightly touched his cup to the top of the thermos lid of water Shane had poured out.

For the first time, Arlo had a hint of a smile, and Cross's matched.

Shane held her breath, feeling like she was on the edge of a cliff high on Copper Mountain. Everything inside of her rose up to make a rash promise—*I'll find a way to adopt you. I promise to take care of you. You will always have a home with me.* She balled her fists. Bit her lip hard enough to taste blood. She couldn't save anyone. She'd proved that three times now—she was the anti-heroine.

"Arlo," Cross said. He waited until the girl's flitting gaze lit upon him again. "I'm not going anywhere."

Two hours later, Shane waited until Remy had buckled up for the ride home to finally uncork the tension that had choked her during the too-brief visit.

"You can't promise her anything," she hissed as she pulled away from the curb after Cross had walked Arlo and Beast back to the front door, given her his cell number and the gift and watched her disappear into the grim, dimly lit house.

"Why not?" He stretched his legs out, looking relaxed, though his expression was tight, and hot as hell—of course.

"A million reasons." She shifted into drive.

"Let's start with one."

"She is a child." Shane's voice rose and cracked. Crap, she hated yelling. She was always calm, reasonable, but now her emotions flew around like they had their own broom.

"So I should walk away from Arlo?"

"I…" Her stomach clenched so hard that the small amount of flavored lemonade she'd drunk burned the back of her throat. "It's complicated."

"Not from where I'm sitting."

She pressed harder on the gas. "That's because you're not thinking."

"And you are?" His voice was deceptively soft, and she absolutely should *not* engage.

"I don't have to explain anything to you." Defensive much?

"Not to me but be honest with yourself. You're as conflicted as I am about leaving Arlo."

She clenched her teeth.

Do not answer.

"Your behavior coupled with your attitude doesn't make sense."

"My state of mind and actions have nothing to do with you, Remy." She pressed down too hard on the accelerator, speeding out of the depressing neighborhood with the tired, droopy, faded homes from the fifties and sixties.

"You obviously care about Arlo. You spent time with her. You packed a picnic for her that included things you knew she liked. You picked out personalized gifts she really loved."

Shane didn't answer. She couldn't. She hit a wider, treelined street with bigger homes, set back from the road.

She felt like each of Remy's words was a knife that peeled the skin off her bones so that it flared out behind her like a tattered, bloody cape.

"Stop," she whispered. "Not another word."

"I'm aware I'm the last choice anyone would make to help Arlo. I don't know how to relate to a teen girl. I don't know how to connect to people."

Remy's self-flagellation hurt her.

"You can connect," she objected, thinking of his quiet and sincere efforts on the lawn.

"But fate chose me." He raked at his hair. "I'm smart. I'm determined. I will learn. You could help."

"I can't." Tears blurred her eyes, and she skewed over to the curb in front of a white, farmhouse-style home. "I can't."

She laid her head on the steering wheel.

"Why not? From where I'm sitting, you're a far better bet. I'm the worst stand-in for Jace. But I'm not walking away. Not again."

"Again?" The one word sliced through her misery and failure. She raised her head and looked at him. He ran a lean hand through his hair, displacing it, but it fell back around his face, caressing those supreme cheekbones, chiseled jaw and teasing his cut shoulders.

He was so strong, and she felt so weak.

"I don't understand you," she said softly. "You have this crazy blend of doubt and determination. I don't know why you think you can do this."

"I don't even know what 'this'..." he waved his hand "...entails—not yet, but I can't walk away and leave another young, vulnerable girl to make her own way in the world."

He stared out of the windshield as if answers waited a block or two away.

"Your sister," she realized, looking at his strained profile.

Pieces fell into place. God, he was brave. And she was such a coward. She shifted in the bucket seat, rubbed her shaking palms down her face and then clenched them in her lap.

"Miranda and I talked about finding a home for Arlo if she didn't have family," Shane said. "Miranda seemed perfect." Shane laughed hollowly.

He turned to face her, listening with his full attention.

"But Miranda's situation now doesn't work. She knows she can't give Arlo the support she would need."

"And you? What's holding you back?"

His voice felt like another whip. One more scar. "I thought this was your mission," she said bitterly. He didn't need to point out that Arlo was not thriving where she was. "Mister I promise riverside picnics and I'm not going anywhere."

"I'm not. But I need to know the terrain, actors and parameters of the mission."

Shane plunked her head back down on the steering wheel.

"This is not the military. Arlo is not a mission. I'm not under your command."

"I need help, Shane. You can help."

She shook her head, feeling the warmed plastic of her steering wheel press against her forehead. Sucking in air, she straightened and faced him. "I'm no one's answer to a prayer, Remy," she said. "I'm really not."

He looked at her. Gray eyes turbulent. She felt like he had some sort of a vortex building in his gaze, sucking her in.

"That makes two of us."

She wanted to smile despite the tension choking them both.

"I can't do kids," she confessed. "I can't."

"You were great with her." He looked puzzled. "You drew her out. She was a kid again. I was trying to stay out of your way and learn something."

"And that's the problem," she said with finality.

"Not from where I'm sitting."

"But it is where I am." Shane shoved her aviator-style Maui Jim sunglasses back on her face, checked her side mirror and pulled back on the street to drive home, but every mile Shane put between her and Arlo's grief, bewilderment and loneliness made it harder to breathe. And Remy's unwavering scrutiny felt like an MRI on her head and heart.

But she couldn't trust herself any longer. Shane to the rescue had twice stumbled and face planted. People had died. Her baby had died. If she tried to help Remy, she'd get sucked in. Committed. And then he'd leave. Or shut her out. Or Arlo could go off the rails, and Shane absolutely could not fail another person.

Chapter Eight

S HANE WAS SHUTTING him out. She had every right, but he didn't like it.

She'd found ways to connect to Arlo. It was obvious Shane cared for her. How could she turn her back on the child when it was clear Arlo needed her?

How can you?

The question hit with the force of a bullet. He'd said he'd taken a vow, but it finally hit him what the vow to Jace and his brothers truly meant. There wouldn't be a few check-ins a year. There wouldn't be a search for another family.

He was going to have to be her family.

Cross leaned back in the seat as Shane hit Highway 89 south. He pinched the bridge of his nose to concentrate. Sam Wilder had done that when he'd been thinking, and for some reason—probably because as a kid he'd tried to emulate Sam Wilder—it had stuck with Remy. Sam had been his example of how a man behaved, and yet, Sam Wilder had ultimately let him down. His mother had made him promise to behave for Sam. To take care of Brianna, but within a day of his mother's passing, the state had come in and taken both him and Brianna away. Sam had watched and then walked off to the barn before the car had pulled out of the driveway.

Maybe him helping Arlo would balance the scales for Brianna.

His mom had believed in God. She'd prayed as she'd died—prayed for her children to be safe, saved. They hadn't been. But maybe, twenty-five plus years later it wasn't totally too late for him to make his own amends even though he was carrying out one of Jace's wishes.

"What do you know of Wild Wind Ranch?"

Shane blinked. "Not much," she said. "I know Sam Wilder by reputation," she said slowly. "Ben Ballantyne, another old-time rancher in town, is a long-time friend of his. He's always trying to get Sam to come out more, engage, forgive his daughter Samara Wilder, or if not that, at least build some bridges with his grandsons. Why are you asking about Sam?"

"I was asking about the ranch."

"I've never been there. I'm friends with Tucker Wilder and also Talon Wilder—all of them really, but they have a separate spread—two smaller ranches they run. Sam's estranged from his family."

"Sounds about right," Cross said. "Take me there."

"The Wild Wind?"

"Yeah."

She seemed to be expecting more information. Cross wasn't used to explaining, but he respected Shane. And he might hate it, but he needed her, which meant the dark lust she effortlessly brewed inside of him just by existing was the last complication he could afford.

It would be easy if he could just give her what she'd wanted that first night—incendiary passion that scorched the sheets and flamed out the minute he hit the door, but he'd known then one night would never be enough.

"My mom was the cook at the Wild Wind when I was a kid. I know Sam, and I know the ranch. I did chores as a kid. Everyone had to pull their weight to eat. Most everything I know about ranching Sam taught me."

He needed Shane on board with his plans, but he wanted so much more.

"I need a job. Maybe he needs a ranch hand. I could start there."

If silence had a sound, it was like the lowest note on an upright bass, softly plucked so that it just hung in the air.

"Remy." She glanced at him. "You're really going through with this?"

"This being?"

"You tell me," Shane said after another long beat of silence broken only by her nervous drumming on her thigh.

He was pathetically aware of her every nuanced move, her breath, the way she swallowed. The long sweep of her pale eyelashes.

"I don't have another path, Shane," he said. "And if you're honest with yourself, neither do you."

"Don't tell me what I feel. Don't tell me what I should

do." She gripped the steering wheel with both hands, but her voice was an ache that reached inside of him and twisted him into one more knot.

"I can't fail again."

"The two of us stumbling together with the best intentions and wills of tungsten will be better than Elaine's barely there attention."

"Best intentions aren't always enough, Remy."

She navigated through a few more hairpin turns as she approached the summit. On the way to Bozeman, he'd been able to ignore the scene of the accident that had derailed his life, because it had been on the opposite side road, and he'd stared into the forest and pretended he was far away.

Now sweat broke out on his scalp, and his breathing shallowed even though he willed himself to not react. He was a man now. Not a boy. There were no ghosts.

"Sam's not at the ranch," Shane said.

"No way, he sold the ranch? That's been Wilder land for generations."

"I don't know the whole story. I heard he was in financial trouble. His daughters caused a lot of heartaches. His grandsons have been trying to help, but…" She shrugged. "He's shut everyone out. But something happened a week ago. Sam's in the hospital."

Remy felt jolted by the news. "Is Sam sick?" He'd been nursing a grudge and the old man had needed someone in his corner to help with the ranch, run interference with his family if necessary. Cross wasn't family, though when he was a kid, he'd pretended that his widow's peak meant that he and Sam—who had one too—were related somehow.

"I don't know. The other rancher I mentioned—Ben Ballantyne—has been visiting Sam. He told me the news after he called the Wilders. A small plane taking a couple of tourists along the route of the Yellowstone River spotted Sam prone in one of his fields near the river. Called it in. He's been hospitalized but tried to escape and so he's in lockdown because he still needs care. Ben said he'd take him to his ranch, The Three Trees. Of course all the Wilders want to take care of him at one of their homes, but he won't even let them visit."

"Who's running his ranch?" And to think if he hadn't discovered that his mission with Arlo wasn't going to be a quick fix, he would have left town, not realizing that the only father figure he'd known, and the man who'd taught him to give his best every day, needed him.

One more debt he needed to pay.

Shane shrugged, an elegant shift of her shoulders. "Tucker, his granddaughter-in-law, said Sam's let a lot go."

"Impossible."

"I don't know, Remy. The Wilders are good people. Honest. They only want to do what's best for Sam and the ranch. The grandsons have been reaching out for years—well, two of them—Luke and Kane."

Remy didn't know either of them, but he intended to

remedy that. He didn't want Sam taken advantage of.

They crested the hill and Shane took her foot briefly off the gas. "This is my favorite spot in the world," she said softly. "Like being on top of the world. I can see all of Paradise Valley and never was a place more aptly named."

He clutched the handle above the door, holding himself rigidly in place. He was being absurd.

"One more road in a world of bad roads," he said, choking on bile.

"Remy?"

He could barely hear her over the thundering of his pulse. His chest felt like a Humvee was on it—something that had nearly happened once.

"Stop," he said. He couldn't do this. He couldn't live with the past waiting to jump out and bitch-slap him. He had to have control. Always. He was a man, not a boy. He was trained. "Pull over. Here. Right here."

Shane ignored him and drove farther down the highway to where the road expanded to two lanes with a wide shoulder and a pull-out spot for viewing. Remy jumped out and stalked back up the road, his vision wavering. He stood on the edge of the road, breathing deeply. He had to come to terms with how his life had shattered so many years ago.

He couldn't have a damn panic attack on a road he was going to have to regularly drive to visit Arlo so she'd know she wasn't abandoned.

Like I was.

He closed his eyes. Breathed in deep. Let the memories flow and hopefully loosen their claws in his spine just a little. Fresh air with a whisper of snow teased his face and hair. Scents of grass. Ponderosa pine. Dirt. And...cinnamon. Shane.

She stood next to him. One arm slipped around his waist, and her head rested on his shoulder.

"Tell me, Remy," she invited.

"Says the woman with so many secrets."

She sighed but didn't retreat—so much strength. Something in him loosened, and he imagined for the first time that his past was a balloon he could release and watch it float away.

"If your past was a balloon what color would it be?" He half expected her to laugh. "Would you let it go?"

"Red." She floored him by answering. "And I'm not sure I can let the past go. Our pasts define us, Remy. Ground us, but the trick is to not let it keep you from also flying."

"Are you flying?" he asked, not to be a jerk. He really wanted to know.

"Some days," she said. "Some days not. I'm scared, Remy. Scared for Arlo. Scared for you. Scared for me."

"Fear makes you feel alive," he said reflexively.

"Remy, this is a young girl's life. When I was training..." she sucked in a deep breath "...I was working with a teen boy. He had many challenges. He'd been in and out of foster care. But he had so many other traumas and issues. I was so young. So confident. We worked together a year. I thought I'd made so much progress. I thought I'd found the magic combination to help him, to unlock his hope. Change his suicide ideation. I thought I was so smart. The savior."

Cross knew what was coming. Her being spooked about kids finally made sense.

"I thought I was magic."

"You are magic." He pulled her into his arms, and she came. Fit. And Cross, for the first time, felt connected and whole in a way he'd never once experienced.

"But I lost him," she confessed.

"We all lose people, Shane. I lost my mom here. Right here," he said. "When I was twelve. My family was in an accident here." His voice sounded rusty. "My mom was driving slowly. Her car was old and had trouble with the mountain. It was slushy and her tires needed replacing," he remembered. "She'd taken me to Bozeman to buy a guitar for my birthday. She let me pick it out. My sister was four. She was with us. Mom took us to lunch—a rare treat for her to not cook."

He stopped. He didn't want to go over the rest.

But maybe he had to. The weight of Shane's head on his shoulder was a comfort. And her arm wrapped around his waist felt strong.

"Usually, I would have been in the front with my mom commandeering the tunes, but I wanted to try my guitar and let Brianna play it. Just as we crested, a jacked-up truck that had been tailgating her for a while, making her more nervous, tried to pass, but there was no place for her to pull over. And someone was coming in the other direction, so it pulled back quick into our lane clipping us and…" He broke off.

"Remy." Shane's hold on his tightened, and she turned her face into his neck and nuzzled him. "I am so, so sorry, Remy. So sorry."

"We went over the edge. My mom survived for a little while, but I couldn't jump over the seat and stop all the bleeding because I was afraid the car would plunge farther down the hill, and my sister was in her car seat, screaming. She made me promise to take care of my sister. Behave for Sam."

He couldn't talk anymore. Didn't want to tell her that he'd held his mom's hand, praying with her, for her, but as he'd heard the sirens getting closer, he'd listened to her last ragged breath.

He didn't know how long they stood there together looking out over the pass, down the jagged boulders and the trees growing up out of the dirt and rocks, like a middle finger to all the doubters of Mother Nature's power, but for the first time in a long time, he felt a sense of peace and belonging.

"I never wanted to come back here," he said.

"But you did it for Jace."

He nodded.

"And you're really going to stay for Arlo?"

"Must seem crazy—a man like me."

"Not crazy, Remy Cross. You are a good man." She looked at him like she believed it. And if she could, maybe he could too eventually.

"Fate has a way of laughing while she spits in your face, doesn't she?" he asked.

"Can't disagree." Shane smiled. "I blame the Greeks and Shakespeare." Shane palmed his cheeks. Her eyes were bright with tears, and something he didn't dare name.

"Let me text Tucker to see if we can visit Wild Wind Ranch. Or meet with them at their ranch. Slay another ghost before sunset."

"Maybe for us both."

The boys and I are at the Wild Wind. Bring your cowboy soldier. It's a perfect time for a cool dip into crazy.

"Quintessential Tucker." Shane looked at the message.

"Probably better for you to drive up in a Jeep than on your bike," she teased. "Although Tucker's been on me to switch to a truck for a couple of years now."

"It is part of the life," he said. "Sam used to drive this old red-and-white, beat-up Ford truck. Had me wash it. Taught me how to service it—change oil, spark plugs, wipers, tires. Taught me to work on the tractor too," Remy mused, stretching his long legs out, and Shane reminded herself to keep her eyes on the road—not on the man next to her. "Taught me to ride."

She heard the pride and affection in his voice, and her bruised heart flipped.

"You liked him," she noted.

Remy's lips kicked up in a half smile. "He was aloof. Watchful. Hard-driving, but he was the closest thing to a father I ever had."

Tension snaked through her and for a moment she wondered why. Then she realized she was worried Remy was going to get hurt. Again. He'd lost his friend, and probably so much more. He was outside of the strictures and structure of the military. And now he wanted to see Sam again—Sam who wouldn't welcome his own daughter or grandsons.

"Don't worry," he said as if he was a mind reader. "I'm a man now. I can take it."

She struggled to corral her galloping thoughts. She'd hoped for one night of dirty, memorable sex. Now she wanted more but knew she shouldn't risk it.

Remington Cross was beyond tempting. Maybe now that she was a woman, she too could take the risk of another heartbreak. Remy was perfect.

But she didn't deserve perfect. She couldn't deliver it back after years of endometriosis, two surgeries, and then the miscarriage. Remy had so much to give, though he didn't know it yet. He might want a family. He needed family. He might not think he was cut out for it. But he was—loyal, a protector, determined. He just needed…

No. No Shane to the rescue. But what if she and Remy and Arlo…

"Turn here." He pointed to a narrow gravel she'd barely noticed, thankfully interrupting her hope before the stupid thing could take root.

"It's federal land. It will cut fifteen minutes off your drive, and the Wild Wind has egress rights."

His voice was low, a thread of tension running through, and he leaned forward slightly as if trying to take in more of the view, one large palm splayed on his thigh.

"Lotta memories," she said softly.

"We all got them." He turned toward her, brushed his knuckles against her cheek. "Thank you."

"For what?"

"For jumping off the bridge with me."

That was melodramatic. Her stomach cramped. She didn't want to hope. "I'm just the driver."

"Baby, you're so much more than the driver." His voice slid deep inside her body like heated syrup. "You're magic. And stop lying to yourself." He feathered his fingers along the pounding pulse in her neck. "And never lie to me either."

The words could have sounded like a threat, but with his hair sliding against her cheek, and the lingering of his lips brushing against her jaw ending with a sensuous kiss along her neck, even as his fingers continued to stroke and kiss, his command sounded like a promise.

"We'll find our way." His lips nuzzled down her neck sending chills skittering down her spine and heat pooling between her pressed-together thighs.

With his teeth, he popped one of the buttons of her western-style shirt. And then another. His fingers found one of her already peaked nipples, rolling, pinching and then his mouth closed over her other nipple through the very thin cotton of her tank.

"I love that you don't always wear a bra. It jacks me up, but why did you have to wear one today?" He sucked her small offering into his mouth and the heat, moisture, and friction had her moaning and her foot off the gas.

They rolled to a stop, evergreens on either side of them standing vigil.

"Remy," she practically wept with frustrated desire. "You're going to a job interview."

"Cuts the tension." He'd tugged her tank down, unclasped her front-clasp lacy white bra and cupped her A-size breast like it was a treasure. He lightly closed over one nipple with his teeth, while his thumb stroked the other nipple into straining alertness. "You're beautiful, so responsive."

She laughed and made a grab for sanity. "Maybe I should have prescribed sex when my previous clients exhibited anxiety before events that triggered them."

"That's a prescription every man would stampede to fill." He raised his head to look at her and his gray eyes glinted silver at her. "But you don't get to play pharmacy when you're with me."

"Remy." She could barely breathe, and somehow her fingers had tangled in his silky hair to tug him closer to her. The lust in his eyes stoked her fire hotter. "We're not together," she whispered.

"Hmmmmm." He kissed the corner of her mouth, and she chased his lips without meaning to, and then his hand closed over her mound, scorching her already radiating heat as he stroked her. "You were saying?"

"We're not dating," she clarified. "Not in a relationship."

"But you'd enjoy sex with me." His smile was cocky and carnal, and he wasn't asking.

"Enjoy is a massive understatement, but..."

"No buts," he said. "Yes or no? Why deny ourselves pleasure when I'm putting down stakes in Marietta."

"It's not that easy," she breathed, wishing she could just shut up and indulge the want that ached through her.

"Doesn't have to be hard." His hand was inside of her jeans, one finger stroking inside her liquid channel while his thumb found her small bud and stroked her dangerously near orgasm. "Don't overthink."

She couldn't think at all. She tried to ride his hand, but he controlled the speed, and his silvery-gray eyes seared into hers, searching, noting her every reaction. And when she tried to clasp him tightly to her, he pinned both her hands in one of his, and held them above and back of her head so that her breasts—her shirt open and tank pulled down—thrust up toward him.

"Remy," she whispered. It was the most intimate thing that had ever happened to her. The most intimate moment of her life, while he pleasured her body and stared into her eyes, and she was trapped into position of staring right back.

She lost track of time and of everything except her body's extreme endorphin rush and the pleasure crashing through her as he cranked her higher than she'd ever been before, just with two fingers and a thumb.

"Remy." Her voice was an urgent confession. And she squeezed his hands holding hers prisoner, short nails digging in as she crested so high it was almost terrifying.

"Keep looking at me." His voice was a whip of command, and her eyes, squeezed shut as if she could somehow still control something, shot open.

"I'm going to..."

"I know."

And then she orgasmed, body spasming, and then he kissed her deeply, drugging her with his taste, releasing his hold on her hands so that she could tug at his shirt, feel his hard hot skin with the sensitive pads of her fingers.

But even as he let her finally touch him, and he kissed her until she had no idea where she ended and he started, his fingers continued to stroke her, expanding and extending her orgasm. Shane had always enjoyed sex, but it had never once felt like this. Not even close.

She gasped for breath, tried to slow her thumping heart.

She couldn't even formulate a thought.

"I like the way you say my name." He pulled back enough so that he could look at her. "I like that you call me Remy."

He pulled his hand up, and Shane saw that his fingers were slicked with her desire. She must have a napkin or something from the picnic. She tried to gather her scattered thoughts, but holding her gaze Remy licked one finger and then the other while she stared at him, still totally turned on.

"Tonight I want to spread you wide open and lick you and bite you until you scream on your picnic table," he said casually.

Shane gasped at the visual.

"And I want to take you from behind as you kneel in that egg chair you tortured me with the other night."

"Remy," she choked out, totally shocked.

"Do you want me to do that?"

Just visualizing that had her moaning. "I've never…been with anyone outside," she whispered.

"That's not what I asked."

"We'd probably get arrested."

"But you like the idea." His glistening thumb stroked over her lip, and then he kissed her. "You taste delicious," he said.

Shane had never felt so carnal in her life. Feeling daring, she reached toward his very long, thick, clearly outlined erection. Her mouth watered.

"I'd like to taste you."

"I'd like that and more, but I have a job interview."

A startled laugh burst from her lips. "That's not awkward at all."

He smiled, and it was so unexpected and beautiful that she reached out, her fingers still trembling as her body slowly bumped down from the rush. "Remy, when you smile…" She touched his lips, and he kissed her fingertips.

"You were saying we weren't together."

"Sex isn't being together." She tried to ignore the stupid stutter of her heart.

"What is?" he asked when she put the Jeep back into drive.

She could be flip, but his question sounded sincere. And he'd brought her to orgasm, staring deeply into her eyes the entire time. He no longer felt like a stranger, but could she trust herself? She'd thought Brandon had been bowled over by her, but no he'd had a different agenda.

"I don't know," she said reluctantly, playing with her keys. She had a carved wood dragon on her keychain to remind herself to be fierce so that she could thrive alone. Remy stirred up wants she'd spent five years vanquishing.

"I thought I did. I was engaged once," she shared. "It was…" So many adjectives. Wrong. Painful. Stupid. Toxic princess fantasy. "It was fast, unexpected. Intense. I thought it was destiny." She closed her eyes at how dumb she'd been. "I thought he loved me and that we were a team."

Remy didn't move. His gaze didn't waver, but she could feel his tension crank up even though his expression didn't change.

"But there was a problem. I was the problem."

Spit it out. Remy deserves to know.

"I had a miscarriage before the wedding," she said quickly before she could take the coward's door to the left. "And Brandon took me to a specialist who said that it was unlikely I would conceive a child, and if I did, it would be a challenge to carry to term because of a medical issue."

Her voice sounded choked, and she dashed angrily at the stupid tears that still formed years later. Remy caught her hand, kissed her palm and then kissed the few escaping tears that trickled down her cheeks.

"Is that why you broke up with him?" he asked as his hand spanned her wrist, covering up her watch.

"No." She bowed her head. She hadn't been that honorable. "He dumped me." She didn't add that he'd done it that afternoon while she was still reeling from the grief and shock of losing their baby.

Remy swore. It was the first time she'd heard him sound angry. His rant ended with the word 'tool.'

"I should have left the lying traitor to rot in that cartel prison."

"No, you shouldn't have," she said, although his leap to her defense felt like a balm to the hurt that scared her battered emotions.

"Still wish I had." He flopped back in his seat, scowling.

Shane laughed, shocked that she could laugh about one of the most painful moments in her life.

"Guy was an idiot," Remy seethed. He leaned over and kissed her lower abdomen tenderly, which made her eyes prick hot all over again. "He was an idiot and a whole lot of other four-letter words."

"Idiot is five letters." She should not be charmed by his defense of her.

"You said I was magic," she said, feeling as exposed as she had when he'd had her half stripped and moaning in the Jeep. "But you're the magic one, Remy."

Chapter Nine

PULLING INTO THE wide, half-circle drive of the Wild Wind felt like one of the most surreal moments of his life and—after twenty years in the service, much of it in places in the world where he and the US military were not officially supposed to be—he'd had many.

His first clue that something was wrong had been when they'd hit the main road to the ranch. The gravel had been ground into the dirt and not refilled, leaving the road pitted with potholes large enough that Shane had had to swerve to avoid them. Some of the western red cedar giants at the entrance to the ranch had fallen or broken off and had not been cleared away, and as Shane steered slowly up the more than two-mile driveway, quite a few of the sentry white barked pines looked near death.

He'd been shocked to see no hands working. No dog ran out to greet them, and the long stretch of white ranch fencing was faded, dirty, and pieces of it were drooping or breaking off. As Shane navigated the final turn, another sight had him leaning forward, staring at a confusing tableau. Two cowboys had their arms crossed while a young woman with deep auburn hair flowing down her back in waves gesticulated toward another woman with black hair blowing wildly in the breeze as she backed up an excavator.

"What is she doing?" Shane stopped the Jeep.

The woman with the witch hair shifted gears and began racing toward a stone wall of the house. Shane gripped the steering wheel, and they both watched the claw of the excavator hit the side of the house hard enough to shake it.

Shane was out of the car at the same time he was.

"Careful." Remy looped an arm around her shoulder, which didn't slow down her long-legged, sexy stride. He kept pace knowing that one orgasm didn't give him a say in Shane's life, but he didn't want her anywhere near the crazy woman.

"What's happening?" Shane whispered, her eyes wide as the bucket of the excavator hit the side of the house again.

The woman reversed, smoothly shifted gears, backed up a distance and then ran at the house again.

"What the f—" Remy broke off. He didn't know any of these people, but were they seriously going to stand around while some crazy woman destroyed Sam Wilder's home? "Is she drunk?"

"Remy." Now it was Shane who held him back. "That's Samara Wilder." Shane held his hand tightly and dug in her boots.

Good luck stopping him. "I don't care. That's Sam Wilder's home."

A large man turned around, arms crossed, expression

closed, and Remy slowed. His brain clicked.

"Slayer."

"Cross, what the fuck?" Colt strode toward him, hand out. He gripped him, pulled him in tight hug and slammed down a meaty hand on his shoulder. Remy did the same.

"You're out." Colt slammed his hands on his shoulders again, rocking him. "Damn. Good to see you alive. Never thought you'd spring the trap."

Remy had served several missions with Colt who'd then been Colt Ewing. He remembered Shane had mentioned a name change—that was a story they'd have to share over a beer. Colt had been a legendary sniper. His greeting was more than he'd heard Colt speak at one time.

"What's up with her?" Remy demanded of Colt even as she watched the woman with the auburn hair and vivid green eyes hug Shane as she threw him some epic side-eye.

The fireball of a woman in the excavator screamed a battle cry and raced over the dried-up dirt, kicking up dust clouds, and made a third run at the house.

The hit made him wince. The house wobbled and some mortar fell out of the stone siding, but nothing had crumbled yet.

"My mom," Colt said wryly. Remy did a double take. He'd always heard Colt was an orphan, living with an uncle on a small spread outside of town.

"That's your mom?" She was exotically beautiful but vindictive enough to star as a supernatural creature in a horror movie.

"I know. Weird." Colt watched another cowboy talk emphatically on a cell phone. "We'll have to catch up. Lot's changed. Good you're home."

Remy hadn't planned on Marietta being a homecoming, but fate seemed to have different plans for him, and having Colt in town could be an asset for him to get some stability.

"You going to stop her?" Remy didn't want to interfere in family matters, but he felt protective of Sam and the ranch, even if it hadn't gone both ways.

"I have a wife and two kids and another on the way," Colt said. "So no, I don't have a death wish." Colt, his arms still crossed over his chest, squinted at his mom's progress, or maybe lack of it.

"You're really going to let her knock down your grandfather's heritage ranch house?"

Everything in Remy was poised to fight. He'd baked cookies with his mom in that kitchen. Done homework at the farmhouse table while she'd cooked, set the table for breakfast and dinner, ladled out stews, soups and chili hundreds of times. But before he stepped in, he wanted to know the players. The cowboy on the phone he could take. Colt was another matter.

"She crazy?"

"Maybe?" Colt shrugged like he didn't care. "Pissed at the old man. Now that he's in the hospital and facing weeks in rehab she carpe diem'd it and raced over here from DC.

Stole Tucker and Tanner's excavator—that's how we knew what was up."

"I swear she needs a leash and a muzzle." Tucker stomped one bright blue boot in the dust as Samara made another run at the house and another primal growl howled over the roar of the engine.

"I'd like to see that," Colt said. "Surprised you aren't up there wrestling her for control."

"Can't." The woman smoothed her hand over her baby bump.

"Definitely stay out of the line of fire when she's in this mood," Shane cautioned. "She off her meds?"

"Is she ever on them?" Tucker vibrated with tension. "Kane's on his way. Not that he's not fed up with her fury. Sky's teaching a class at Harry's House. She's the only one who can calm Samara when she's raging like this."

"My brother Luke," Colt said, nodding toward the cowboy who still held his cell phone but walked alongside the excavator, his hands gesturing appeasingly.

"A weird twist of fate gave me three brothers, and she blames the old man for me and my twin not growing up together with her. She blames the old man for a lot of things. Never met him. Don't want to."

"Samara Wilder is destroying her family home while Sam Wilder, her father, owner of one of the top ranches in the country is in the hospital?" Remy still couldn't believe this. Family was supposed to have your back, not watch while your legacy was torn apart.

"Look around. The ranch is falling apart. Sam's nearly bankrupted himself tilting at one windmill or another, and his daughter's a land, mineral and water use rights attorney. She usually works with tribal councils, but she's made her daddy's life hell over the past five years."

Colt sounded like he was narrating the history of someone he didn't know.

"We've been trying to negotiate peace," Tucker said, tucking her arm through Shane's and giving Remy a long, calculated stare. "Obviously not successfully. Hey, do ex-shrinks carry tranq guns?"

Shane stifled a laugh.

"Talon does," Colt deadpanned. "Should I call her? I've seen her nail a rampaging bull at fifty yards."

The Wilders were joking about the destruction of their granddad's home? Another hit shuddered the house.

"The Wild Wind is a legacy ranch. The Wilders were in Montana before it was a state. Sam Wilder is a rancher to his soul."

Colt stared. "You know Sam?"

"Lived here as a kid off and on until I was twelve," he amended not wanting to dig up the past again. "My mom was the ranch cook. Sam was a good man."

"Tell her that," Colt invited, just as the shutters and framing broke free with a shriek and a crunch and glass shattered as a large window in the front caved in.

Samara whooped it up from her seat in the excavator and backed up again farther away this time. She shifted into gear, and a smile lit her lips. She looked like a beautiful demon. She didn't look big enough or old enough to have birthed Colt or anyone else. She might be a high-powered DC attorney, but Remy had had enough. She was trespassing and destroying property, and he wasn't going to stand around and watch.

This time as the excavator rolled fast past the huddled group, Remy jumped on the machine, reached in, jerked the gear and slammed it home, and then put his hand over the swing gear as she reached for it.

"Stop," he said, his voice cutting over the rumble of the engine. He seized the keys and tossed them out in the dirt at Colt's feet.

"Get off my property," she barked, her voice fierce as the deafening silence.

"Not yours. Not yet. Maybe not ever."

"I'm ripping down this hellhole prison. I'm leaving him in the rubble just like he left me. You can't stop me."

She reached out and slapped him hard. He let her, but when she brought up both hands in fists for round two, he grabbed them both in one hand and held on, letting her feel his strength and determination, but also that he had no intention of hurting her.

"No more."

"You can't stop me." She struggled and kicked up as if

she could kick the heavy machine back into gear.

"I have zip ties in my pocket."

"You wouldn't dare."

"Try me," he invited, a bit surprised neither of her sons had stepped in to help her.

"Get off my rig."

"Not yours, but good idea." He hopped backward dragging her with him. She struggled, twisted, kicked and even, Remy thought, bit him. Damn. He'd thought Sam Wilder had no back-up in him. His daughter was just as tough. Remy was reminded of an escaped young ram goat he'd once had to wrestle into submission at the county fair. The memory nearly made him laugh and drop her. He wondered how she'd like being compared to a farm animal.

He released her, poised to stop her again if she made a move for the excavator. Adrenaline still flooded his body, and the sizable hole in the side of the house pissed him off anew.

"I'm going to tear this whole house of horrors down," she announced as calmly as if she were telling them all that she was going to do a load of laundry. "And no one here had the balls to stop me."

"Mom, you've made your point," Luke said. "Granddad's in the hospital, but he's coming home eventually, so he'll need a house, and you don't want to go to jail."

"Jail," she spit out the word, her hands on her skinny hips. "He stole my life. He stole my children. He kidnapped my love and threatened him. He had him arrested. Deported. Kidnapped and sold his grandchildren, and now he's selling part of this ranch to a developer. A developer." She spit on the ground, closer to Remy's custom boots that Wolf had ordered for all of them one Christmas to celebrate surviving another dangerous and highly classified mission.

"And he's giving away another huge chunk—the still-fertile part with the river cutting through—to a stranger. Probably a love child. Sanctimonious ass. Hypocrite. A love child. He never loved anyone in his life."

Her words continued to flow, fast and furious. "I'm saving us from his vindictive hate," she said. "This is my land. Your land. I'm not letting him sell an acre. And he's definitely not giving anything away to a bastard, especially not a soldier bastard, a man of violence and destruction."

She pushed at Colt's broad chest with both hands, but he didn't budge.

"My sons should be helping me."

"Even the bastard former ex-soldier?" Colt looked and sounded bored.

"I wasn't talking about you." She stomped a boot in the dust. "I'm going to tear this house down. I'm going to hire a helicopter to salt the land. And then I'm going to light it all on fire and laugh while it burns, and you—" she pointed an elegant finger with a turquoise ring at Remy "—are not going to stop me."

She ripped off her designer shades. Her eyes practically

shot sparks at him, but it was the color that froze him to the spot. Mercury. A pale, silvery gray that glittered eerily in the sun.

Remy nearly swayed with shock. He saw eyes like that every day in the mirror. No. Impossible. He was grasping at straws. He was wrong. He had to be. None of it made sense.

Remy removed his shades and tucked them in his pocket. He moved slowly, with deliberation. He'd been here before when a mission went sideways. A soldier had to flow with the change, think on his feet, seize the opportunities to shift the tides back in his favor.

"Yes, I will stop you, Samara Wilder," he said, staring into the woman's beautiful, furious face. "I will stop you. I will protect Sam Wilder's land until he is able to do so himself."

She stared into his eyes. Hers were nearly hypnotically beautiful. He'd been told that his eyes were cold. 'Like death,' but those had been rumors whispered by enemies, so he'd done nothing to shut that down. Remy felt dizzy with the suspicion whirring through his brain. He rifled quickly through his usually suppressed memories of his childhood at the ranch, but nothing jumped out that he'd been anything special to Sam. Yes, he'd spent time with him, but it had had a purpose—to teach him chores. Check on his work. He'd been the only kid on the ranch.

And his mom had said nothing as she struggled to draw her last breaths except to behave for Sam as if it was a done deal that he would keep Remy and his sister on the ranch.

Samara's expression was open disdain, edged with shock, speculation, but she pulled back, wrapping herself in contempt like it was a pair of wings. "So you came home, soldier," she said.

Remy felt everyone's attention fix on him now like he was in a play, which he'd never been. He'd always operated in the background. Even as a child he'd tried not to draw attention to himself.

"Wanted to see if you were named in my father's will and what you might get. Nothing." She stepped in close to his body, radiating fury. "You're going to get nothing, Remington Cross. But I welcome the fight. Give it your best shot." She held her arms wide and smiled. "But you can't beat me. I'm ruining Sam Wilder. I'm destroying the Wild Wind Ranch. I'm bathing in vengeance. And I'll happily add you to my list of destruction."

With that she made a fist and took another hard shot at his jaw, and the sound of her fist slapping Remy's open palm was loud.

SHANE FELT LIKE the director of the wrong play. She'd brought Remy here to meet with the Wilders in hopes that he could find meaningful work so that he could build a life, follow his dreams and find some peace. Now he seemed full-body-slammed into a Shakespearean family drama.

How had Samara known Remy's name? She did the math in her head, certain Samara was long gone when Remy would have lived here as a child. And she was ranting about a will.

"Mom." Luke sounded appalled. "Please calm down. You'll hurt yourself." To Colt, Luke mouthed, 'You know him, right?'

Colt nodded imperceptibly and checked his phone like this destruction derby and wrestling match was a normal predinner ritual. Maybe with the Wilders it was.

Cowboys.

They took everything in stride. Even Tucker seemed more entertained than worried. Shane had noticed the dust cloud racing toward them and wondered if it was Kane intent on trying to de-escalate their mom.

"I'm happy to release you so we can discuss what's bothering you like adults."

"Discuss," she shrieked.

"No more Power Ranger moves, and no more demo."

Samara swore and tried to reverse head-butt him, but she was so small that her head just plunked hard against his rock-solid chest. Then she hung down, using his grip to hold her up, and tried to kick him first in his ass and then in his boys. Remy easily maneuvered her so it looked like he was managing a tantrummy child.

Remy looked at Shane, an odd light in his eyes. "I know

you're retired, but a little help would be nice. Couldn't you step in with some shrink mind control or advice? A meditation perhaps?"

Wait, was he having fun?

"Bartender," she reminded him.

Tucker gave her a hard look before refocusing on her brother-in-law Kane's arrival in his tricked-out black truck. A former bull rider, he popped out agilely.

"What's going on?" He surveyed them all, hands on his hips. His silvery-blue gaze crackled with energy. Then he looked at the hole in the side of the house and the excavator. "This looks crazy even for us," Kane noted, his attention shifting to Remy. "That's my mom you're restraining."

"Take her. Hope you're wearing a cup."

Kane laughed. "C'mon, Mom." His smile widened—the famous smile that had been on countless adds for the pro rodeo and too many products to count. "I know you're pissed," he said. "And you've got every right, but my kids need their nana not to be in jail. I don't have a cup with me, and Sky and I might want to go for five someday. Give it a rest." He held out a hand.

Samara looked up, ceasing to struggle. Her hair blew around her like it had its own dance track. The midnight waves cascaded down to her tiny waist.

"My beautiful boy." Samara's gaze softened.

"My beautiful mom," Kane said easily. Tucker had always said that Kane was her favorite because he looked the most like her, and she was as vain as she was arrogant.

"Kane Wilder." Kane's voice hardened a little as he refocused on Remy. "I'll take it from here." His gaze was as hard as his words.

Remy stared at Kane. His expression revealed nothing, and Shane was so busy focusing on Remy that it took her a moment to notice Kane. To really see him. Smaller build, but just as muscularly honed. But it was the black hair, the widow's peak and the eyes that fisted her breath.

What was going on? Dismay clattered down her spine.

"Mom," Kane said, his gaze never leaving Remy's. "We having a family reunion you didn't tell me about?"

Samara faced Remy. "No. Never. Get. Off. My. Land."

Shane felt like she'd been slapped, but Remy didn't recoil or react.

He released Samara close to Kane and stalked back to Shane's Jeep, his stride fluid, strong with just that hint of swagger. Shane's heart wept. To be hit with something so shocking and private yet so public had to be…she couldn't even think how awful the shock, the suspicion and the angry rejection must feel. And this had been shoveled on top of the emotional meeting with Arlo.

Her sexual buzz earlier that had made everything seemed more vividly alive fizzled and now seemed obscene. He'd given her intense pleasure, and she'd given him nothing back except doubt and reasons why she didn't want to be involved.

Remy climbed into her Jeep, closing the door firmly like nothing out of the ordinary had occurred. Tucker touched her arm—in question or sympathy, she didn't know. She shook her head. Her choice was made before she knew she had a choice. She walked to her Jeep, hopped in, closed the door and started the engine.

Colt was there, his massively cut body blocking her path unless she wanted to rack up a manslaughter charge today— and destroy her Jeep.

She looked at Remy, who nodded. Sighing, Shane rolled down the window.

"You looking for work, Cross? You staying in town?" Colt's tone said Remy better be staying.

"Yeah," he said. "But I'll find something." Remy looked straight ahead, not at the ex-soldier he might have more in common with than he'd ever dreamed.

"Ranch? Construction?" Colt pushed.

"I grew up ranch—here." His lips twisted. "And then at a ranch outside Bozeman for high school. Was hoping to work as a hand when I got out, but I can do construction. Don't want your land. Don't want your mom on my ass."

"Me neither," Colt admitted just as Tucker ran up and jumped up on the runner on Shane's side. She rolled down her other window and caught a glimpse of Luke talking to his mom who gestured back furiously. Kane's body posture was relaxed. Nothing to see here.

Colt tossed the keys to the excavator to Tucker over the

roof of the Jeep and she caught them and did a little dance.

"You ride?" Tucker demanded.

"Haven't in years," Remy said. "But I rode nearly every day until I joined the service. Know how to fix most ranch equipment, fence, repair the barns, take care of the animals, cattle round-ups and vaccinations, lay pipe. Did it all. Want to do it again. Want the space. Want the responsibility. Want to be a part of something. Build something."

Honesty bled from every syllable, and Shane hoped that Colt would give Remy a shot.

"Let's meet tomorrow seven a.m. at the Wilder Dreams Ranch." Colt put his number in Remy's phone. "We'll show you around. Hook you up."

"Don't need charity," Remy said firmly. "Don't want anything I don't earn."

Tucker rolled her eyes. "Yeah, yeah, we get it," she said. "I train horses. My twin and Kane breed bulls. Luke runs the ranching end of things. My husband is a distiller and brewmeister, and he leads survival and adventure courses for fun. Economy the way it is, we need all the help we can get. No favors, but if you're a hard worker, you'll have your choice of jobs."

Tucker reached in and squeezed Remy's bicep like he was a loaf of bread.

"Yup! Prime of life." Tucker stuck her tongue out at Shane. "Gotta look out for my bestie and my ranch. See you tomorrow, Remy Cross. Bring the zip ties. With this family you never know what the day will bring."

"Seven a.m.," Colt confirmed, tapping lightly on the Jeep door.

"That means an early night, kids." Tucker made a sexy face and licked her lips. "Shane, I'll teach you how to rope so you can keep Mr. I Got Zip Ties In My Pants in line."

Shane choked back a shocked laugh although she should be used to Tucker's teasing by now.

"You solid?" Colt took up the entire window as he bent down, peering in.

"Getting there," Remy said. "Obliged about the job."

"'Course. You got digs?" Colt looked at Shane.

Heat flushed through her again. Did she have a tattoo on her forehead saying *wanton woman*?

"I will need a place to live," Remy said. Then he finally looked at Colt. The tension radiating off him was tangible. "The leader of my unit, a good man, died in the field. Should have been me. He left unfinished business. We're taking care of it—the brothers in my unit. There's a young girl, Arlo. He was her godfather, but now her mama's dead."

"Arlo Holt." Colt nodded. "Friend of my son Parker's from school. He's been asking about her. Didn't know the mom, but Parker and Arlo were in some art and science camps together at Harry's House."

"She needs a home. A family. I'm going to make sure she has it."

"Let's make it happen." Colt's hand was large on Remy's

shoulder. He squeezed once. Then stepped back. "We got a cabin on some property I inherited. One bedroom but also a loft. It's yours as long as you need."

"Paying rent."

Colt nodded. "We'll get you set up." Colt and Remy made some sort of a hand-slapping, gripping move and ended up with a "Together," at the end.

Colt stepped back in line with Tucker and waved goodbye alongside Kane and Luke as Shane drove out. Samara Wilder stared and spit on the ground.

"Remy?" Shane asked after they exited the ranch. It had taken her that long to process.

He caught her hand in his, and she tried not to read anything in it other than comfort.

"How are you?"

"Not sure. But I want the job. I want the cabin. The rest I'll think about later."

She tried not to feel rejected. It was stupid. They weren't in a relationship. Even if they did…no. Too soon to go there.

"Do you want to stop at the store?" She grabbed for an easy topic. "We could pick up something to grill—maybe run by Marietta Western Wear to get a few more shirts and a hat since you're going all cowboy on me?"

"Yes, ma'am," he drawled. "I will need to cowboy up. But first, stop off at the hospital. I want to have a little talk with Sam Wilder."

Chapter Ten

REMY HAD FACED many dangers in his life. Walking down a hospital corridor to visit a man he'd desperately wished had been his father or grandfather shouldn't be one of them. Sam Wilder had refused visitors, but Remy had spent the past five years finding people who didn't want to be found or who had been hidden for money or political capital. An old man, badly injured in a fall from his horse, recovering at a small regional hospital didn't even nudge his skills.

His reaction did.

In the space of an afternoon, Remy had slipped back into Cross. Stealthy. Calculated. Heart of stone. Nerves of titanium. Shane had just begun to tame him—hell, he'd purchased a gift for a teen and was now thinking of asking Shane out for dinner.

If Jace could see him now... A reluctant smile tugged on his lips. This mission was wildly out of control, but damn, he felt alive. And sick to his stomach when he paused several feet away from room 208.

His past. Maybe his future. All tangled. But he had to work through the knots. Learn to live as a civilian. At first, he'd been resigned to go through the motions of creating a life to help Arlo. But now he was curious about the Wilders and his maybe place in the family. He'd thought with his sister Brianna's death the door to family had been slammed shut.

The door to room 208 was cracked open. A baseball game played low on the TV. Remy stood still, breathed in deeply and relaxed the muscles in his body. Another breath in, hold and out. Square breathing. Every soldier knew it. Every soldier had their own method of facing battle. And this one had the advantage of him likely not being shot at.

Although maybe not. As a kid, he'd never seen Sam without some firepower at his side. Ranches held many dangers. And it must burn Sam's ass that his horse had been the one to take him out.

Remy raised his hand to knock and then changed his mind. He didn't want to draw attention to himself, not yet. He pushed down the irrational wish that he'd said yes when Shane asked if he'd wanted company. Habit. Shutting himself off. Could he change? Would she want him to?

Remy slipped through the door, stood behind the curtain and listened. No voices, just the game on low. Crack of a bat, muted commentary. Remi stepped all the way inside the hospital room.

Remi thought he was prepared to see Sam again— diminished by age and his injury. Not even close.

Pale silvery-blue eyes that veered toward a stormy gray

glared at him. The face was leaner, deeper lines. The black hair was now threaded with gray. And in the hospital gown with tubes going in and out as if Sam was some sort of transitioning cyborg, the electric physicality of the man—the strength of purpose that had always snapped around him like a lightning storm—was muffled to the point of silence.

Remy didn't know what to say. His mouth was desert dry. His throat felt garroted.

Sam reached for a remote and raised his bed a little, wincing as he did so. Guilt crashed through Remy. Why was he confronting an injured man? What did he hope to gain from this visit? An explanation? Acceptance. Pretty late for that. Sam couldn't change the past. Bring back his mother. Bring back his sister—those failures were on him.

"I always hoped you'd come back someday, Remy," Sam said, his voice hoarser than he remembered, but still surprisingly strong. "I just thought I'd be dead when you did it."

"Surprise," Remy murmured.

Sam had always been larger than life. The ultimate man Remy had looked to even after Sam had rejected him and left him to pack up his and Brianna's small life in two trash bags while a stranger from the county urged him to hurry.

"You out of the service finally?"

He nodded. He didn't want to talk about his career. "Stopped by the ranch. Didn't see any hands." He didn't want to tell him what he had seen.

For the first time, Sam's intense stare shifted away, and

his expression settled into shame.

"Out of the cattle business."

The shock felt like a lightning bolt. Sam Wilder had once run one of the largest herds of cattle in Montana. His beef was legendary and organic before organic pinged anyone's radar. Remy didn't want to embarrass Sam by asking if he needed money. What he had would be a drop in the bucket of what Sam's needs might be, but Remy would gladly share. He was strong. He could earn more. Sam shouldn't have to worry in his later years, especially when he had family. Anger against Samara Wilder stirred. She was lucky to have a father, sons, grandchildren. Looked like Sam had no one.

"Your choice?"

Sam wheezed a laugh. "That's a complicated story we'd need a bottle of whiskey for, and that damn Dr. Witt Telford tells me whiskey is out for the foreseeable future."

"I'll take you out for a drink when you're up and about," Remy said automatically, before he remembered that Sam Wilder might not want to see him.

And would he want to see Sam if he learned the answer to the question he may or may not ask? Remy hadn't yet allowed himself to think about Sam walking away when the county came in. He'd been desperate as a child to stay, pleading, promising, but he'd thought he was trying to negotiate with his mom's employer, not a relative. Bitterness coated his tongue. Had Sam really let the county take away his son? It seemed impossible, and Remy shut himself down—plenty of time later to feel. Now was not the time to let his long-buried emotions dominate. He'd be overwhelmed by the what-ifs.

"You stop by the house?" Sam asked after a long beat of silence where Remy warred with whether or not he should ask the question he'd come to ask.

"Yeah."

"It still standing?"

"Any reason it wouldn't be?"

"Samara. Always was contrary. Trouble from the day she was born. Hates my guts. Hates everything to do with me. Passionate like her mom. Temper like me. Too smart and too independent for a girl growing up in conservative ranch town. Lived to shock everyone. Vengeful as the devil when thwarted." Sam actually sounded proud of his offspring. "Could barely control her when she was a toddler and when her mama walked out for good with my ranch foreman?" His face sunk into lines of bitterness. "No reasoning with her. She went off the rails. And I…"

Remy let the silence steep. He felt Sam still had more to say. He toed a chair over so he could sit, not loom.

"She's been slapping me with lawsuits. Her vengeance. Bloodless. But with me laid up, I figured one of her sons would tell her, and she'd come flying in here on her broom screeching like a banshee with the fury of Missoula's Hellgate winds on her heels. Figure she'd rent an excavator and level my house and dance on the rubble before lighting the remnants of her past on fire."

It was eerie how well Sam called it. But Remy didn't interrupt. Sam's relationship to his daughter was his business. Remy didn't know if he even had a right to ask any questions. Was Samara's anger justified? Had he really separated her from her children? How?

Same way he let me go?

Sam laughed a little, but ended up coughing, and Remy fought the urge to help him. They didn't have that kind of relationship. Even when he'd been a kid and had dogged Sam's footsteps craving a crumb of attention, Remy had been in awe of him.

Screw it. He poured Sam some water from a pitcher and held it while he drank through the straw.

"You know your daughter," Remy admitted. "Couple of your grandsons arrived to stop her."

"Doubt it. They don't know how to handle her any better than I did. Kane does okay because he doesn't care about anyone or anything but that pretty little wife he has and the stream of kids they keep popping out. Women," he grumbled. "Got yourself one?"

'No,' teetered on his tongue, but he immediately pictured Shane and didn't shove her out of his thoughts this time.

"Thinking on it."

"Don't. Heartbreak. Soul crushers. Life suckers."

"You should put that on a coffee mug."

Sam wheezed a laugh. "Better luck with a coffee mug."

"Could get lonely without a woman," Remy said, the truth resonating for the first time. He wondered where Shane was now, what she was doing.

Had she gone grocery shopping for the dinner she'd offered? He hadn't committed to anything for later today, not sure how this meeting would go, but he found himself hoping Shane would expect him, wanting to cook a meal with him, shop for ranch work clothes. When was the last time he'd done something normal?

He wiped his damp palms on his one pair of jeans. He was in deep before he'd realized he'd stuck a toe in the water.

"Lonely is peace." Sam Wilder leaned back against the bed as if his low burst of energy had already seeped out of him.

"Not so sure about that anymore," Remy admitted.

"You staying in Marietta?"

"Thinking on it. This place always felt like home, even when it wasn't."

Sam Wilder's eyes closed. A pained expression swept across his face. His weathered hands clenched into fists on the top of the sheet.

"I got a job offer at one of your grandson's ranches. Colt's going to show me around," he said carefully, watching Sam's reaction. "I ran a few missions with Colt back in the day." He wasn't sure why he was sharing—an olive branch?

An open door?

Remy was unfamiliar with all of those things, but he didn't want to end up here—in a hospital bed alone, bitter, angry and estranged, which meant he'd have to learn to connect. His mind turned again to Shane. Arlo. The Wilders, and he realized it was too late to remain in control and indifferent. He already felt the first unfurl of hope.

He didn't understand why Sam wouldn't want his grandsons in his life. They seemed like good, hardworking family men. The questions mounted, but did he have a right to any of them?

"I should let you rest. Just wanted to give my regards," Remy said after a long silence where Sam's eyes remained stubbornly closed.

"Ask what you really came to ask, son."

In the act of standing up, Remy's legs wobbled, and he sat down hard. The walls closed in.

SHANE GATHERED THREE different types of lettuce from her garden, one red pepper, and a couple of leaves of basil for seasoning. She told herself it was best if Remy didn't show up. She was already too emotionally involved with him and his budding plans to make a home for Arlo. She wasn't fully sure of all the obstacles and terrified to have her heart ripped out again. But still her imagination leapfrogged and she'd pictured herself cooking with Arlo, answering her softly spoken questions, taking her for riding lessons with Tucker.

She couldn't do this to herself.

But where was the joy in life with no risk?

Her mind spun round and around while she waited and hoped for the growl of Remy's bike. When she heard it turn down her street, she had to fight the urge to run to her back gate and fling it open. Instead, she tucked the lettuce into the bandana-lined basket she used to gather veggies from her garden and tried to quiet her pounding heart. Her body warmed, felt soft and sexy.

You have it so bad for that man.

And she was tired of fighting it.

Remy pulled up close to her gate and cut the engine. She waited for the sound of his footsteps even though she knew he walked so softly for a big man.

Probably why he was still alive.

And that made her heart clench.

As Shane held her breath waiting for Remy to appear, her mind raced with questions about Sam, but as the seconds ticked by and the silence expanded, Shane's curiosity morphed to worry. What was he doing out there?

She walked to the gate, briefly wrestled with her conscience to give him privacy. Finally, irritated with her rioting thoughts, Shane unlatched the gate and stepped out of the sanctity of her small backyard.

Remy sat on his bike, head down, hair obscuring his face,

his body slumped to the point that he looked defeated.

Shane didn't bother with words. Many times in her life words had not been enough—her sister Dare's terrifying teenage grief and depression; Connor, the housing insecure teen with substance abuse issues she'd counseled but lost; and then finally Ethan, the young soldier with the deep moral injury he'd hidden with humor and a love of jazz. Her words had been studied, educated, cultivated by experience and empathy and delivered with best intentions, but her efforts had fallen flat.

But she couldn't leave Remy to fight his fight alone.

Shane closed the distance between them in a rush and wrapped her arms tightly around his strong shoulders and pressed her body around his.

REMY DIDN'T REMEMBER leaving the hospital. He'd felt like he was drowning. He'd climbed on his bike, desperate to clear his head, but instead of gunning it down the narrow ribbon of highway, he'd come to Church Street, the Hozier song mocking him. He was a shard of metal buried in layers of dirt, and Shane was a magnet pulling him up and into the light.

He knew he shouldn't be here. He was too hollowed out. Too far from the man he needed to be to build a new life. Shane deserved a man who was whole, but still he'd been lost and had come here to her.

He smelled her first. Earth. Green. Life. Cinnamon. He greedily inhaled as if his lungs had just been jump-started. She straddled his bike behind him—effortlessly with her long, toned legs—and wrapped herself tightly around his body, hips aligned, breasts pressed to his back, her cheek between his shoulder blades. She held him like she'd never let him go.

Remy breathed her in. And just let the clock run. He'd never found comfort in the arms of a woman. He probably didn't deserve it, and yet he relaxed into her embrace, wanting to howl at the twilight like the lone coyote cowboy he was—separated from his pack.

"There you are." Shane's voice was soft in the twilight. She buried her face in his hair, and he felt her lips on his neck. Despite his truncated talk with Sam. Despite the unknowns surrounding him, his cock woke up. Blood rushing in, bragging. It was the only part of him that had ever worked right.

"I have salad; potatoes, peppers and corn are roasting. Kebobs made, just need to be grilled. Peach-infused iced tea. But it can all wait," Shane said as if she sensed the change in him.

Maybe some men would have taken the high road. Talked it out over dinner, but Remy wasn't that man. Not tonight. Probably not ever. Shane was offering more, and he wasn't man enough to walk.

"Dinner later." He swung off the bike and held his hand out to her. "Dessert first."

"I have a peach and blackberry cobbler with homemade vanilla ice cream for dessert." She smiled, but her eyes were worried. "I bake when I'm wound up."

"Sounds good." Maybe he'd eat the cobbler off her body. "But I have a different idea for unwinding."

He laced his fingers with hers and opened her gate, swung it wide and indicated that she should precede him.

"Yes or no, Shane?"

He stood at the entry, not sure what the hell he'd do if she told him no. Sex was her choice. But he wanted so much more than that, although his question wasn't fair, as he had no idea of what he was really asking her to take on.

He felt like this was a momentous moment. Life-changing, but Shane again surprised him. She stood in the middle of her small glowing garden. A secret smile teased her lips. Her fingers popped one of the snaps of her western-style blouse and then another. He followed her progress. His blood roared when he saw she wore nothing under her shirt. Just the silky ivory skin he hadn't begun to explore properly yet.

"Your turn," she invited.

He dropped his jacket.

Her shirt slid off her shoulders and pooled at her feet that were already bare. She had a small jeweled charm that glinted in her belly button, catching the light.

He pulled off his T-shirt, and her hiss of an inhaled breath jacked him up more. He knew women liked what they saw with him, but they'd only seen his body. Shane had marched into his head. He thought she'd cracked open his heart. He should probably try to save himself and ride away, but he knew he wouldn't. For the first time since he was a kid, he felt home.

"I want to take off your jeans."

Her gaze glowed with desire. She popped her first button.

HE STALKED TOWARD her, the focus on his face and the sensuous curve of his hard mouth totally thrilling. She'd never felt a man's desire burn her from across a room, or in this case, a patio, before. He pounced, and Shane didn't even try to stop the moan of joy. She expected his kiss to burn, but instead his lips were tender, his hard hands gentle as they palmed her jaw.

Shane returned the kiss, her fingers spearing through his hair like she'd been fantasizing about since the first night she'd seen him across her bar. He continued to kiss her, exploring at first, and then his kiss deepened. His tongue stroked along hers, and she returned the fire, almost feeling like she had to hold herself back from stripping off the rest of his clothes, breaking the kiss so she could taste the rest of his body, lick a trail along the outline of his tattoos. He was so hard and so hot that she just wanted to jump in all that fire and burn with him.

He licked along the seam of her lip like she was ice cream. Shane blinked, her focus totally on him, and she was unable to describe the expression in his eyes. It was thrilling but so tender and she was so awed that tears pricked her eyes. Remy sweet would utterly undo her.

She had imagined that Remy would conquer. Be intense and quickly drive her out of her mind. But instead, he touched her as if she was brand new, fragile, important. He read her as he kissed her, and his desire to please her made her feel as if a bright yellow primrose of the evening bloomed in her chest, reaching out toward him.

"I like that you keep your eyes open when we kiss."

"I don't want to miss anything," she admitted, shyly.

His fingertips touched her blush, which made her more self-conscious. She'd been holding so much of herself back for the past few years, and now this man had broken her dam and everything she was, everything she wanted to be, seemed poised to burst out of her chest.

Remy gently tugged the elastic from her hair, slid it over her wrist and began to unweave her braid. She felt like she was unraveling along with her hair.

"I feel like we're moving too fast and too slow."

He stilled. "You set the pace, Shane."

She covered his hand, still in her hair, with hers. "If you

don't kiss me again and touch me and peel off your clothes, I'm going to die."

She brought his hand down to her jeans. The smile that briefly kicked up was so unexpected and beautiful that she'd barely caught her breath, before he deftly unbuttoned her jeans and peeled them from her body, leaving her only in her pale blue lace thong and unbuttoned shirt and tank. Her shirt fluttered to the ground and then he kissed his way up her body, pulling the tank up with his teeth before he swished it over her head.

"Now there's a fantasy I never knew I had," he breathed, startling a laugh out of her as she stood before him in a thong and cowboy boots.

"You are exquisite." His voice rumbled to a lower register, pebbling her nipples. "A treasure, a gift."

She'd been engaged, and her fiancé had never said anything so sweet. Nor had he ever looked at her like Remy was—with heat, but something more: awe.

"Tell me about this." He traced gentle fingers around her belly button, the few small scars there, faded now, and her hummingbird charm.

So much history, but her body's flaws, its failure wouldn't stay firmly in the past, she tried to remind herself. Remy was such a spectacular man. He'd want a son— something she couldn't give him, but it was hard to remember that when Remy was on his haunches, his breath warm against her delicate skin as he inhaled her and exhaled.

"You smell as delicious as you taste," he said, looking up at her, before his lips traveled the same path as his fingers.

She shivered, feeling undone by his words, by the way he looked at her, by the way he touched her.

"Hummingbirds symbolize that hard times are behind you. They can also be harbingers of good luck."

He played with the charm with his tongue, and she couldn't help the moan of pleasure that escaped. She gripped his shoulders to balance herself as moisture slicked her panties and her legs trembled.

He inhaled deeply, and it was such a turn-on that he was scenting her like the coyote that he'd told her he had been nicknamed after.

"What else?" he asked.

She could barely hear him over the blood roaring in her ears and her ragged breaths while he seemed almost studious as he explored her belly button, her scars and the charm. Her core muscles quivered. She'd hidden her body since the last surgery, and part of her felt so exposed that she wanted to run, while the other part craved his meticulous and sexy perusal.

"Ummmm..." She could barely think. "People in many cultures believe that hummingbirds indicate the spirit of a loved one is near."

His tongue drew circles around her belly button and then he teased her with the tip.

"And...healing," she gasped, shocked that she was building up to an orgasm, and he hadn't yet touched her clit or her breasts, which though small, were super sensitive.

His hands cupped her bare butt, angling her closer to his mouth as he kissed her belly, and the rasp of his stubble sent sensations cascading through her.

"Remy, oh my God," she breathed.

"That's quite an elevation." He looked up at her, and she felt like some primitive woman, naked except for her thong and cowboy boots in her backyard while a full moon danced in the passing clouds high above them. "I want more," he said. "I want all of you."

She wanted him thrusting inside of her, and she was about to start begging if he didn't get on with it.

"Yes, or no?" He rose to his feet, and she pressed herself against his cut strength, reveling in the determined press of his erection near where she wanted him the most. Desire made her clumsy as she fumbled with the buttons of his jeans. He kicked off his boots but caught her wrists as they slid inside his jeans and tugged.

"Need to hear the words, Shane, and see it in your eyes."

"Yes," she said forcing power into her voice. She would have agreed to almost anything to have him naked and powerful above her in her bed.

His smile was feral, and his eyes glittered silver. She pulled off his jeans, and he kicked them away. She reached for the part of him she wanted most, but he shocked her by picking her up and tossing her over his shoulder. Her breath whooshed out, and at the same time, he lightly swatted her bottom.

"Whaaaaat..."

His answering laugh and palms brushing a soothing circle on her butt startled her into silence. She'd imagined sex with Remy would be hot and memorable and maybe even mind-blowing, but never once had she imagined he'd be playful.

He carried her into the house and into her bedroom and laid her gently on the bed.

"Remy?" She now wanted to make sure he was okay with this, but the hard desire stamped on his face as he looked at her was all the answer she needed. He stood above her, and another flood of heat soaked her panties. But instead of peeling off her last item of clothing, he wrapped his fingers around her calves.

"Any chance you'd keep the boots on for me, cowgirl? I think I've discovered I have a fetish."

His smile was the sweetest thing she'd ever seen, and the way his hair fell into his face leant his angular features a softer tone.

"Any chance you'll get your prime ass up here and give me what I want right now, cowboy?" she sassed back.

His eyes looked like mercury in the light from the moon blasting in her window. He pushed his fingers through his hair and knelt on the bed, easily lifting her higher so that she was propped up on the pillows. Then his hands pushed her legs up and apart so that her boots were on either side of his shoulders.

He shook his head. "Not a chance," he teased. "I'm taking my time. Savoring my meal."

"But you were so generous this afternoon, Remy. It's your turn." Her hand fluttered in the direction of his cock—beautifully shaped like the rest of him. "I want to—" she moistened her dry bottom lip, and was pleased when his gaze flared with answering heat "—taste you."

"You'll get your chance," he promised, levering himself between her thighs. "But I'm feeling very selfish and hungry and incredibly turned on."

And then his mouth and hands made her forget her own name, and any modesty she might once have possessed died as she writhed under him, shouting his name and begging him to fill her empty spaces. She had no idea how or when she'd lost her panties. She suspected he'd ripped them off with his teeth. She'd never met a man so oral or so skilled, but when Remy, his face slick with her juices, finally lodged himself at her weeping entrance, he linked their hands together and kissed her once, sweetly before he slowly entered her.

He paused when he was finally buried to the hilt. She wanted to touch his face, hold his body, but his hands pinned hers to the mattress.

"You okay, Remy?"

"Better than that." For a moment his eyes shut, but then

they burned into hers again, and she felt like he was asking a question she didn't know how to answer. "I feel perfect. You are perfect."

She was a long way from perfect. His sweetness was turning her into a crier, something she'd never been. A tear escaped, and he caught it with his tongue before he began to move, slowly at first, but as Shane tilted up her pelvis and clenched her muscles in her sheath and her thighs, wanting to feel all of him, Remy's control finally broke.

Chapter Eleven

A S THE SWEAT cooled from their still-naked intertwined bodies, Shane's tongue traced a line of sweat over his pec.

"We never got to dinner," she said. "I need to feed you. Keep your strength up to work the ranch and...other things."

"Let me do the work," he said. "I can bring you dinner in bed."

It was ridiculous how pleased she was with his offer, but she felt like she needed some space to come to terms with what they'd done. And what this might mean, if anything.

"Most of it's cooked," she said. "We could grill the kebobs and do the last bit together." She felt shy suggesting cooking together. She never had that with a man. "And we can eat at the dining room table since it's a bit chilly tonight."

"Letting me eat at the table." He kissed along her collarbone, and she shivered with pleasure. "Progress."

Who would have guessed he was so oral?

"I let you into my bed."

"Yes." His eyes darkened. "You did."

Shane didn't want him to think that meant anything, but who was she kidding? It did, at least to her, but she needed to proceed with caution. Remy was dealing with a lot. He'd lost a friend. Mustered out. Was taking a new job and possibly considering fostering a teen girl. She couldn't lay any of her expectations or hopes and dreams on him.

"Okay," he said. "Let's make dinner."

To think was to act with Remy. He stood up and pulled on his jeans, leaving half the buttons undone. Remy retrieved her silk kimono from the back of a chair and fed her into it.

"This is only a temporary reprieve," he murmured in her ear.

Shane couldn't shake the feeling that his words sounded as much like a warning as a promise as he grilled the chicken she'd marinated. She warmed up the veggies she'd roasted and soon they were seated, enjoying the meal.

"Why'd you quit being a therapist?"

The question, casually delivered, was unexpected. But really, she should have been prepared. Shane continued chewing and then sipped her sparkling water.

"I got burned out."

Remy watched her, chewing the whole time. Shane chased a piece of cauliflower around her plate.

Remy speared another piece of chicken. "Try again."

"That's my answer."

"What are you afraid of?"

"I'm not afraid," Shane denied, staring at him, appetite

gone. "What's with the role reversal—women always take the hit for being all emotional and confessional after sex."

"You saying I'm a girl?" he asked around a bite of chicken.

She laughed at the absurdity. He was all man.

"What's with the twenty questions?" She pushed her plate away.

"I don't have twenty. Just a few."

Well, she had some of her own.

"Tell me about Sam, what he said at the hospital," she challenged.

"Nothing. He told me to ask what I'd come to ask, and while I thought about if I wanted to know that he was my biological father, but had kept it a secret, and also why he would have let social services take me and Brianna away and separate us, and if his answer would make any difference to me now—how I would process how different my life would have been—he fell asleep."

"What?" Her mouth dropped open.

He closed it with his finger under her chin. "I can help you."

He switched conversation direction so fast, she felt dizzy. "With what?"

"Did he hurt you? Threaten you?"

She stared at him, anxiety stirring. "Who?"

"You were hospitalized. You quit your job. Left your townhouse fully staged with your furniture and sold it fast and at a bargain and moved to a blip on the map in Montana."

"Do. Not. Research. Me." She jacked up to her feet. "I want you to go."

"I had to know what I'm dealing with so that I can best protect you."

"By spying on me?" Her voice rose like she was auditioning for an opera.

"I didn't know it was you." He continued eating as if his betrayal was no big deal. "You were Shane Knight, a job I wasn't really interested in taking. Now I'm interested in protecting you so talk. The chicken's good."

"Thank yourself. You grilled it." She crossed her arms. "What was the job?"

"Your marinade is fantastic."

He was maddening. She was pissed, and he wasn't even noticing, and she'd told him to leave, and he complimented the meal. And she didn't know what he was talking about.

"Why do you think you need to protect me? I'm a bartender in a blip of a town in Montana." She tossed the description back in his face. "And who hired you to do what?"

"You're wearing a watch that retails for six figures. The owner wants it back."

Shane's legs gave out, and she sat back down. The silence felt like a language.

"I can help," he said. "I take care of problems."

She so did not want to know what that meant. She looked at the watch face. It was so beautiful. But haunting. A reminder of all that time stole. The indifference of time and it tracked her failures.

"The owner's dead," she finally said looking up at him. "So, I don't need your help."

"How is he dead?"

"He hanged himself in his parents' boathouse while they were out cruising the harbor," she said flatly.

"That's dead."

So now Remy was a medical examiner. Fabulous. "He was a patient. A former officer. He'd never been suited for war or for his role in his family. He'd only been trying to please his family in taking the traditional West Point route. I worked with him over a year, and thought he was making progress."

She hated Remy right now. Hated him. "And that's why I quit. I failed again. I missed the warning signs. Just as he wasn't cut out for war, I'm not cut out for objectivity. I'm not cut out to help anyone. Not patients. Not you. Not Arlo, and I want you to leave. Now."

He stood up. Finally. But instead of walking out the door like she'd been anticipating since she'd first seen him, he wrapped his arms around her and held her against his body. His strength and warmth broke something in her.

"You were in love with him."

"Yes," she admitted, "but nothing ever happened." She

buried her face against his neck. "I fought the attraction. I was young. Recently out of my training. He was so smart. Charismatic. Engaging. He loved jazz. I played the upright bass, gigging in a club a few nights a week in a group. He'd come watch. In session he talked about so many things— books, politics, music, the morality of war and responsibility of leadership. His family. The poetry he wrote that no one knew about but me." She couldn't stop the words that had been bottled up for so long.

She'd never even told her family any of this. "I had admired the watch. We had talked so much about art and time and family dysfunction and legacies. I had no idea it was so expensive," she breathed.

"When I felt like I was sliding down the slippery emotional slope, I met with a few colleagues to find a better therapist to match him with. We had our final meeting, and I told him I felt like I could no longer be an effective therapist for him. He agreed that we'd 'run to the end of our rope.'" She gulped in a couple of breaths.

"He said that exact thing. Then he left. Later I learned that he placed his watch in a gift bag with a card at the reception desk so I didn't see it until the end of the day. I called for a welfare check but it was too late."

He kissed the top of her hair, and she pulled away.

"God, Remy, I hate you. I hate you for making me relive this."

"Seriously." He barked a laugh. "You're wearing a shackle to remind you of a perceived failure, and I'm the bad guy? You don't want to forget."

"Maybe you should be the shrink," she said bitterly. "Because I absolutely sucked. I was so unsuited, and yet I thought I was so smart. So attuned to my patients. The arrogance of twenty-five."

"Try the arrogance of thirty-eight he said. "That's when it gets interesting."

She tried to cling to her anger, but it had evaporated, leaving her feeling wrung out.

"Still want me to leave?"

"I don't know what I want."

"Join the club."

"I was in a groove," she said. "Happy. Thriving, before you showed up."

But even as she spoke the words, she realized they were hollow. Three of her sisters were happily married and moms. Her two best friends in town were married and now moms, and Shane had felt like she was treading water. Even fostering the dogs no longer brought her joy because she would have to give them up once she'd socialized them enough. Healed them. She felt like everyone was moving on with their lives and she was treading water.

"Still hungry?" Remy asked.

"No."

"Let me clean up then," he said. "You relax."

"There's more," she said dully, wanting to get it all out.

She'd always seen how much talking had helped her patients, but she'd never taken her own training to heart. "I'll tell you as we clean up."

The sound of water always soothed her.

"My patient made a will—months before he killed himself. He named me a beneficiary. He left me his Philippe Patek watch. His family lost their minds, filed a lawsuit and wanted me investigated for professional misconduct."

"Did you get fired?"

"No, but Connor's brother, Brandon—you call him the major…"

"Former major, and I have a lot of other names for him."

"He showed up. He was so kind and helpful. He didn't blame me for his brother's death and blah, blah, blah. He took me to dinner. Told me he'd sort his family out." She rolled her eyes. "I was stupid. I believed him. He was so…into me, and I felt like someone understood how much I was hurting. A few months later I got pregnant; we got engaged. I lost the baby, and he dumped me and set a second lawyer on me to return the watch."

"You don't want to give it back and just be done with that chapter of your life? It's probably full of bad juju."

She smiled. "That is not a word I would have predicted that you knew."

"I know a lot of words."

"Good. You'll need them later." She turned off the water. Remy dried the roasting pan and started the dishwasher.

"I've thought a lot about the watch," Shane mused. "I can't tell you much because of privilege, but Ethan's family is competitive and toxic in a way I didn't see until too late. The watch had been given to him on this eighteenth birthday by his grandfather. He and his grandfather had been close. He felt like his grandfather had supported him and loved him for who he was, not what his family wanted him to be. Brandon, his older brother, had, I imagine, always resented that so if I give the watch to Brandon, I'm going against Connor's final wishes."

"Son of a bitch," Remy breathed. "Baby." He took her hands. "Sorry I pushed. But I had to. I don't trust Brandon the Third."

"Smart man."

"I'll talk to him."

"No." Shane was decisive. "If I want to see him to discuss the situation, I will talk to him. You can come and look scary if you want, but I'll do the talking. You have a range to ride and cattle to lasso."

"And a cowgirl to please."

"Bartender. And I was more than pleased," she said and paused. "I do feel...lighter. So thank you, Remy, for pissing me off and for listening."

"And for what I'm going to do next."

SHANE WATCHED THE moon climb higher in the sky, moving out of view from her bedroom window. Remy's hair was soft on her breasts while his fingers toyed with the hummingbird charm in her belly button.

"Do you think the hard times are behind you?" he asked.

She stroked her fingers in his hair. "Some are. More will appear. I need to trust myself to be strong."

"Why are you so reluctant to bond with Arlo?"

It had been a night of confessions, and she no longer felt like she had to hide.

"Did you not listen to anything I said tonight? I lost my objectivity with a patient, and he died. I lost a patient when I was a student. My body couldn't even keep my baby safe."

He was quiet for a moment, then he pushed up to one elbow.

"You are empathetic and passionate and filled with kindness. Everything you did was with best intentions."

"Those weren't enough."

"Maybe not," he agreed. "But your patient had made up his mind to suicide before you severed your ties as a therapist. And your time counseling the teen you spoke of, I'm sure you helped him in many ways, but his problems were so large. It's not healthy to hold on to all the bad, Shane."

"Can you let go of your bad?" she asked curiously, wishing it were so easy, when she knew it was hard. "Losing your mother and your sister. And whatever's going on with sleepy Sam." She didn't want to push him like he'd pushed, but maybe she should. But they were so new. They weren't even a couple yet, not really. "Can you forgive Sam? Can you forgive yourself?"

"I don't know." His palm spanned her stomach.

"If you are determined to try to have Arlo in your life, you'll need to accept that you will make mistakes."

"I'm going to make a ton of them."

"You'll learn, but you'll also need to forgive her when she messes up and kids do, especially kids who are hurting. You'll also need to forgive yourself."

He rolled onto his back, but his palm stayed resting on her stomach. "I'll need help, Shane. I don't know how to build a life like you have. I've never had to do it. I had my mom. Then I was a foster punk, always running away and in trouble. Then I was in the group home ranch for troubled boys. The military. I haven't had to structure my days, my life. I have no idea what to do, but I'm not running away."

She turned on her side and traced the tattoo of the coyote in front of a mountain.

"One obstacle at a time. The job. The cabin. Making appointments to visit Arlo. Getting to know her. Letting her know you. Meeting her social worker. There will be paperwork. Interviews. If you decide to adopt her, you'll need a lawyer."

"Still not running."

"You're the bravest man I've met, Remy, except for my dad. He'd take you on."

He looked at her, his expression unreadable, and she felt like she'd gone too far, like she was pushing for a relationship when she'd only known him for a weekend.

"He would? A dad. I've never met a woman's dad before." His eyes glittered silver in the night. "Totally feeling my way now."

"That's good," she said. "In the words of Tim McGraw, stay humble because you'll need to be open to stumbling. I know you made a vow, Remy, but ultimately proceeding with operation Arlo isn't about Jace or your friendship with him. This is about Arlo—who she is, what she wants, what's best for her. And if it's right for you."

"Operation Arlo. I like the sound of that. You're already talking me off the wall and putting me in my place."

She sighed, tension easing a little. "You have such a big heart, Remy," she said, knowing her own heart was likely in her eyes for him to see.

"Careful, you'll ruin my rep."

She pretended to zip her lips and smiled.

"Why didn't you fight for Arlo?" he asked. "You were so good with her and learning that you might not be able to have a biological child seems like it would have been a natural fit."

"I didn't feel I was suited. Or that I had a right to try to adopt her. We didn't know if they'd find more family, and my career isn't conducive to being a mom. I work nights."

"You were thinking of raising her alone. I'm planning to

enlist the help of the town."

Shane blinked, not sure if she felt amused or slighted, and that right there told her what she really wanted—to have Remy and Arlo in her life. Once again: goodbye, objectivity.

"I pictured you more of a lone wolf."

"Nah." He flexed to show his tat. "At heart I want a pack. Coyotes are scrappy, smart, flexible, innovative, territorial. Adaptive. They hunt in packs. They raise their young in packs." He tangled his fingers with hers. "I don't want to be alone anymore, Shane."

It felt like her heart jumped to the base of her throat. What was he saying? He wanted a relationship with her? Or more as a surrogate mother for Arlo?

"I'm not trying to pressure you." He leaned up on his elbow so they could be eye to eye. "I'm just stating my intentions. I'm not expecting you to adopt Arlo or take responsibility for her, but I'm tired of being alone. I think we're good together. I'd like to see where this could go, but I want you to know that I am intending to ensure that Arlo has a good home. Safety. Love. Opportunities. Support. All the things my mom tried to give me."

And all the things Shane had had without being aware of how lucky she'd been.

"But I'm hoping that you will want to be a part of our journey. One day or one step at a time."

Shane stared at him. God, he was so…so…everything.

She hadn't realized how lonely she was until just now.

How empty. How frightened when she thought of herself as brave.

All Shane could see were the obstacles ahead. Remy was way out in front of his horse in so many ways. But he was still determined to ride.

"I know what I want," she said, willing to be honest. "I don't know if that's possible, but if you're asking me if I want to see you, be with you and be a friend to Arlo, then the answer is yes."

Shane tried to push down the wave of panic her answer unleashed. It rose up like a rogue wave eager to knock her off her surfboard and drag her under and out to sea.

Chapter Twelve

"CROSS, HOW LONG'S it been since you've been on a horse?"

"Been a while," Remy said to Colt the next morning.

He hadn't had time to cowboy up with a Stetson after yesterday's drama and his heart-to-heart with Shane. If he didn't feel so drained, he'd be amused that he had been the one pushing for conversation and truth, not Shane. He'd tried to leave without waking her this morning, but when he'd finished his shower and dressed in her guest bathroom, she'd already made him a breakfast burrito.

"You didn't have to."

"I wanted to," she'd said, and she'd looked so vulnerable for a second that he'd felt as if his sternum had been cracked open.

He'd expected Colt to greet him and act as an intermediary, and he thought his interview would be with Luke, but it was Kane standing next to Colt at the main barn.

"Tell me about your time at the Wild Wind," Kane prompted.

"I was a kid. We lived there almost five years. My mom was the cook for the ranch. Sam and his foreman set me up with chores—everyone had to pull their weight. I helped feed the animals. Mucked out the stalls, groomed the horses, took care of the tack, washed the saddle blankets, helped my mom in the garden and orchard and kitchen. Sam taught me how to do basic repairs on the ranch trucks."

It still felt like a punch in the gut to have seen the ranch so diminished, disheveled and deserted. And he hated having to talk about his past like this, but he needed the job, and he wanted this one.

"My mom died when I was about to turn thirteen. I bounced around in foster group homes for a bit, caused some trouble because I kept running away to find my sister, so I ended up at a working ranch for boys outside Bozeman and was there for three and a half years. I can't talk much about my time in the military as most of it's classified, but I can get letters of rec from my superiors and commander."

Kane's expression didn't change, but Remy could feel him trying to get his measure.

"I've been in the military a long time, but always intended to come back to the land," Remy admitted. "I'm used to working on a team. I've also had to work long stretches on my own. I want hard, honest work. Open space and a purpose."

As he finished, Luke joined them.

"Let's ride." Kane, the shortest of the three brothers—he hadn't met the fourth yet—rocked up on his toes.

"You do realize we're heading out on horses, not bulls."

Luke looked amused.

"Least I can keep my ass planted on a bull."

"I stuck my fair share," Luke's low voice rumbled out.

"Retirement." Colt walked alongside him to the massive red barn that was a few hundred yards off from what the main house. "Those boys are always jawing about who was the best bull rider."

"Kane was world-famous," Remy said.

"He's still adjusting to the *was* part." Colt frowned. "Maybe not that exactly, but for nearly a decade he was just on—touring, promotion, just commitment after commitment, and when he quit, he was thinking he'd be an announcer or do something with the tour or be a stock contractor, but the pull of his family was too fierce, and still he has so much energy. Hard for him to sit still."

"He work the ranch?"

"He works more with the bull-breeding program with Luke's wife, Tanner. We're going to show you that after we ride. Because your help there will occasionally be required even if you're a hand on Wilder Dreams."

They arrived at the stables. He chose a horse without their input. They just watched him greet each horse, spend some time talking to it. Colt gave him an apple for treats and then held out a Buck 119 Special Pro knife that he'd likely used in the service.

"Bit of an overkill." Remy, pulled out his own Buck GCK to indicate he had apple slicing, and pretty much anything else, covered.

"We are not comparing knives because I will pull mine out." Kane's grin had an unholy humor to it, and Remy found himself relaxing a little. Camaraderie. He hadn't realized how much he'd missed it since Jace passed and how much he needed it.

He chose a horse named Shadow and saddled up. He was aware the men watched him without seeming to watch him. But the movements came back, achingly familiar. The feel of the hard leather of the saddle, the lay of the blanket, the flexibility of the cinch, the testing of the fit, and then looking into the eye of Shadow, talking to him in a low voice, letting the horse take his measure, while he got a feel for his new companion. Strength and eagerness shined in the sideways dance of hooves.

"I'm beyond ready too." He stroked his hand down the strong neck, finger-combed the mane a little. "It's been a long time," he said softly. "But I'm game if you are."

He swung himself into the saddle, and as his ass plunked down, a feeling of rightness flowed through him. No one said anything else, and by the time they were riding across the first field, closest to the main barn, the sun's rays were just starting to stretch up the back of the Absaroka range.

"This was my...I'll call him my uncle's land," Colt said. "I inherited it, and we pooled our money and all bought more to fill out the ranch so we can run cattle, build houses, build business, whatever we want to do. We also have another ranch that's come to Tanner and Tucker, Luke and Laird's wives. That's where the bull-breeding program is. Tucker breeds and trains horses on this spread. We run cattle at both. We'll ride this portion, then you and Luke will drive to the other ranch, take its measure and yours."

Remy inclined his head. He'd not been expecting to be handed a job. He'd heard Colt did his best to help vets get work and get settled into the valley.

"After we tour the ranches, I'll show you what I got going on in construction, and you can see what suits. All of us pitch in on the ranch—especially around calving, vaccinating the new calves, moving the cattle to the upper pastures and back down."

Anticipation licked through his blood. He hadn't expected a choice of jobs. Remy was willing to do pretty much anything to make a living, but as they rode over acres—the land spreading vast and beautiful all around—Remy felt himself settle into Shadow's rhythm, and he felt like there could be nothing better than being a cowboy again.

They rode for a couple of hours—Luke playing tour guide talking about the cattle, the ranch, the work. Colt's face was stoic. He was as silent as he'd been as a sniper. Kane was much more personable and not reticent about asking a few personal questions.

"You go by Remy or Cross?" Kane demanded.

After a brief hesitation, he decided that going by Remy might help him settle in sooner, accept his new surroundings, identity and reality.

"Remy," he said. "Shane calls me Remy, though I haven't really been called that in over twenty years."

"You and Shane Knight, huh, Remy?" Kane asked as they dismounted at a particularly scenic spot shaded by an oak savannah and a creek offshoot from the Yellowstone River meandering through. The horses drank. Luke handed out ham and cheese sandwiches. Colt poured the coffee from a thermos stashed in one of the horse's saddlebags.

Remy drank deeply, cut up another apple, sharing slices between each of the horses, before they lowered their heads and grazed.

"Too soon to tell," he answered cryptically, not wanting Shane up for discussion.

Kane snorted at that. "That's what these dimwits said. Now look at them. Married. Fathers. They bought into the whole American dream. Hook. Line and Sinker."

Both Luke and Colt shrugged at their youngest brother and his attempt to goad them.

"Heard you say you were married with four kids," Remy reminded him mildly.

Kane's face shone with pride, and Remy had the feeling he'd pull out his phone and start showing pictures next.

"He took his time too," Colt said. "He saw his ex, Sky, at a Scottsdale gallery and kidnapped her on the spot and drove all night to New Mexico to ride in an American Extreme Bull Riding final round the next day."

Remy stared at Kane, waiting for him to refute the crazy story.

"And she married you?"

"What can I say? I got persuasion skills." He crammed the last bite of his sandwich into his mouth. "What did Sam tell you?" Kane asked, the question they'd all been avoiding. "You kin? You angling for a piece of the Wild Wind?"

"He said nothing," Remy admitted. "I went to ask him, but he fell asleep. Doubt we are," he said. "When my mama passed, social services came to pick me and my sister up. Packed our things in trash bags. Sam watched it all. I…I pleaded with him. Begged him to let us stay. I promised to work full-time, watch over Brianna."

Kane swore and kicked the dirt.

Luke glared off in the middle distance.

"Fact he let you be taken away doesn't make it less likely you're kin," Colt said after a long while when none of them spoke. "He watched me play high school football, never said a thing."

"Long story," Luke said. "Maybe we'll hit Grey's sometime."

Remy nodded.

"Or the Graff," Kane said. "Watch your girl make some magic."

It was an olive branch and Remy grabbed it.

"I came to Marietta to fulfill the promise of a friend," he admitted. "And I will do that, but I'm here to work. To contribute. Not try to take a piece of what's yours, kin or not."

Luke stuck out his hand and Remy shook it.

"Still, you want a DNA test, we'll comply."

Remy shook his head. He didn't feel ready to open that can of worms.

"I want to know," Kane said. "Family sticks together."

"Maybe later," Remy said. "I'm still trying to figure out who I am now that I'm not a soldier," he admitted.

"You're a cowboy," Luke said. "You ride like one, and you picked a horse that Tucker said we should call Demon Seed, not Shadow, and he's accepted you."

Pride flashed through Remy, something he'd rarely felt. He'd been good at being a soldier, but he had never loved it. What he did was necessary for his country and unit and team's safety. An obligation. Being a cowboy felt more like destiny.

"And I'm going to apply to foster Arlo Holt, a thirteen-year-old girl I barely know, and she doesn't know me."

He sounded demented.

"All the more reason to do the DNA test since Sam won't admit to anything," Kane said. "You show the courts that you got a big family to back you, a ranch, a home, brothers and sisters-in-law and cousins for her, that can go a long way with a judge."

Remy hadn't thought of that. He'd been alone for so long. He'd been thinking maybe he and Shane might be able to be a family for Arlo if he didn't screw it up because he was floundering. But Colt had done it.

"Let's put that aside for now," he said slowly, finishing his sandwich. "Show me the rest of the ranch. Tell me where I can help the most."

"Saddle up, cowboy." Kane grinned. "You do realize that if Sam's your dad, you might be our uncle." Kane started laughing. "Welcome to Wilder Dreams Ranch, where everything just maybe got a bit wilder."

REMY SAT IN the chair at the lawyer's office and forced himself not to fidget.

"You don't have to make any decisions today." Shane sat at his side, although she'd initially balked at coming with him.

"I definitely would counsel taking your time, not rushing." Attorney Mia Zabrinski spoke in cultured tones that Remy wondered if they taught in law school.

"Taking my time is not an option." It had taken him three days to get this first appointment.

"In matters of family law and minors…" the lawyer began calmly.

"Every day, every delay exposes that girl to more risk, more trauma, more isolation. She needs a family. She needs a home. She needs someone who is watching out for her, putting her interests first, keeping her safe."

Mia Zabrinski blinked. "I researched the group home. Ms. Hammond has no complaints against her facility or accusations of abuse. She has another adult in her house, her sister, so her residents are supervised. It's true that her home is at capacity with her residents…"

"She's dialing it in at best," Remy interrupted. "She's in it for the check. She's trying to get permitted to…"

"There are easier ways to earn money, Master Sergeant Cross," the attorney said, proving she too could interrupt and do her homework.

Heat flushed through him, hearing his title spoken aloud. He wondered if this title would help him provide a home for Arlo or hurt him.

"Remy," Shane said softly, but firmly. "It's important to remember a child is involved in this process—a child you have at present no relation to, and you have just met."

"I made a vow." Remy's jaw cranked tight. "To my deceased commanding officer. He'd made a promise to a friend. I intend to honor that promise no matter what it takes."

Shane's hand was warm, brushing against his. "I know. But this is about what is best for Arlo, not you. I never met Jace, but the way you speak of him, so honorably, seems that he too would want the best for Arlo."

She was right. He loved that she called him on his crap. Love. He didn't want to go there. He'd never been there before. Had no idea how to get there or stay there. And would a woman like Shane even want to try with a man like him? He hated that word: *try*. It was so half-assed.

"So that I best understand your goals, Master Sergeant Cross..."

"Remy's fine," he said restlessly, interrupting again. He stirred in the chair, stretched out, then sat up straighter. Nothing felt right, and he hated revealing that to the attorney.

Shane smiled, and he felt his temperature and discomfort drop.

"You want to apply to be a foster parent with the goal of fostering Arlo Holt, age thirteen."

"Yes, ma'am."

The attorney blinked. "Do you intend to apply to adopt Arlo Holt legally?"

He heard Shane catch her breath next to him.

Coming from the attorney, it made him feel like he was about to jump off a bridge.

"Yes, ma'am." He could feel cold sweat trickle down his neck—him, who'd been ice-cold calm in the middle of an enemy camp, ghosting in, doing his job and ghosting out again, losing his cool in a Marietta, Montana attorney's office.

He clung to Shane's hand, so he had no idea if she wanted to pull away from him or not.

"If you qualify to become a foster parent, and with your

past ties to the community, your service to our country, your relationship to the child's godfather, who had been named legal guardian in the deceased mother's will…"

The attorney kept talking, but Remy couldn't hear any more. There had been a legal arrangement. No one had known. Did that help him or hurt him? He didn't think a judge would be impressed that he'd picked the task of taking care of Arlo out of a helmet. He felt chilled to his bone.

"If Arlo remains in the foster system while living with you, she will be under the control of the county and could be removed at any time," the attorney said.

"She needs a family," Remy reaffirmed, feeling like he had an unexploded IED planted in his chest. Who the hell was he kidding? How could he give her a family when he'd lost his?

Could he build that with Shane? Did she want that? She wasn't meeting his gaze at all. Maybe she too was lost in a private freak-out. And maybe he'd have the Wilders, but he was afraid to hope. He'd told them he didn't care, that being related wouldn't change anything. But he'd been lying to himself and them. And now that lifeline had been dangled, he desperately wanted to lunge for it. Him. Needing support. When he'd always been his own rock. So alone.

"How would you suggest we proceed?" Shane asked softly, her aquamarine gaze was fixed on the attorney. He saw her swallow and her fingers tightened on his for a moment.

"I would suggest meeting with Arlo's case worker. Discussing your intentions. I can help you proceed with the paperwork—the applications, the legal work. There will be background checks. A home visit. Court dates. Interviews. But I'd also suggest working with Ms. Hammond and Arlo. I'd see if you could arrange regular visits with Arlo at her residence and see if you could bring Arlo for a visit to Marietta. Does she have contact still with friends?"

Yes, Arlo had had friends. A girl needed friends. And maybe cousins.

"Details. Hoops. I can be a poodle if I need to."

Shane smiled. "I can't envision that at all."

She brushed at his hair that he wondered if he should cut when he went for his interviews with social services, but Shane often played with his hair in bed after, and it occurred to him suddenly that he should probably check with her before he did certain things. Warmth spread through his belly.

"It will be a longer and more complicated process than you want," Mia Zabrinski said dryly. "I'm good and can expedite certain parts of the process, possibly, but I'm not a miracle worker. Despite often being criticized in the media, social services does want to protect children."

"I don't just want her to survive. I want her to thrive."

Mia Zabrinski glanced down at her notes and eyed them seriously again. "Arlo is thirteen. There is no set age in Montana for a child to go before a judge and have their wishes given preference," she said. "Sixteen is generally considered the age of capacity, but not always. Some judges will take in a child's wishes. Some not so much. But yes, I will take you on as a client to shepherd you through the adoptions process."

"Thank you," Remy said. They'd already discussed her retainer and her hourly fee.

"I don't need to tell you that if you were married and both applying to adopt her, the process would be far easier."

Shane's fingers spasmed in his, and that sexy little pulse fluttered faster in her neck.

"Shane is established in town. She owns a home. She has a good salary, a managerial position. Your military service is a strong indication of character and stability, Remy, but I don't have to tell you that only being in town a week and a half and having a job for a week is not going to impress a judge, so you will need patience."

"Remy." Shane spoke softly, her other hand covering their linked ones. "Arlo is Arlo, not Brianna."

"I know."

The emotive look on her face stopped his fast assurance. But what else could he do but go forward? Yes, Jace would have been a better man for this job, but you went into battle with the soldiers and equipment you had—not what you wished you had.

"I would like to proceed," he said gulping in a deep breath. "With the adoption."

"The adoption application."

"Adoption," he said firmly. "There is no try for me."

The lawyer eyed him, her gaze steely. He let her see him—who he was. The man who got things done no matter what obstacles life or fate or terrorist or warlord or cartel kingpin threw at him.

"Arlo is a young girl who's lost her mother, Remy," Mia Zabrinski said. "She lost what amounts to her life—family, home, school, friends, activities."

"I can't bring her mother back," Remy said, but didn't dare look at Shane. "But with determination and help I can help her build a new life."

He'd be doing it for himself as well.

"I don't doubt you." For the first time his attorney smiled. "That's why I'm taking you on as a client."

Chapter Thirteen

S HANE HAD NO idea what to say as they walked out of the attorney's office. Remy had enlisted her help. He'd pushed for a chance for them to build a relationship, and he'd shoved for her to open her heart to Arlo, but in the attorney's office, he'd said 'I.' Not 'we.'

Remy put his Oakley shades back on, looking like a ba-dass, while Shane avoided looking at herself reflected back and instead fumbled for her Maui Jim's in her small back-pack-style purse. He helped her, sliding the sunglasses on her face, and his hands covered her shaking ones.

"What scares you the most?" His deep voice rolled over her, sucking her in and under like he was a powerful Pacific Ocean wave.

"Nothing."

Everything. She was becoming the biggest coward.

And that metaphorically snapped her spine straight be-cause she didn't want to live that way. Her confidence had been shaken, but she didn't want to hide for the rest of her life.

"You used 'I' with the attorney." She heard the accusa-tion in her voice.

All around them, Main Street was a buzz of activity as merchants had begun the process of decorating their windows for the Copper Mountain Rodeo in a few weeks. A city crew hung banners announcing the rodeo. This year the Graff was sponsoring a Rodeo Cowboy contest where merchants or groups would create a cowboy 'scarecrow,' that would be placed around town and voted on in several categories and then auctioned off at the rodeo's steak dinner Saturday night.

It was so much easier to think of the contest she and Miranda had pitched to the hotel's marketing and events coordinator Walker Wilder and Langston Ballantyne to add something new to connect the historic business core to the rodeo this year, rather than think about this man and the life he was tempting her with and that she might lose.

Remy looked at her, and even through his Oakleys, she could feel his gaze pierce her as if he could read her thoughts.

"I don't know what you want, Shane. You're like water through my hands."

"Water," she protested that analogy.

"You're right. I did disrupt your life. I rode into town intending to ride back out again once I'd made contact with Arlo and her mother in a laughably ignorant misunderstanding of what I'd committed to. I made contact with you under false pretenses, and my loose plan to carry out Jace's wishes, and see if the major was jerking my chair, fell apart."

His hands were on his hips. "Yeah, we need to talk, but I

don't feel like I'm on solid ground, yet, and I'm hungry and don't want to have this conversation here."

It was such a man moment—the focus on hunger along with deftly shoving aside a conversation.

"Let's eat. What's good?" He looked up and down Main Street as if the restaurant's rodeo decorations and signage would announce something delicious.

"We can go to my house," she offered, feeling too antsy to push the conversation off. She had to head to work in an hour.

"You're always cooking. I want you to relax."

How could she relax when she felt sick and like her skin would peel off? There was so much churning inside her, she wasn't sure she could eat anything. And it was an awkward time—too late for lunch, too early for dinner.

"Colt and Parker have a Friday morning ritual breakfast at Main Street Diner," Remy said. "That's probably good."

"It's lovely, but Flo, the head server tends to be chatty and very observant, and if you don't want everyone to know your business it's a no-go."

"Luke likes the sandwiches and coffee at the Java Café."

"Perfect," Shane agreed, and they walked toward the coffee shop, and Shane cataloged who she might run into at this time of day—nearly three in the afternoon.

"Are you going back to work after this?"

"Yes," he said, holding the door open for her. "And then Colt and I are going to look at the cabin to discuss what we'd need to do to make it work for me and Arlo."

No mention of her.

Her emotions seesawed, making her nauseous. She knew she was being ridiculous. She'd asked for space. She'd cautioned him to go slow. She had her own house and her own life, and she hadn't jumped up, hand waving wildly to adopt Arlo. So why did she feel so gutted?

"What would you like to eat?" Remy prompted while Shane stared blankly at the large, colorful chalkboard menu.

She ordered a peach iced tea and nothing else, convinced she'd never be able to choke down food, plus she could leave faster. Not fall foolishly apart over a reason she couldn't logically explain.

"Not a tuna melt?" he asked. "You said you loved those."

He not only listened to her, he also remembered. No man had ever taken that much interest—even more reason she was being an idiot.

"No thank you."

Remy ordered a tuna melt and a turkey club sandwich on rye. She looked up at him. "I'm hungry."

He also ordered two dozen cookies to bring back to the ranch.

"You're really jumping right in," Shane noted as they sat down.

"Have to. What's bothering you?"

"It's stupid," she said, balling up her napkin then smoothing it out again. "I complained when you were pushing me, and now I'm disappointed you're putting on the brakes. I know. Dumb." She finally met his eyes.

He'd taken off his sunglasses so she could really see him, really try to read his expression, divine his thoughts.

"What would you say if one of your former patients said their feelings were stupid?"

"I think you're a closet therapist." She felt the first flicker of humor all day.

"Pretty sure no one who met me would ever make that call."

"I just feel like everything is moving way too fast," she admitted.

"And?"

"That's not enough?"

"Not if it's not everything."

She gnawed on her straw instead of drinking her tea. Their order was called, and Remy returned with one sandwich wrapped to go and the tuna cut in half and plated on two small plates.

"Eat half a sandwich first and talk."

"Bossy," she said without heat, trying to clarify her thoughts. She cut the half into quarters. "I'm feeling like I have to make a decision soon, like I'm running blindly toward the edge of a cliff," she said.

"That's my fault," he said, pausing before he took a bite. "I can't push you. The decision to adopt Arlo, to fight for her, no matter what that looks like is on me. Not you.

Would I rather you be on board? Yes. Do I realize I'm asking a lot? Yes. I trust you, Shane, and I don't trust many people, but you don't trust yourself and that's on you. Your decision—to be with me or not to be with me is yours. Your decision to be a part of Arlo's life is also totally on you."

Remy took a big bite and chewed like it was a job, and all the time his silvery-gray eyes analyzed her.

"You just got out of the service. We just started dating. You've just met Arlo. You have a new job. So many new things in your life."

He took a sip of his water and then another bite, nodding for her to continue.

"That's it," she said, feeling exasperated at his calm and his focus on his food. "You're dealing with a lot."

"Yeah." He eyed the quarter she'd left and she nodded. "And I'm dealing," he said, cramming the bite in his mouth.

"How can you be so calm?" Shane demanded. "There are so many changes coming. I feel like I'm standing on a train track and feeling the rumble and the whistle screaming."

He reached out and covered her hand that was shredding another napkin.

"Thank you for telling me what's bothering you."

He wasn't mad. He wasn't minimizing.

"I haven't had a lot of choices in my life." He wiped his mouth. "I haven't had downtime to think in my life. Or quiet. It was constant motion. Lots of chaos. Survival was my focus—mine and my team's—so I'm reading this situation differently, not as a threat, but as something necessary to be managed with planning. But I have faith in myself and I have faith in you."

"Me?"

"You're strong. Smart. Kind. You don't have to save anyone, Shane. It's not ever going to be all on you. It will be on us if we choose to be a team. That's the decision you need to make. Do you want to be a team with me? I can't make it for you."

"SO," TUCKER SAID as she and Shane entered the kitchen of Luke and Tanner's ranch house. "I've been so patient. It's been weeks, and I want deets."

"Of course you do, nosy woman." Shane pulled out the three pies that she'd made for dinner tonight at the Wilders'. She was trying to take her own advice about not feeling too pressured to solve every potential problem all at once. But Remy had been full steam ahead—meeting with the social workers. Filling out his paperwork for background checks, working full time at the ranch and then at night working on the cabin before meeting her after work.

"I'm happy," Shane said as she trayed two of the pies so that they'd be easier to carry.

"Why does that make you nervous?" Tucker asked as she gathered plates. "And you sound...I don't know sad or something."

"Not sad." Shane added forks, and napkins and a large scoop for dishing out ice cream to the basket that Tucker was carrying with the plates. "I am a little nervous, though—dumb, but I feel like it will all poof away. I'm not used to relationships feeling so right, so easy."

"Everything about that man looks like he'd go down easy." Tucker winked and laughed, giving Shane a glimpse of her once legendary bad-girl flirt.

"Seriously Remy is amazing. The boys are all impressed and convinced he's one of them, although Laird is a bit freaked out to have an uncle who's only a few years older. He thinks we could start our own rancher reality show and cash in big so we can buy the Wild Wind before the bank seizes it and auctions it off to some Russian oligarch or Chinese national or a developer." Tucker pretended to gag herself.

"Is he going to take the DNA test?"

"I don't know," Shane said.

"What? Why? Are you too busy banging?" She made a circle with one finger on her left hand and then with her right index finger...

"Stop." Shane laughed playfully and slapped Tucker's hands away. "You. We aren't in high school anymore."

"Praise be to any god who will listen," Tucker said. "Amen."

She followed Shane out to the large farmhouse table where many of the Wilders were sitting. The kids had their own separate picnic table and were running around.

"You must really like him if you won't rate his performance." Tucker hip-checked her walking past. "Eight? Nine? We have pie and ice cream," Tucker sang out. "And fixings for sundaes if Parker will help me carry out the goods."

"On it." Parker with one of his cousins bouncing on his back and shouting giddy up ran into the house.

Shane began slicing the pies and Remy scooped the vanilla ice cream and distributed the dessert according to who called out for what.

When she went to sit back down, he pulled her between his thighs. "I'll share." His breath warmed her ear, and she saw that he had a thin slice of each pie that she'd made.

"This is nice," she said looking around at everyone relaxed, enjoying their dessert. Luke had brewed coffee, and the sun was just starting to set, casting a purpled orange hue over the yard, scattered with kid toys.

Remy fed her a piece of apple pie, and she sighed as the flaky crust dissolved in her mouth, mixing with the apples and cinnamon.

"Like a dream or something someone would see in a magazine," Remy agreed.

"Pinching yourself?" Shane fed him a bite of the strawberry rhubarb.

"No, but sometimes it does feel like a mirage, and I'm going to keep walking and find out I'm back in a cold and dusty mountain pass."

She laid her head on his shoulder. In a way it made it easier that they both couldn't believe their good luck. Shane had always been the strong one, never giving voice to her doubts, and she loved, loved, loved that Remy was starting to share with her more.

"I'm still working on scheduling a visit to bring Arlo to the ranch for an afternoon so she can have a riding lesson with Tucker, but Kane suggested me bringing Arlo to the Wilders for the rodeo weekend. She could spend the night here with the Wilder kids and Petal and attend the rodeo."

"She'd love that," Shane said. She would be working the steak dinner, but she could attend the Friday barbecue and Sunday finals. Remy had the weekend off.

"I thought so too. I emailed Arlo's social worker and Ms. Hammond with the plan as soon as Kane suggested it, and it's a go."

"Wow." Shane pulled back a little so she could look at him. "How are you feeling? Excited? Worried? It's the next step."

"Yes it is," Remy admitted. And having the other kids around and the rodeo will ease everyone through her first visit here. I was thinking, if you're willing tonight to visit the cabin, maybe give me some advice for how to make it look more like a home instead of a shell."

"Sure," Shane said. "Although I don't know if it's a good idea for you to show the cabin to Arlo yet until you have more certainty that you will be able to foster her as you go through the adoption process."

"Understood, but I have an ulterior motive."

"Really?" She could feel the shift in his motives against her back.

"I wanted you to feel comfortable there if you wanted to visit." His breath tickled her nape. "So I thought you could suggest colors for things like a bed."

"Remy Cross, are you propositioning me?"

"Is it working?"

He seemed so lighthearted that she felt like some of his strength and confidence was rubbing off on her.

"I'll let you know."

Chapter Fourteen

REMY DROVE SOUTH on I 89, determined to not break out in a cold, prickly sweat at the top of the pass this time. He'd driven this road twice more with Shane and once to pick up supplies in Bozeman for Colt, but this time he'd picked up Arlo for her first visit back to Marietta without Shane.

"Petal will be there?" Arlo asked, staring out the side of the window, her fingers stroking Beast, who no longer wore a cone of shame, but still looked rather battered and beat up, though well loved.

"Absolutely," Remy said to Arlo. "Petal and Parker."

He hadn't met Arlo's friend, Petal, but he'd had a lot of exposure to Colt's oldest son, Parker, whom Colt had adopted when he and Talon had married six years ago. Parker with dark hair. Intense, adult gaze and mile-a-minute mouth and who might, just might be his...what...great-nephew?

Remy was determined to not think like that, but still the thought that he might be related to the Wilders continued to ping his conscience when he worked the twelve- and four-teen-hour days, both at the ranch, and then renovating the cabin so that it wasn't so rustic. He was hoping it would prove suitable for Arlo when the home visit from the social workers happened, and yeah, he continued to try to draw Shane into what Colt described as 'design decisions,' so that she too would like it.

Between working at both of the Wilder Dreams' spreads during the day and working on projects on the cabin at night, he'd never been happier, although the paperwork for the county and the meeting with a social worker and psychologist who cautioned him to get to know Arlo at her pace, not his had made his skin crawl with anxiety that he'd never experienced during a mission. Probably something was wrong with him, but he didn't have time for it.

And he was still irritated that Sam Wilder wouldn't allow his grandsons to start caring for his ranch in his absence. Maybe it was worth another visit to Sam, who was due to be released any day now—not that he thought he'd have any sway with the man, but he didn't have quit in him. Luke had approached him about a drive-about to catalog needed repairs to the Wild Wind, so maybe going rogue was a Wilder thing.

"Arlo, you can choose something on the radio," he invited for the second time as the silence stretched out. "Got the satellite package just so you'd…we'd have more options."

"Really?" Arlo's face creased into momentary interest. She looked at the audio system but didn't make a move to touch anything. It was the second time he'd offered, and his confidence dipped. He should have insisted Shane came. He wanted to respect her boundaries, but he was having trouble adjusting to her speed. When he made up his mind, he was all in. Shane needed to process. He tried not to chafe against what he saw as delays, but he knew, especially when Shane discussed Arlo's needs, that he needed to listen and respect what Shane called 'the process.'

"Give yourself time," Shane had said gently to him this morning. "Enjoy the moment and connect with Arlo and yourself."

Easy to imagine being patient when he and Shane lay in bed or relaxed after a long day around her firepit. Impossible while alone with a nervous, silent thirteen-year-old girl, and he was trying to be so casually strong and not intimidating.

Remy, driving his new Ford 250, was still trying to not feel claustrophobic in his own damn vehicle. "Or you could use music from your phone," he invited.

"I don't have any."

"We'll have to change that." He relaxed. He could put Arlo on his cell plan so she could access music and other things.

"Really?" It was the first time she'd looked at him, even if she quickly looked down at Beast.

"Today, if possible," he asserted feeling his confidence surge.

"We'll have music maybe, Beast," she whispered to the dog.

"You like music? There's a music store in town."

She goggled at him like he'd suggested they fly to space, and he inwardly flinched. Shane had reminded him to go slow. So had the social worker and psychologist. Not overpromise.

"I like music. Are you sure Petal's coming?"

"As sure as I can be." He looked ahead at Highway 89 unraveling ahead of them. He'd driven this road a few times during the past week—once to Bozeman for some building supplies for Colt, and twice with Shane to visit Arlo and her social worker.

"Why didn't Shane come?"

Remy blinked. Kids sure could keep brooding to a minimum.

"She's getting supplies and setting up for the activities for the three of you." He wasn't completely sure what Shane had planned—something she called cowboy scarecrows and rodeo seltzers. "A craft project for the rodeo."

He liked his life now. Meaningful outdoor work in a beautiful setting. Quiet. A hard, honest day's work. And then after quitting, he'd shower, head into town, sit in the Graff bar, drink a coffee and watch Shane, help her clean up, walk her home and make love. It was what he imagined a normal life was, and he'd never dreamed he'd have a shot at.

Arlo nodded and cuddled Beast along with the plush horse he'd bought for her at Marietta Western Wear where he and Shane had shopped for some clothing appropriate for his new job. He'd never paid much attention to what he wore or looked like. Function was what mattered. Not standing out had ensured his survival, but Shane wasn't interested in him blending in. She'd chosen shirts that 'brought out the color of his eyes.'

He'd felt like a damn fool, but seeing the admiration in her gaze, feeling her hands as they'd adjusted a button or a collar or smoothed down him as she'd looked at the fit of the fleece-lined Carhartt barn jacket he'd bought because his leather jacket wasn't going to cut it on a Montana cattle ranch, he'd purchased far more than he'd intended. What had been a utility trip had turned into something fun, a bit of a game that had left him more content and relaxed than the random sexual hookups over the years.

He looked at Arlo, holding the plush horse tightly to her chest, and moving its head as if it was talking to Beast.

"I was right," he said. "I hoped you'd like the horse. Shane thought you might be too old for a plush animal."

It had been the other way around when Shane had plucked the horse off one of the displays and put it on top of his stack of boots, jeans, shirts and jacket, but he'd steal a win.

"You were right," Arlo said. A smile teased her lips when she looked at him. "I just hope Beast isn't jealous."

Remy had bought a crate for beast to keep him safe during the drive, but Arlo had clung to the pup so desperately when he'd suggested they crate him, that Remy had capitulated, not wanting to start off wrong, especially since Shane wasn't around to smooth over his rough edges and mistakes.

"We can stop and get Beast a bone and a chew toy on the way into town, and you can pick a bed for him that fits in the crate so he's more comfortable next time."

"Really?"

"Sure."

Arlo smiled a little wider this time and nuzzled the dog. "See, Beast, I told you today would be fun. You didn't need to be nervous."

Remy didn't need a psych degree to know projection when he saw it. He slowed down as he crested the pass. His heart rate sped up; sweat broke out on the back of his neck. He had to get over this. He had to.

"I'm also thinking since I've been working on a ranch that I could take you riding sometime."

She looked at him, her expression such a painful clutch of hope and doubt.

"If you'd like."

She stared down at her plush, stroking it. Her head-nod was nearly imperceptible.

"I used to ride with my sister," he said, bringing up the painful memory. "She was little—lots younger so she rode up in front of me. You'd have your own horse to ride."

Another small nod. He felt so lost. Was he terrifying her? Overwhelming her?

He glanced at Arlo who still held the plush like it was a

lifeline and made a split-second decision. He'd made many as a soldier. Many of them had saved his life and the lives of others. Perhaps by facing his demons, he could help Arlo face hers.

He pulled over at a viewpoint, but he didn't look at the view.

"I want to tell you something about myself," he said softly. "And show you if you're willing."

"Huh?" Arlo looked up.

He probably looked serious. Scary. He'd known having Shane stay behind was a bad idea, but she'd insisted, said she had things to do, but that was a thinly veiled cop-out that meant: 'you need to get used to being alone with Arlo if you're really going to do this crazy thing.'

And she wasn't wrong.

But she was wrong about one thing. It wasn't crazy. It was atonement. Redemption. A fresh start when he hadn't even known he'd wanted one. But it was also, he hoped, another chance for a young girl.

"We need to walk back a little ways, up toward the curve."

"Can Beast come?"

"Of course. Keep his leash retracted so he's off the road and safe and walk behind me. It's not far."

They walked in silence and stood vigil at the curve, looking down the steep, rocky drop-off. It was beautiful—trees, birds singing, the air smelled pine-fresh, mountains still with snow playing sentinel.

"My life changed here," he said. "I was your age. My mom and sister and I were driving back from Bozeman. A guy in a black truck had been tailgating her up the curves, but she wouldn't speed up. She wanted to keep us safe like moms do, but the guy was impatient. He tried to pass her at the wrong spot and clipped our car. We spun around, jumped the guardrail, flipped over and fell down about fifty feet before a tree and a rock outcropping stopped us."

Somehow, telling the story again, while Arlo stared up and him, eyes huge, it felt for the first time, as if it was a story, a memory, not jail imprisoning him. Even Beast sat beside Arlo and looked up at him as if sensing the seriousness of the moment.

"My mom died," he said. "It took a little while for help to come, and she tried to reassure me and my sister, even as she died."

Arlo didn't say anything for a while, but she didn't look away from him. Her eyes swam with tears.

"I'm sorry," she said. "My mom died too. You're right. Moms want to take care of you. Even when she got too sick to take care of me, she kept telling me that I would be okay. That I was strong."

"My mom said the same thing to me, that I was strong. I was. I am. You are too."

Arlo rubbed the plush against her cheek.

"The thing is, losing your mom sucks," Remy said. "I

know that. I experienced it. I can't help with that. My friend Jace was going to help her with you—be in your lives. I'm not sure if he knew she was sick, but that wouldn't have made a difference to him. He made a promise to your mom. He was a man who kept his promises."

Arlo turned back and stared out across the valley, her slim fingers stroking the plush. "But he died too." Her voice hollowed out, quavered, and he almost lost the thread of it in the wind that whistled over the ridge to tear down into the valley. It was the first hint of autumn that he'd felt to his bones.

"He did. A huge loss to so many people."

The next words were a little harder to form. But they were real.

"But he was thinking of you. He wanted me to take care of you just as he would have. I want you to know, Arlo, that I am also a man of my word. I didn't know your mom, but I knew Jace, and I made a promise to him, that I would do what he no longer could."

She nodded, still looking out to the valley. There were probably more words he should say. Explanations. Reassurances, but the social worker and the counselor had told him not to promise anything that he couldn't guarantee—as if life had any guarantees.

"So maybe I could come live with you and Shane?" she finally asked, turning to look at him again—her face was full of doubt, but also tinged with what looked like hope.

"I'm working on it," he said firmly. "There's lots of paperwork and meetings so it will take time, but I am committed to doing everything I can to make it happen, but also, it's your decision too if you want to come live with me out on the ranch or if we get a place in town."

"What about Shane?"

"I'm working on that too," he said, realizing that the words were just as true as the ones that had come before.

Who would have guessed?

Maybe Jace, with his sunny optimism, determination, relentless sense of humor and huge welcoming heart that had never, ever given up on anyone, even him.

SHANE WATCHED THE three young teens, feeling totally amused and unnecessary. She'd put so much thought and planning into the activities wanting Arlo's first visit back to Marietta to be perfect, and yet all she'd needed was Parker and Petal. Just like she'd been cautioning Remy to let Arlo lead, she needed to take her own advice.

"Whipped cream is essential."

"Whipped cream should be its own food group," Petal Telford tacked on to Parker Wilder's pronouncement.

"We should call it the Patriot because it's red, white and blue." Arlo looked at the drink they had created at Shane's.

"There's lime in it, but you can't see the green." Petal

swirled her glass around and held it up to the light. Then she took a deep drink, giving herself a whipped cream mustache, which made her and Parker laugh.

Arlo fisted her hands and rested her chin on them and looked at her drink with the sparkling lime-flavored water, muddled raspberries, a few blueberries and a dollop of fresh whipped cream on top with red sprinkles.

"Maybe we should add blue sprinkles too," Parker said, looking critically at his drink.

"It's for the rodeo; it should have a rodeo theme," Arlo mused. "The Cowboy Patriot." She looked directly at Remy, who stood next to Shane in the kitchen after she'd helped the three kids narrow down some flavors that they liked. "What do you think?" she asked Remy and then her gaze slid thoughtfully toward Shane, who'd helped them make the refreshing take on lemonade to sell at their lemonade stand during the rodeo weekend to raise money for Harry's House and their local 4-H club. Cowboy and cowgirl cookies were also going to be sold, but they hadn't decided yet which two recipes to use.

"What about cowgirls?" Parker licked the whipped cream from his upper lip. "We don't want to be sexist."

Remy snorted a laugh that morphed to a cough when Shane elbowed him.

"We want to keep it simple," Shane added, "since we want the kids to do most of the work—making and selling, but with a few changes, you all could have two separate drinks—maybe with a different base, since muddling blueberries won't be as pretty as the raspberries."

"So..." Petal wrinkled her nose. "The Cowboy Patriot and the Cowgirl Patriot or the Barrel Racer Patriot."

"The Rodeo Queen," Arlo suggested, totally focused on her drink. Beast sat at her feet, and the plush horse Remy had purchased hadn't yet left her lap.

Shane wondered if she should switch up the conversation or get them started on their scarecrow design. The cookies might have to wait until next time.

She caught her breath. She was doing this. Committing, and even though a thrill of fear ran through her, she felt good. She felt like this was where she was supposed to be, who she was supposed to be.

"We should have patriot in the name since my dad and your dad were soldiers."

"Remy's not my dad," Arlo said quietly.

"He could be," Parker said. Shane felt Remy stiffen beside her, and she felt like she'd been hit with an arrow. Remy was all in on adopting Arlo, but if he stuck with her, adoption would be his only option for more children. It might seem that a man like Remy didn't care as he'd told her he'd never thought he'd marry or have children, but with him making so many inroads with the Wilders, who certainly seemed to treat him like family, he might change his mind.

"I heard him and my dad working together on making a bathroom upstairs in the loft in the cabin where Remy's going to live. Remy said teen girls should have their own bathroom, but I don't think that's fair, because I don't have my own bathroom—" Parker broke off as if just realizing that he should not be airing what had been a private conversation between adults. "Sorry, sir," Parker said, contritely. "I was in the tree house reading, and I had to pee, and my mom doesn't like me peeing outside so I ran to the cabin, and I…"

"Ew, you pee outside?" Petal demanded.

"No."

"You better not." Petal turned to Arlo as Parker took a long sip of his seltzer.

"Will you come back to school next week with us?" Petal asked, sliding closer to Arlo on the bench and slipping her hand into her friend's.

The tension Remy radiated was tangible, and she could hear his teeth grind.

"Let's make a second sample with lemonade as the base," Shane smoothly intervened. "We'll use the same fruit and try a different flavor of spritzer to add color and use a different color of sprinkles. Petal, why don't you choose the color of sprinkles this time. Parker, you muddle the raspberries like I showed you, and Arlo, you can help me squeeze a few lemons."

"And whipped cream?" Parker asked.

"What do you think?" Shane asked Arlo, who'd stood up, her plush toy in her hand, and Beast's leash looped around her skinny wrist. "Should we have whipped cream for our Cowgirl Patriot Spritzer?"

Arlo looked at her friends, whose expressions were full of entreaty and then nodded.

"Okay we have our recipe. Remy, why don't you head outside and make sure everything for the scarecrows is in the right place and that nothing has blown away."

She didn't know if she wanted to laugh or cry at how quickly he fled. She and Remy had talked about how seeing Parker and Petal could create nostalgia or trigger memories that would be bittersweet, but talking about it and seeing it in real time were two different things.

"Ready, sous chef?" She smiled at Arlo remembering something her sister Sutter had always said about performing on stage—'the bigger the mistake the bigger the smile.'

"How's it going?" Shane asked, sorting through the various art and recycling supplies she'd collected and laid out on a picnic table to create the scarecrows.

"My blood sugar has likely tripled with all the taste testing," he said.

"Extra exercise for you tonight." She kissed his jaw, and he felt the lick of her tongue. "Delicious."

"No fair when I can't retaliate," he murmured.

He felt a tap low on his back.

"Yeah." Remy turned around.

"What do you think?" Arlo asked, holding a drink that was heavy on the whipped cream and dark with blue sprinkles.

"Mmmmmm." Remy sipped the drink. The lemon was tart, but the sweetness of the raspberries balanced the face-cringing tang.

"We should share with the master," he said, handing the drink to Shane, who sipped it like it was a fine wine—not that he'd know what that would look like other than a few people he'd seen order wine in the Graff pub.

"A bit heavy on the whip, but I can't blame you." Shane smiled. "And if I were doing this at the bar, I would add a strawberry on the side, but we want to keep this simple."

"Why isn't a strawberry simple?" Parker and Petal had joined them in the backyard, to surround him and Shane.

"She means not expensive," Petal said. "We're raising money for 4-H and Harry's House, so we have to keep our costs down."

"Well said, daughter of a successful merchant." Shane smiled.

"What if we do strawberries not raspberries?" Parker asked.

"No we have to do raspberries in the cowgirl drink to make it pinkish," Petal said, with authority. Arlo looked between Petal and Parker.

"Why can't the cowboy drink be pink too?" Parker said. "Or pinky red. We could muddle strawberries. I love smashing things."

Parker and Petal discussed the gender message of fruit, which was hilarious, but Remy noticed Arlo grew quieter.

"Ready to start creating a scarecrow sample for the Graff?" Remy asked.

"Yes," Petal and Parker shouted, fist-bumped the air and then each other and made an exploding sound.

Arlo's drink wobbled in her hand, and she scuffed her toes on the cement. Remy took the drink and then crouched down so he was closer to her level.

"What's on your mind?" he asked.

"Will I even be able to sell the cowboy and cowgirl spritzers? I'm not in 4-H anymore."

Her whispered question felt like a direct hit to his heart.

"Of course, you will." Petal slung her arm around Arlo's shoulder. "You were a member for four years with us, and you will be again—right, Shane?"

Shane looked at him, eyes wide.

"I...we..." He broke off. He didn't want to rush her, and he didn't want to shut her out, but it was getting harder and harder to find a middle ground.

"We're doing our best," Shane said, curling her fingers around his.

"That's all you can do every day, is your best," Remy said, bringing their linked hands to his chest.

Hope glimmered on Arlo's face and Petal nudged her and gave Parker a smug look.

"Told you so."

"I was going to save this for later," Remy said, "but today I got the final okay for Arlo to spend the rodeo weekend with all of us at the Wilder Dreams Ranch. She can attend the rodeo with us, and camp out with the two of you and all the Wilders on the ranch. That's where I work," he told Arlo, hearing the pride in his own voice.

"Can Beast come?"

"Where you go, Beast will come too if legal and possible."

He felt like he could breathe again when Arlo's shoulders relaxed.

"And can we walk in the pine forest and listen for the owls that you told me about?" she asked.

"Definitely on the agenda," Remy reassured her.

Parker and Petal whooped it up.

"You're camping with us too—right, Shane?" Arlo slid her hand through Shane's, and Remy could see the surprise and pleasure light up Shane's beautiful aquamarine gaze.

"I'm free on Friday, but I haven't been invited," she said casually.

Arlo rounded on Remy, and he laughed.

"I'm working on that," Remy said. "Do you have any ideas how I can persuade her to join us?"

"Shane, come camping with us. Come camping," Petal and Parker called out.

"Please?" Arlo picked up Beast, who licked her chin. "I

have Petal and Parker and Beast. I don't want Remy to be lonely."

"Hard to resist that invite." She pretended to consider.

"Then don't," Remy advised, his lips brushing her ear sending warmth throughout his body.

Chapter Fifteen

THE BORDER COLLIE ran the perimeter of the herd, barking and dashing toward one of the curious calves that started to stray. The calf then bellowed and ran toward its mother. Remy sat atop Shadow, keeping the left side of the herd moving in the direction of the new pasture. This morning, like many mornings, he found himself smiling and happy that the Wilders still were a bit old-school—having the cowboys ride horses instead of ATVs or Gators. He could appreciate the sounds of the breeze in the trees, the birds, the livestock's hoofs hitting dirt.

He breathed in deeply—pine-scented air, dirt, animal and a hint of cool that rolled down the mountain range into the valley. His restless gaze tried to take it all in—make his brain believe this was real. He was home. He wasn't going to have to ship out on another mission in the middle of the night.

"You settling in?" ranch hand Dane Morgan, another army vet who'd been working Wilder Dreams for the past two years, asked as if reading his thoughts.

"Feels good," Remy said. He liked working with Dane. He didn't talk as much as some of the other hands. Just told you what needed to be done and didn't make it obvious he was checking your work.

"That's because you arrived after most of the work had been done." Kane Wilder grinned. Kane had decided to ride with them. His horse—no joke called Trigger—was jumpy as if to justify its name. Kane had arrived shortly after the morning meeting with the foreman who was handing out assignments for the day. Remy had been filling his thermos with coffee and a second with water. He'd flashed that trademark smile, held up several bags of pastries from the Java Café that he placed next to the coffee, and then told Remy and Dane he'd be riding with them.

Kane wasn't their boss. He didn't usually work on this ranch. But he was a Wilder and had provided most of the seed money for Wilder Dreams, although all the Wilders— the men and their wives—contributed to the ranch.

"How you figure that?" Remy asked Kane now. He and Dane and a crew had been checking and relaying pipe in several fields all week in the mornings and cutting, bundling and stacking hay for the winter for the past couple of afternoons. And tomorrow they'd ride the north section of the ranch and check the fence line. His job in the army had required him to be in top shape, but after a few weeks on the ranch, even he felt muscles twinge when he'd shower at the end of the day.

"You missed calving, vaccinating, castrating and dehorning. Fun times." Kane grinned.

"Next year." Remy marveled he could say it and mean it. His work in the army had given him purpose and direction, and he'd worried that if he left the service he'd have no idea who he was anymore or what he should do. A man like him who was lost could be dangerous, but now he knew what he wanted and where he wanted to go. Shane, Arlo, the ranch, had become his North Star.

"Don't have to wait that long. I've put you on the list to help us with breeding. You haven't lived until you've been part of a team collecting semen from a bull and inseminating a cow," Kane said, causing Dane to snort a laugh.

"Sounds like a party," Remy said. "I grew up ranch but never worked an operation this large."

Dane looked pleased. "We're expanding while other operations are cutting back on cattle due to the expenses and drought."

"We've had some luck," Kane said placidly riding closer to Remy.

As if preplanned, Dane moved positions, riding away and up toward the front of the herd. One of the border collies headed out with him to guide the herd to the more verdant pasture they wanted them to graze now that summer was beginning its death dance.

"You going to see Sam Wilder again?" Kane asked.

Straight to the point. Remy appreciated that.

"I am," he said. "Not asking for any favors. Not because he might be..." Remy broke off. He hadn't been willing to think about Sam maybe being his father. He'd avoided it, especially the night Shane had brought it up. He'd always admired Sam, wanted to emulate him. To think that he might have been his father, but let the state drive away with his kid…that was not a man he wanted to be.

"I don't know if I want to know anything about my parentage," Remy admitted to Kane. It surprised him that he found Kane the easiest to communicate with out of the four Wilder brothers. "Doesn't seem like it would make anything right but could stir up a lot."

"I rejected my biological father when he finally came around once I was rich and famous, and he wanted something," Kane admitted. "But you could take the test for yourself. Doesn't mean you have to welcome Sam in your life."

The rhythm of Shadow soothed him, felt right. "Not sure how I feel or what I'll do," Remy admitted, and it felt good to be honest with a colleague, maybe a nephew, which still seemed weird to him, and he was afraid to even admit hope. "Still feel like I want to check in on him. Make sure he has a place to go while he heals."

"There's a place in town," Kane said. "Another rancher, Ben Ballantyne, has offered to take him in; see that his needs are met. He might have better luck than us." Kane's eyes narrowed, and his voice hardened, and Remy saw the competitor in him, the alpha, instead of the easygoing cowboy.

"Sam was never a warm man," Remy remembered. "But he was fair. Gave people a chance. Showed me how to do things—fix machinery, care for animals, use tools. He taught me the value of hard work and a love of the land and wouldn't let me ride or do chores till my schoolwork was done, so I always got it done on the bus home."

"He acted like a father figure."

Remy didn't respond.

"He should come here." Kane's voice was tight. "Stubborn man. Vengeful. Unforgiving, but he should come to us. We're blood. Ben's a good man, but we are blood."

"I don't understand the rift," Remy said, surprised by Kane's openness. "And I'm not going to poke my nose…"

"Poke away," Kane fiercely interrupted, his jaw tight and his eyes sparking silver. "You're family. We don't need a test. Your eyes. Your hair. The way you move like Colt. The way your jaw and eyebrows are totally Luke. But the rest I don't get. How can a man hurt his own daughter? How can he cut her out of his life? Cut his grandkids and great-grandkids out of his life? What could possibly be a transgression large enough for that?" Kane demanded.

Remy had been asking himself the same thing.

"And selling his land away from family. Four generations could be on Wilder land. Four. He should come home. We should care for him and be the ones to bring the Wild Wind back to its prime."

"I'll do my best to get a feel for what his plans are," Remy said after he digested all that Kane had to say. "See if I can persuade him to come here to heal and if he'll let us at least repair the fencing and irrigation on a few of the fields."

Jace would have relished Remy stepping up and trying on the role of peacemaker. He closed his eyes and said a silent thank you to Jace for bringing him home, guiding him to family and purpose and what felt like love.

LATER, EARLY IN the evening, Remy stopped by the hospital with a couple dozen rodeo-themed cookies from the Copper Mountain Dessert Company.

He left the bigger bag with the nursing staff, earning a round of applause that had had him heel-toeing it fast to Sam's room amidst the nurses' teasing laughter. He paused a moment outside the door, bracing himself for...what? He wanted to get over his impulse of pulling back from engaging with people.

He'd been slightly delayed when Colt had invited him for a beer at his house after he'd finished up at the barn. They hadn't discussed much beyond how he was settling in and the work at the cabin, which Colt often helped with. Then he'd asked how the paperwork was going with Arlo— he and Talon had been interviewed over Zoom as had Kane and his wife, Sky. Luke, as Remy's official boss, had already been interviewed.

"I'm going ahead," Remy had told him. "Sometimes I feel like I'm flying blind, but I look at you with your kids, Kane, Luke. I see Shane with Arlo, and this feels good." He looked out of the house's living room window to the outdoor living space, the sports court, the tree house barely visible in the distance and the cabin that would be his just beyond.

"But this path I'm on feels good. Feels right."

Colt had looked at him a long time without saying anything. Remy had the same skill with silence. Then Colt had drained his beer, clapped him on the back and stood up. Remy had followed, wanting to install some lights at the cabin before taking off.

"I had the same habits of disconnecting," Colt said. "Like it's genetic." He didn't crack and smile, and Remy wasn't sure if Colt was joking or not. He'd never known him to attempt to be funny or anything other than bluntly honest. "Talon tamed my beast, but it was becoming a dad to Parker that really guided me back to life."

Remy had felt too choked up to answer.

"And if you're feeling really confident, we could blow out the back wall of the cabin since you're not staying there yet, and double the square footage, but we'd have to get the foundation poured and it framed up before mid-October or wait until late spring."

Colt's look had been pure challenge.

"Let's do it." Remy jumped off the edge into his new life.

"We'll look at some designs. I'll get a crew in to ready

the site, and we'll fast-track. Welcome home, Remy," Colt said even though Remy had been in Marietta over three weeks.

Remy had left feeling almost dizzy about his decision. But it felt right. He belonged on this ranch with the Wilders and so did Arlo. He'd implemented operation Arlo. Now he just needed to double down on operation Shane because he couldn't imagine his life feeling complete without her by his side and in his bed.

He rapped his knuckles against door of room 208 and pushed it open but stayed in the doorway, partially hidden by the curtain hanging open by the hospital bed.

Sam was not alone. He was glaring at another man who could have been a model for a seasoned Montana rancher with his worn Wranglers hugging his wiry frame, very broken-in boots, crisp white western-style snap shirt and thick gray hair streaked with dark. A straw cowboy hat was in his hand, hanging loose at his side. A memory stirred—a freak summer hailstorm and riding with Sam and a crew over to his friend's ranch to help repair a heavily damaged pole barn. He remembered how proud he'd been to be included in what he'd thought at the age of eleven as 'men's work.'

The man stared at him for a long time. Remy stood for the scrutiny. He knew who the man was now. Twenty-five years had aged him, but Ben Ballantyne still looked strong. Capable. And pissed.

"Stop being a damn fool," Ben said to Sam, who sat up

in bed courtesy of the hospital bed's remote. An untouched meal congealed on a side table.

"Stop being an interfering fool," Sam growled back.

His voice was stronger than the last time he was here, and his color was better. The relief that coursed through Remy caught him off guard.

Another much younger cowboy, with a long lean frame and longish hair leaned against the wall, arms crossed, expression carefully neutral. As Remy fully entered, all three men turned to look at him now, and he felt like a bit of a fool carrying the smaller bag of cookies. Did the uneaten dinner mean that Sam wasn't up to eating anything, or did he just hate hospital food?

"Bodhi Ballantyne." The younger cowboy stepped forward, hand outreached. "This is my granddad Ben Ballantyne owner of the Three Tree Ranch. Here to negotiate a peace treaty with these two elderly warring ranchers."

"Elderly," Sam scoffed, glaring at both Remy and Bodhi now.

"Warring," the older rancher muttered.

"I'll check out what treats you brought." Bodhi took the bag out of Remy's too loose grip. "I love that Rachel gears up early for the rodeo." He plucked a boot cookie out of the bag. "Much obliged." Bodhi bit into the cookie.

"Give it here, thief. The cookies are mine." Sam sat up a little higher.

Bodhi grinned as he chewed. "Come and get them, old

man."

"Bodhi," Ben Ballantyne said, his voice threaded with a combination of amusement and exasperation.

Bodhi took another bite and tossed the bag of cookies to Sam, but before Sam could react, the cookies were caught by Ben, who held the bag close to his chest.

"Here's the thing, Sam," Ben said in a warm, deep bass. "You need to go to the Maybell Center for rehab or to us, and we'll hire you a nurse and have the physical therapist come out to the house," Ben said. "You are not going home alone, Sam. Not this time."

Might as well jump in.

"Remington Cross. I'm here as an intermediary for the Wilders to offer…"

"Here's another one sniffing around to steal my land." Sam's still-dark brows descended.

"I'm not here to steal land, nor are the Wilders attempting to steal from their kin." Remy stared deep into Sam's eyes, and felt eerily as if he were looking into a mirror, slightly distorted, forty some years from now. "We…they," he corrected, "want to offer you a place to heal and stay as long as you want on the Wilder Dreams spread."

Sam couldn't have looked more pissed, but Remy continued, undeterred.

"The Wilders would also be happy to send a crew to your ranch to implement necessary repairs and maintain the ranch for you while you are healing. No charge. No games. No expectations. No criminal masterminding in sight."

"Stand in line," Bodhi muttered. "Rejection is good for the soul."

Remy doubted Bodhi had experienced much rejection in his life. He looked more like a movie star than a cowboy, although he was dressed the part and his boots had definitely seen work. The wedding ring on his finger was thick and etched and looked like platinum, not the simple gold band that most married cowboys sported in town. And it was clear that he and his granddad were close.

"Why are you butting in, Bodhi?" Sam glared. "Last thing I heard that beautiful wife of yours was supporting you while you studied medicine in Seattle."

He made the words *medicine* and *Seattle* sound like curses.

"I pay my way." Bodhi's teeth briefly gritted. "And yes, I'm in my second year at the University of Washington, but I flew out this weekend with Nico so that I could help Granddad and Bo and Beck retrofit a room in the main house for you while you heal, so don't waste my time or Granddad's money."

Sam glared. Bodhi didn't seem perturbed, but he did seize the bag of cookies again and plucked a hat from the bag, bit into it and held Sam's hostile gaze.

"I'll let you hash it out between Granddad and Remington and the Wilders while I wait in the truck. But Sam—" Bodhi pointed his cookie at him "—I might be doing your hip replacement in a few years so you play nice with Ben, now."

Sam's growl was impressive, but Bodhi laughed. "Stop being a coward. Face up to your responsibilities, Sam." Bodhi pierced him with a deep blue-eyed gaze, and then glanced at his granddad, who also looked at Remy briefly and then almost imperceptibly shrugged.

Family—the thought staggered him. It was like they were speaking without words, totally connected. So much history. And Remy wanted that so much.

"I ain't funning, Sam." Bodhi's voice slid country. "You can go to the Maybell, Three Trees or Wilder Dreams to heal. Granddad and I will get you there, and we can call up Bo and Beck to help, but I figure the Wilders will come in force. Makes no difference to me." Bodhi took another bite of cookie, chewed and waved the cookie in Sam's direction. "But you are not going home alone, besides..." Bodhi looked at Remy. "I heard the house had a big hole in the side so you may want to take the Wilders up on their offer of repairs."

"Who do you think made the damn hole?" Sam demanded of Bodhi's back as he left the room, tossing the bag of cookies over his shoulder like it was a game of keep-away.

Sam's voice, hoarse from the feeding tube that had been removed several days ago, gave out, and Sam coughed.

Remy handed Sam his water, and he waved it angrily away, but Remy held firm and finally Sam took the plastic bottle and sipped through the straw.

"None of your boys have any manners," Sam accused.

"And you're the expert?" Ben retorted. "If the Wilders want this stubborn old bag of bones, they are welcome to him," Ben told Remy. "But we are nearly done with the main floor bedroom and bathroom refitting and there is an alcove we carved out for the physical therapist to work with this stubborn fool. Likely will need to bring the sheriff with him," Ben said as if Sam wasn't there.

"Come out to the ranch sometime, Remy. I remember you when you were small dogging after Sam wanting to learn a man's work before your hands were big enough to hold the tools. Remember Sam bought you a kid's tool set at Big Z one Christmas?" Ben looked at Sam, as if urging him to speak.

Instead, Sam just glared at the hospital sheets.

"Last time I saw you was at the stock auction after the rodeo. Sam bought you a quarter horse to learn how to saddle break."

"Winston," Remy murmured, although the piercing sorrow of loss and disappointment had finally faded over the years. He had no idea why he'd named the horse that—likely because it had sounded regal. But he'd never had more than a week with his horse because his mom died.

"I'll let you two visit," Ben said. "Sam, my offer stands." He lightly rested his hand for a moment on Remy's shoulder. "Good to see you again, son. Thank you for your service.

Welcome home."

Ben Ballantyne paused at the door. His hat was in his hands, and he turned it round and round, hesitating. Then he took a deep breath and turned back to face his old friend.

"You need to let go of the past, Sam. All the anger and bitterness is eating you alive and destroying the only thing that mattered to you—your family's land." He glanced at Remy and then back at Sam. "It's only too late when you're in the box."

Ben walked out, tossing the bag of cookies over his shoulder with excellent aim to Remy.

The silence felt like a clap of thunder and Remy found himself bracing for an imaginary lightning strike. Finally, he toed a chair over so that he wasn't towering over Sam.

He picked out two cookies from the bag and held one out to Sam. He didn't think Sam would take the offering as the older man stared straight ahead, the lines on his face etched deep. Remy could practically feel the walls growing taller, thicker. But then Sam took the cookie and after an eloquent pause where his gray eyes glistened with a pain that Remy himself felt, to cover his vulnerability, he took a bite.

Remy took a bite of his own cookie savoring the sweetness and happy for something for his mouth to do while he searched for words.

"Not sure why you came back here." Sam's voice sounded hollow.

"Marietta always felt like home," he said, although that

had driven him away, "even though there were so many ghosts. Didn't think I'd come back, but fate had other plans."

No bitterness laced his tone. Maybe it had been fate— the wrong prison cell, learning about Shane and being curious and captivated enough to stop in at the Graff, Jace leading the mission instead of him. Arlo. Fate not his fault. Something in his chest eased, and he took a deeper breath and another bite of cookie.

"You believe in fate?" he asked Sam.

"No. I own my mistakes."

"So do I," Remy said, meditatively. "But I don't want my mistakes to be the only thing I hold on to."

"You were robbed of your birthplace and your birthright," Sam said, dully.

"That you owning your mistakes?" Remy asked.

Sam glared for a moment and then looked back at the end of his bed. He took a small nibble of the cookie.

"I don't have a birthright," Remy said. "No one owes me anything. I work for what I want. I make my own choice and pay my own way."

"You always were fierce," Sam said after ring of authority in Remy's voice silenced. "Independent. Determined. Even when you were little, before your mom…left the first time."

Remy didn't remember much before he was eight or so. He remembered his mom in the hospital having Brianna. He'd slept in a recliner that first night in her room. And then instead of taking Brianna home to the small apartment they had in Missoula, they'd driven to Marietta and the Wild Wind Ranch. He had snatches of memories from before when he was little. Horses. Cattle. Dust. Running in the grass and falling and being picked up and placed on wide shoulders.

He glanced at Sam. "Before?"

"I made my fair share of mistakes."

"Sounds like," Remy said. Normally he wouldn't have said anything else, but he'd learned from Shane and also from the therapist the social worker had recommended because they were an adoption and parenting expert, that he needed to open up more, share, in order to establish bonds. And he wanted connections—family, home, a future. "Any in particular you want to share?"

Sam glanced at the door as if hoping a nurse would interrupt.

Tough luck, old man.

"No."

Remy finished his cookie and wiped his mouth with one of the napkins, and then took a calming breath, surprised that he didn't feel more nervous.

"Then I'll say my piece first. I came home to Marietta as a favor to a friend, but I am getting far more than I intended to give. I only thought of duty. Getting the deed done and hitting the road for somewhere far from here. But I found me. I found love. I found family even if the Wilders aren't blood."

He waited to see if Sam would respond—say something, do something to let him know if he was on the right track. Sam had his head bowed, the cookie forgotten in his hand.

"I'm creating a family, a home. I have a new job and a new life that I intend to hold on to with both hands. I'm starting my life over."

Too wound up to sit, Remy stood and zipped the wadded-up napkin across the room to the trash can.

"You can stay alone and stuck and choking on your mistakes and anger and fear or you could take the first step to start over too."

He wasn't sure what he expected. Personally he felt as if he'd run up the side of a mountain at night, taking cover behind boulders as he came under heavy fire. But Sam still sat in the same position.

Remy tried to swallow around the lump in his throat. "We don't have to talk about the past. I'm fine letting it all go." He heard the resolution in his voice. "But I did want to thank you."

"Thank me?" Sam's head shot up. His voice was incredulous.

"When I was a kid, you taught me a lot. I began to have an idea of what a man was. And now that I'm an adult, you're teaching me about the man I don't want to be." He walked to the door, almost jubilant. He'd said what he wanted to say and he was free. "The Wilders' offer stands. So does the Ballantynes'. Or lock yourself up in your house alone, afraid and waiting to die."

Remy gripped the door handle and pulled it wide open, feeling no resentment, hurt or regret. He was truly free to start over. He lightly touched his coyote tattoo thanking Jace, thanking Wolf for pushing them.

"I don't know if you're my son," Sam said.

Remy froze. Damn. He'd been so close. And now what, Sam Wilder was slut-shaming his mom? Remy's fist curled and he stared at it, willing it to relax.

"Becca said you were. But I don't trust easily."

"Doubt you trust at all." Remy closed the door and pressed his back against it, determined to let Sam say his piece just as he'd said his.

"Got that right. Came to that honestly. My wife—Samara's mother—ran off with my ranch foreman. Left his wife and son. Her family was third generation working on the ranch so she stayed, raised her boy who helped out as he grew and then he ran off with my daughter."

No doubt it had been a double blow. Humiliating. Infuriating.

"Can't cage people, Sam."

"Thought Becca was the same way. Should never have touched her. She worked for me, but she was young, talented barrel racer and magic with horses. So much life, and I was so cold and alone. Let her stay and train horses and compete a bit. Saw you looked a bit like my Samara, and even though

I didn't want to, I took an interest in you. But…" He crumbled the cookie in his hand. "I wouldn't claim you or… Becca offered a paternity test, but I was more worried you wouldn't be mine.

"Then she had enough of me and left me for a nephew of mine who was working on the ranch to learn how to be a stock trainer. They fell in love and left taking you with them, and I let her go, convinced that you weren't mine, but she came back four years later a widow with a baby. Daniel had died in a pile-up about six months before Brianna was born."

Remy remembered Daniel, dimly. He'd played baseball with him and soccer, but he was on the road a lot. His mom had never talked about him and as Brianna grew, the memories of the apartment in Missoula had faded.

"So Brianna was kin too," he said, not sure how he felt about that. She'd been his sister. He'd never cared who her father was or wasn't.

"And I let the county come take you both away."

He stared at Sam. He'd told Kane he'd try his best. He'd act as an intermediary. But this was one hill he wasn't going to climb, and he wasn't going to die on. Kane had told him the story of how Samara had come back to the ranch as a pregnant teen with her boyfriend who wanted to marry her. They needed Sam's permission because she was so young. But they'd been in a serious car accident, and he'd had his grandsons, born prematurely, while his daughter was in a coma, adopted out and the boyfriend arrested.

Samara had eventually recovered thinking her babies had died, and when she'd learned the truth, she'd never spoken to her father again.

"I don't understand you," Remy said. "Not sure I want to."

"You are my son," Sam Wilder said. "You're a Wilder."

Remy would have said that that quiet affirmation was something he'd waited for his entire life. But now the words fell flat.

"I am so much more than your son," Remy said.

He opened the door. "You don't have to be alone, Sam Wilder, but you will need to change. You will need to forgive your wife for loving another man, and your daughter for falling in love with that man's son. You will need to make amends to your grandsons. Try to earn their forgiveness so you can have them in your life."

"I don't know how."

The quiet words spoken to the hospital bedsheets were laced in frustration.

"Learn."

Remy walked out of that hospital room, posture straight, head unbowed, knowing he wouldn't come back. Even though it was customary to wait until a man was outside, Remy placed his new Stetson on his head. It felt right. Symbolic. He was home. He was a cowboy.

Chapter Sixteen

S HANE RESTOCKED THE bar. She could have waited until
tomorrow, let Lachlan and Just do it, but the work
soothed her. The different hues of the liquor lit up by the
recessed lighting in the shelves still looked so visually pretty
to her even after three years. With the kick-off of the rodeo
activities on Friday, the town buzzed with activity. Restaurants were booked. The boutiques were busy and the
scarecrow competition had been friendly and fierce. Many
merchants had entered a design and displayed their scarecrows in their store, but other organizations or businesses
without storefronts had showcased their scarecrows in the
Graff lobby and outdoor garden, which had brought in more
foot traffic—most of whom seemed to be hungry and thirsty.

Already the rodeo-themed cocktails she'd introduced this
past weekend were a hit. Shane loved to create new drinks
and pair different ingredients for holidays each year—it was
the favorite part of her job—but she kept a specialty cocktail
bible from previous years in case a local requested an old
favorite. Miranda had been on her to collect them in a Graff
cocktail book, and the Graff PR and event team of Walker
Wilder and Langston Ballantyne were all in.

The Graff Hotel management had approached her today, and Shane had already talked with the hotel's pastry chef and chocolatier to start brainstorming ideas. And she'd need to hire a photographer. And invent more hours in each day if she and Remy were successful in welcoming Arlo into their life.

Said every working mother everywhere.

That thought jump-started her heart.

She'd been trying to take each day at a time. She'd been cautioning Remy not to jump too far ahead, but she was lying to herself and Remy. Each day her thoughts spun faster than a hamster on a wheel. Should she and Remy get engaged? Would that make it more likely the adoption would be approved? Should they marry and apply to adopt Arlo as a couple? Should they live in her house or on the ranch where Arlo would be surrounded by other kids and animals and quite likely family?

It was scary how much she wanted to jump on the family bus Remy had jump-started.

"Stop stalling."

Shane took one last swipe at the very clean, gleaming bar. It was the first night Remy hadn't showed up to walk her home. So what? She was a woman, not a baby, and he deserved his own life and friends outside of her.

She checked her phone.

No text.

Shane looked around the bar one last time—she kept a

few of the mood lights on so that the bar looked like a stunning secret gem adjacent to the Graff's lobby and would intrigue guests into returning when it was open.

Then she grabbed her small backpack and cropped denim jacket, slid it on and walked out the side entrance into the garden. She breathed in the fragrant night and exited through the side gate.

Her heart flopped over. Remy stood there. Tall. Silent. Radiating a tension she hadn't felt from him in a long time.

"What's wrong?" She rushed up to him, searching for clues in his silver-gray eyes. "What's happened? Is Arlo okay?"

She was relieved when he took her in his arms. She pressed her palm against his chest, feeling the slow, rhythmic thump of his heart and looked up into his angular, shuttered face.

"I'm good now," he said, taking her backpack from her. "Better than."

He always did things like that—carried her packages, groceries, even her books from the library once.

"Such cowboy manners." She touched the brim of his tan Stetson with one knuckle. "You look good. I missed you."

I've been thinking.

But she kept the musings that kept tangling up in her mind to herself, feeling a spurt of shyness.

They walked home. "I'm sorry for not coming in tonight. I went for a ride. Needed to sort some things out."

Her heart thudded to her cowboy boots, but she kept her tone light. "No worries."

They continued to walk in silence. It was peaceful, the night enveloping them—this was why Shane chose to walk to work until the weather no longer permitted. But questions continued to burble up in her mind, spoiling her pleasure.

"I am Sam Wilder's son."

She tucked her hand in his. "He admitted it?"

"He said that he had a relationship with my mom, and that she said that I was his son."

"But why didn't he…?" she began but bit her question back. This was Remy's story, and clearly it had impacted him.

"Looking back, Sam acknowledged me in his own way, but he's not very trusting. He broke off with my mother, feeling guilty about the age difference and being her boss, or maybe she wanted someone younger, more responsive. His nephew came to work at the Wild Wind soon after their affair had ended. He and my mom ended up falling in love and left together. Sam's reasoning was that I might be his nephew's, even though my mom had told him she was expecting his child."

Shane kept quiet, feeling like she was breathing for both of them. She tilted her head against his shoulder and let the quiet of the night surround them. So Sam had known or at least known it was possible that Remy was his son, and he'd stood by and let social services take Remy away. Anger burned, and she was glad she was no longer a therapist, trying to remain objective.

"I thought I'd feel more," Remy admitted.

"You might later."

"I hope not," he said. "I don't want him in my life. A man who could turn away from his grandsons, his daughter and his son is not a man I want to be."

His voice sounded hard. But he stopped walking and rested one hand on her hip and the other gently combed through her hair so that it tumbled messily around her shoulders.

"I have you. I'm not considering failure as an option in adopting Arlo. I have the Wilders and a home. I don't need anything or anyone else."

As a promise, it sounded as absolute as one could be. But he might change his mind—want a child of his own.

"I'm not fully closing the door," he said as they walked the rest of the way home. "But I realized tonight that it's on him to walk through it if he wants a relationship with us."

Us, Shane thought. Remy and the Wilders? Could she be part of an us? It hurt how badly she wanted to be an us with Remy, Arlo and the Wilders.

FRIDAY NIGHT A campfire blazed and about a dozen kids sat

on hay bales around the fire, roasting marshmallows. Shane leaned against Remy, content, tired from the day of hectic fun on Main Street viewing all the rodeo scarecrows and participating in the kid activities that many of the merchants—including the Graff—had for the kids. Tomorrow was the parade and then the opening of the rodeo. She planned to join Remy, Arlo and the Wilders who weren't involved in the rodeo, during the morning. Then she needed to peel off in the afternoon to set up the beer, wine and cocktail booth for the rodeo steak dinner. Laird Wilder and some of his tasting room employees were helping to staff the booth.

But tonight, the calm before the storm, felt idyllic. It turned out that all of the Wilders had decided to camp out in what they called the grove. It was fairly close to where Remy's cabin was. She'd been to the cabin a few times to weigh in on some designs when Remy asked, but she was surprised when he told her tonight that it wasn't yet finished, and he'd been vague when she asked about why, but then Arlo had called out to Remy and Shane to show them the tree houses in the grove.

Colt had built one for Parker when he'd first come into his life. One had become five as Colt and Parker had created new designs, and Colt had turned tree-house designing into a side business of his construction company. Some of the kids would be camping in the tree houses tonight, and Arlo was glowing with excitement as she and Parker and Petal discussed the benefits of each tree house.

While Colt checked the roasting sticks for splinters before handing them out to the waiting children, Luke supervised the fire, and Kane told the kids a couple of lighthearted ghost stories. Remy kissed her forehead and rose up to help Colt.

"Arlo seems happy." Tucker joined her, jamming two marshmallows on her roasting stick. "It's almost like she never left."

"She does seem lighter, more confident, more how I remember her before her mom died," Shane said. "But she's still grieving. Healing will be a long road." She said the words louder than usual, hoping Remy would be tuned in enough to hear. She didn't want him or the Wilders to expect miracles, as if coming to live on the ranch would be a magic wand.

"Yes, of course," Tucker said. She and her twin, Tanner, had lost their father a couple of years ago. Tanner had taken his death much harder than Tucker. "Everyone grieves differently, and it comes in waves and blah, blah, blah." Tucker grinned and stuck her tongue out at Shane. "Not letting you get too broody tonight—at least about death."

"What can I brood about?" Shane asked flippantly, not able to look away from Arlo sitting with Kane and Remy and several other children. Arlo was trying to help Kane's oldest daughter Montana blow out a flaming marshmallow, but they kept dissolving into giggles. Remy extinguished the blackened mass, and proclaimed it was perfect, but Kane swiped it and pretended to eat it, which made the kids squeal and laugh harder.

In one month Remy had changed so much.

This could be my life.

"Broody as in you know, the British broody like a hen about to lay an egg. Earth to Shane. Stop drooling over the hot soldier cowboy."

"Huh?" Shane focused back on Tucker. "Eggs?"

"Broody—you know the British meaning—wanting babies. Soon you'll be living on the ranch with Remy and be one of us Wilders with a big ole belly and chasing after a little one while you're helping Arlo with her high school biology or chemistry homework, although we can probably rely on Talon and Tanner to help with the kids' science homework." Tucker laughed, patting her small bump while her beautiful eyes flashed fire and amusement.

"What? Why are you staring at me like that?" Tucker asked. "Anyone can tell he's crazy about you, and your gaze is forever glued to his fine backside or his finer front, or the kids. It's crystal clear where your mind is. You're in love and ready to start popping out babies. Happens to the best of us. I met Laird and then timber. I was a goner. Do you think Remy will change his name to Wilder like Colt and Laird did?"

Shane could barely swallow. "I have no idea," she managed to say through her stiff lips.

The picture Tucker painted of her and Remy married, living on the ranch, wrapped up with the Wilders and raising little ones was so seductive. But she could never give Remy a child—his child. He hadn't seemed to mind when she'd told him that because of her severe endometriosis and several surgeries and scarring, it was unlikely she could conceive or carry a child. But that had been before he knew he was a Wilder. Before he was part of a large family with four nephews, all of whom were happily married and parents of young children, and their families were growing. Before he had adjusted to his new life outside the military. Before he really gave himself a chance to settle in and understand what was really important to him. Remy was a man's man. He'd never hold her infertility against her, but she knew he would want to continue his bloodline. Hold his own son. Nurture him. Teach him. Be the kind of father he never had.

She would hold him back.

"Why isn't Shane at the parade?" Arlo asked after the high school band marched past showcasing their loudness more than musicality in Remy's opinion.

He'd been asking himself the same thing when he'd woken up alone this morning shortly after the birds had started singing and he'd caught the first whiff of coffee.

"She had something unexpected come up at work." He

made sure to not let any of his own worry color the words. They'd been fine yesterday and last night. Better than fine. Sure, she'd been quiet when she'd rolled her sleeping bag next to his in the tent last night, but he hadn't been expecting anything else. They were directly below a tree house with four children—Montana being deemed one of the 'big kids' which at almost nine had delighted her. And spending a day with so many people—adults and children—had exhausted him. Give him a horse and a task alone on the ranch and he had energy and focus for hours.

"She wasn't supposed to work until later this afternoon," Arlo continued.

He looked down at his phone, hoping for more explanation but her simple *'enjoy the day, I will help you and the kids set up their lemonade stand. I emailed the volunteers' shift schedule'* hadn't been supplemented.

"Sometimes plans change, and we have to adapt," he said, wondering if this was one of those teachable moments. Judging by Arlo's round eyes and quivering lower lip he thought so.

"She'll help you get settled with the lemonade stand, and Colt and I will be there to supervise," he reminded her.

Arlo nodded. "But she didn't go on the owl walk, and she told me that she was looking forward to that the most last night."

"I missed her too," Remy said as the suspicious niggling that something was wrong blared into a full alarm. He forced himself to stay relaxed, but the longer the morning stretched out, the more he felt like he was missing something, and barraging her with texts wasn't going to help.

But it occurred to Remy that he didn't have to passively wait for Shane. He snapped a few pictures of Arlo with her two friends holding small American flags and each of them biting into the edge of a chocolate boot just as the rodeo queens trotted by holding different flags—the US, Montana, and what he thought was a Copper Mountain Rodeo flag.

As a backdrop, it was bright, beautiful, and symbolic. The kids had fun thinking up funny poses. He took a few more pictures, realizing that Arlo might not have much remaining from her childhood. He made a mental note to ask her social worker about that. He didn't have anything, just one framed picture of him with his mom and Brianna at a pumpkin patch.

When the only response to the pictures of the kids he'd sent was a heart-faced emoji, he knew something was wrong. And as he shepherded the three excited kids, jacked up on candy thrown from the parade floats, to the rodeo grounds, he speculated uselessly about what the problem was. He told himself repeatedly that he'd find a solution, no matter what.

No, *they* would find a solution. He wasn't alone anymore. He and Shane were a team.

"You're here." Arlo rushed forward, arms out to embrace Shane, who was already working with Colt to organize the pieces of the booth as they loaded them out of her Jeep, which was parked in the loading zone.

"I am." Shane enveloped Arlo in a hug. "How was the parade?"

Arlo started talking, Petal and Parker chiming in. Colt and Remy used a drill to quickly assemble the booth, while the kids unfolded the table and added the red-and-white checked tablecloth. Shane brought out the supplies from the supersized cooler, asking the kids how they wanted everything set up, and he tried not to notice that she hadn't looked at him once.

Something was definitely wrong, but this wasn't the place. Today was for Arlo and her friends. And maybe this was his first test as a potential parent—put his child's needs above his own, no matter how much it burned, or how desperate he felt.

THE OPENING COUNTRY music band following the steak dinner played their hearts out. Shane kept the beat as she and several other bartenders pulled mugs of beer, poured glasses of wine and quickly made one of the two different cocktails offered. The team had all worked together before. They were fast and smooth, and the tips that piled up were all part of a donation to the Cattlemen's Association, which made everyone extra generous.

She'd always loved working the steak dinner. Tonight

she hated it. Her thoughts continually arrowed toward Remy—where was he, what was he doing, did he miss her? She hated keeping Remy at a distance. It physically hurt to not be with him and Arlo today. But it was going to hurt even more if she continued to drift along in the beautiful fantasy Remy had woven of them being a family with Arlo.

She didn't doubt he meant it. Now. But he had no perspective on what he was going to want in a couple of years or five or more. His life out of the service was so new. Remy was a man who'd lost his mother and sister, close buddies in the service. It was quite likely that he would fall deeper and deeper into the Wilders' close fold. They were so clannish. So into family. Remy was such a man's man. He would want his own son to love and nurture and teach to be a man.

He couldn't guarantee that he wouldn't want that.

And she'd already been dumped for being defective—not that she thought Remy would dump her. But she didn't want to hurt him, diminish his chances of living a full life and pursuing happiness.

Tucker had done her a favor last night waking her up to the future expectations.

As if her tumbling thoughts manifested him, Shane looked up to serve her next customer, and it was Remy.

"Hi," she breathed, unable to stop how she looked around, seeking an escape. He was so beautiful and so potent that it hurt to look at him, and now she was going to have to rip out her heart and break up with him. She'd been trying to work her courage up all day to tell him it was over.

"I need to talk to you," he said.

"Is Arlo okay?" she asked breathlessly.

"No."

"What?" Shane pulled at the ribbons on her apron. "How? Where…?" Panic closed her throat.

"She's confused as hell and so am I," Remy said grimly.

"Remy, I…" Her voice failed. "This isn't the place." She looked around quickly. Her co-workers were smiling and shooing her to go. She was the only one of them who hadn't taken a break to eat so no help there.

"Do you want me to hop over the bar—you know I'll do it, and toss you over my shoulder and disappear into the night, or would you rather come out of the booth, and you can tell me what the hell is wrong?"

"I…fine," she said and slipped out of the booth. She held out one hand—fingers spread wide—to Laird indicating that she'd be five minutes.

"Really, that's all you got?" Laird teased Remy. "Five minutes. Dang, I am so sorry, Shane. I'll get him a book or something." He laughed.

Remy looked around and then subtly flipped Laird off, which amused Laird even more, but even the men's teasing didn't ease the constriction around her heart.

Shane walked quickly away, but it was hard to find a place without an audience. She knew so many people in town, which was only one of the many reasons she loved living here, but privacy was scarce. Many people called out for her to come join them. She smiled, waved and kept walking needing to get to the far side of the park away from the buffet, booths, band and long tables under the party lights strung through the old oak trees.

Finally, she felt like she'd put enough distance between them and the steak dinner guests, but the fast walk had done nothing to settle her heart rate or organize her thoughts.

She spun around, arms crossed, ready for battle but was completely unprepared for him to pull her against his hard, strong body.

"Tell me what's going on, what's scared you," he said softly.

She tried to hold herself stiffly and away from him. But he smelled so delicious and felt so good that every part of her wanted just a minute more before she made the final break.

"We talked about this—sharing when something's bothering us."

"I can't be with you." She forced out the words and stepped away from him, bereft that he let her go. She looked up into his starkly beautiful but utterly masculine features.

His hands remained anchored on her hips, but loose enough so that she could cross her arms over her breasts.

"It's not fair to you," she said.

"Isn't that my decision?"

"But you don't know. You're still adjusting. You're making so many huge changes in your life—a new career, coming to terms with your past, trying to carry out a duty to a fallen comrade, working on bringing a teen into your life— So much is going on with you. You can't possibly make a long-term commitment."

"Arlo's long-term."

"Yes, but you've found your family now. You're going to…"

"I love you," Remy interrupted her verbal stumbling.

Shane gulped. He sounded so sure. Solid.

"I want to build a life with you and Arlo. That's what I want. The rest of it—my job, the cabin, the Wilders—those are unexpected bonuses. But you, Shane, are absolutely essential in my new life."

She gaped at him. She shook her head as if some of her training would break loose to help her out.

"Changes in career, home, death of a loved one, a move, becoming a parent are all huge stressors," she said, grasping at facts. "You have jumped in feet first to four of life's biggest stressors, so you shouldn't…we shouldn't begin to consider…"

"What freaked you out last night?" he asked.

"I don't think I would qualify it as freaking out," she said with dignity. He was making her sound like a panicked, immature teen.

"You're running. Again. From what?"

"I'm trying to be the voice of reason."

"By dumping me—the man you're in love with, and the

teen who desperately needs you as much as you need her."

"I..." Her mouth dried up. She was in love with him. She was. She had been for a long time. And Arlo was an answer to a prayer. A precious gift she never thought she could open. "This is so hard, Remy."

Why couldn't he see that? "Don't make it harder."

"Don't be noble."

"You're such a...a...good man. I don't want you to make a decision rashly when you are reeling from leaving the military, learning about your family, honoring a vow to Jace and adjusting to the idea of becoming a father."

"Because the last twenty-five years of my life have been one hell of a psychological roller coaster, and I dealt. Now I have a woman I love and want a future with. A job I've dreamed about since I was a kid, men and women I respect who are welcoming me into their lives, and a kid I'm surprisingly growing attached to. So why are you freaking out? Because I'm not—or I am now because you are. But what we are building—you and me and us with Arlo—feels right. It feels hella good. You and Arlo are the best things that have ever happened to me."

"You're the best thing to happen to me," she said. "But I can't be selfish. You are all about family. You have a large one now. You may want to have your own son someday or a daughter, and I don't want you to miss that opportunity. I don't want to stand in your way."

He stared at her, his hands on her hips, hard, clearly

waiting for more. But that was it. She couldn't guarantee him a biological child. In the distance she could hear the band kick into a slow song—'Every Rose Has its Thorn,' she thought.

Yes, it does.

"You really think I'm that narcissistic?"

"No." She didn't like that he phrased her concern like that. "I know you think it doesn't matter now, but in the future…"

"To hell with the future." He slashed his hand in the air. "I have faced challenge, change, uncertainty and peril almost daily for twenty years. I live my life in the now. I don't know how I'll feel in five years. You don't know how you'll feel. I could be dead in a highway pile-up."

Shane flinched and felt the blood drain from her head, leaving her cold and dizzy.

"Remy." She couldn't stand the thought of him being hurt. He was too precious. Too much of a fantastic man. He was needed in the world, in her world.

"And then I would have missed the time with you and Arlo and us as a family if the adoption application goes our way—time wasted. For what? Because of how I might feel in a few years? And if we want more children in the future, we'll deal with it then, and who's to say I'm fertile after all the places I've been and the chemicals I've been exposed to? Would you dump me if I couldn't get you pregnant?"

"No."

"And you think my love is less? The thing is, Shane, we don't know what will happen in the future. But what I do know if that I love you. I want you, not some random woman with a smooth, sparkling womb. You. Only you."

She couldn't breathe. She could barely see him through the sheen of tears curtaining her eyes.

"So, the question you need to answer for yourself, Shane, is do you want to take a shot at happy with me?"

"Yes."

The taut tension Remy had held whooshed out of him and he pulled her in a tight hug and then he was kissing her, and she was kissing him back, not even worried if anyone was watching them.

"You want kids," he said between kisses, "we'll have kids—foster, adopt, surrogate, in vitro, whatever. You want it, I want it—we'll make it happen."

"You're so sure of yourself," she said, looking up at him.

"I'm sure of us."

"Then I'm with you, Remy." Shane cast off the last of her doubt and looped her arms around his neck. "I love you," she said against his lips. "No matter what the future brings. My answer is yes. Yes to you. Yes to us. Yes to everything."

Epilogue

A MONTH AND a half later before the first snowfall, their application to be foster parents to Arlo was approved and they married. The wedding was simple on the Wilder property in one of the barns tricked out for events. The Wilders were there, except Sam. Shane's family all flew in for the ceremony where they wrote their own vows and a justice of the peace married them.

Their honeymoon was in Sweet Tea so that they could have more time to visit with Shane's family, who got to know Arlo better. Shane got to show them both where she'd grown up.

They road-tripped to Charleston to show Arlo a little more of the country, and so that Shane could finally let go of her past.

"You sure?" Remy asked as he drove the rental SUV up the circular drive with the huge trees lining it and the moss dripping like they were on a movie set. "Could be a sweet college fund."

"I'm sure," Shane said as he stopped the car. "And I hope you're joking."

"Kinda sorta. But since I'm getting the better end of the

deal, I'll zip it."

Shane looked down at the celestial watch face. It was beautiful and tragic and somehow no longer felt like it was holding her in place. She'd held on to Ethan's memory and wishes, but it was holding her back. She unbuckled the wristband and palmed the watch. She would never hold anything with such a monetary value again, but looking at her husband and daughter, the watch's value was negligible. She had everything she wanted.

"Want me to walk up with you?"

"No," she said. "I want to do this last thing on my own. Close my chapter before you, and before becoming a mom." She smiled into Arlo's curious gaze.

He took a deep breath and looked at her as if memorizing her face.

"I'm ready, Remy. I'm done with the past and holding on to my failures."

"Failures make us stronger." He winked at Arlo who sat beside Beast, who now had glossy fur, and a sparkling curiosity in his eyes.

"And we reframe them as wins," Shane said.

She left the car door open. That seemed symbolic. She mounted the wide circular steps and used the lion's head door knocker. A Ring camera was off to the side.

She took a deep breath and squared her shoulders, not sure of her reception but not worried. Remy had worried Brandon would send someone else for the watch, but Shane hadn't thought Brandon would take that risk.

A beautiful, coiffed woman opened the door, not a housekeeper.

"Hello, Alyssa," Shane said.

Brandon's mother stared at her as if she'd risen from the dead.

"What are you doing back here?"

Shane held out the watch, face up on her palm.

"My father-in-law gave that to Ethan," she said, but made no move to take it. Instead she stepped back as if the watch might be haunted.

"He gave it to me the day of our last session as a thank you. I worked with him over a year as his therapist, as you know."

Shane looked at Alyssa Huntingdon. She'd once been intimidated by her. She'd once wanted desperately to connect with her. Now Alyssa looked diminished. The huge elegance of the house made her seem more like a doll than a woman who chaired many charity boards.

"He gave you the watch as a gift, but he also thought to list it in his will. Clearly he wanted you to have it."

"It was a gift I did not deserve," Shane said sadly. "But I had trouble going against his wishes. I was thinking…" She broke off. Alyssa likely had no interest in Shane's ideas for starting a foundation or something for vets with the money possibly.

"Why would you think you didn't deserve the gift of the

one thing that meant so much to Ethan? He was so close with his grandfather."

"I didn't help him."

"But you did," Mrs. Huntingdon said. "You did. Ethan struggled with depression as a teen and longer. It's a family curse." Her lips tightened briefly. "But we never talked about it. He kept the journal you'd told him to. He'd written how for the first time talking with you that he'd found pieces of peace. Not enough, but you gave him comfort during a terrible struggle. Something that I..." She looked around the beautifully appointed marble foyer with the expensive artwork. "That we and all of our money never managed to give him."

"But..." Shane didn't know what to say. It was such a different story from what she'd thought, from what Brandon had told her.

"Keep the watch, Shane," Alyssa said. "It was a present in good faith. Ethan wanted you to have it."

"Brandon said it's a family heirloom."

"Brandon always wants what others have," she said. "Yes, it's an heirloom. But it was not ever going to Brandon. It was always Ethan's, but Brandon has always wanted more. Keep the watch. Leave it to one of your children."

"I can't have children. You know that." She was surprised that it didn't hurt the way it used to.

Mrs. Huntingdon looked over Shane's shoulder toward SUV. Remy stood outside the vehicle, long hair ruffling in the breeze off the harbor. Arlo hung outside of the open window, Beast next to her.

She turned her attention back to Shane, her blue eyes still holding pain, but also a kindness shone through that Shane didn't remember from before. "There are many ways to make a family besides blood and bone." She took the watch, held it to her cheek and then buckled it around Shane's wrist.

"I didn't learn that until too late. People are more important than things. Keep the watch. Wear it or don't. Pass it down to your daughter or a future son. Live your life. But don't let things tether you—only hold people to your heart."

And then she hugged Shane like a mother, like she should have before when Shane had received news that had ripped her already battered heart in two. Surprised, Shane slid her arms around the delicate shoulders of the woman who had almost been her mother-in-law, but Shane knew now that that marriage would never have lasted.

"Live your life, Shane. Ethan saw something in you much deeper than your beauty. He saw your soul, something Brandon and I ignored. Ethan suffered for years, trying to please us, struggling with his disease. He wanted you to live your life and remember him and how much he admired you. Go live your life, Shane."

Shane briefly squeezed her eyes shut to control the emotion, but it was too late. She gently touched Mrs. Huntingdon's delicate hands. Her skin was cool and paper-thin.

"Thank you," Shane said.

The moment felt epic though she hadn't done what she'd come to do, but that was okay. The watch no longer reminded her of failure. Instead, it was a reminder of second chances. Hers. Remy's. Arlo's. Maybe one day Arlo would wear the watch or maybe she'd take Remy up on his jest, and it would pay for Arlo's education or kick-start a program. But today it was a promise. A connection. Past to future.

"Take care, Alyssa," Shane said and then quickly walked down the stairs and into her future.

"You okay?" Remy met her halfway, his arms as always strong, warm and safe.

"You helped me blow by okay a long time ago." She looked up into his familiar face.

"What do you want to do next?" he asked, and she saw how he noted the watch still on her wrist, curiously.

"I want the three of us to go home and find out together."

"I like the sound of that," Remy said, taking her hand and bringing it to his lips, holding her gaze. "Let's go home."

The End

Don't miss the next book in The Coyote Cowboys of Montana series, *Marry Me Please, Cowboy*!

Join Tule Publishing's newsletter for more great reads and weekly deals!

If you enjoyed *The Cowboy's Word*,
you'll love the next books in…

The Coyote Cowboys of Montana series

Book 1: *The Cowboy's Word*

Book 2: *Marry Me Please, Cowboy*
Coming in September 2023

Book 3: *The Cowboy's Christmas Homecoming*
Coming in November 2023

Available now at your favorite online retailer!

More Books by Sinclair Jayne

Montana Rodeo Brides series

Book 1: *The Cowboy Says I Do*

Book 2: *The Cowboy's Challenge*

Book 3: *Breaking the Cowboy's Rules*

The Texas Wolf Brothers series

Book 1: *A Son for the Texas Cowboy*

Book 2: *A Bride for the Texas Cowboy*

Book 3: *A Baby for the Texas Cowboy*

The Wilder Brothers series

Book 1: *Seducing the Bachelor*

Book 2: *Want Me, Cowboy*

Book 3: *The Christmas Challenge*

Book 4: *Cowboy Takes All*

The Misguided Masala Matchmaker series
Book 1: *A Hard Yes*

Book 2: *Swipe Right for Marriage*

Book 3: *An Unsuitable Boy*

Book 4: *Stealing Mr. Right*

About the Author

Sinclair Sawhney is a former journalist and middle school teacher who holds a BA in Political Science and K-8 teaching certificate from the University of California, Irvine and a MS in Education with an emphasis in teaching writing from the University of Washington. She has worked as Senior Editor with Tule Publishing for over seven years.

Thank you for reading

The Cowboy's Word

If you enjoyed this book, you can find more from all our great authors at TulePublishing.com, or from your favorite online retailer.

TULE
PUBLISHING